THE GOOD THE BAD AND THE INFERNAL

First published 2013 by Solaris
an imprint of Rebellion Publishing Ltd,
Riverside House, Osney Mead,
Oxford, OX2 0ES, UK

www.solarisbooks.com

ISBN: 978 1 78108 090 0

Designed & typeset by Rebellion Publishing

Printed and bound by CPI Group (UK) Ltd, Croydon, CR0 4YY

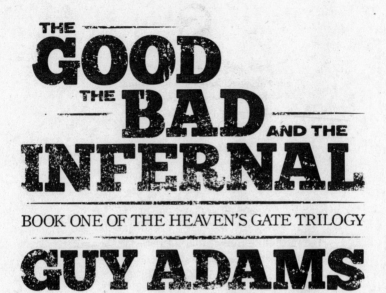

THE GOOD THE BAD AND THE INFERNAL

BOOK ONE OF THE HEAVEN'S GATE TRILOGY

GUY ADAMS

SOLARIS

To Michael George Adams,
who fathered the outlaw that wrote this book
and taught him the difference between
good, bad and ugly.

IN THE BEGINNING

1. THIRTY DAYS AGO...

"THE ATLANTIC IS a cruel and venomous woman, Father, just as likely to snatch you to her bosom, body and soul, as deliver you to your destination."

"No mere ocean is capable of taking the immortal soul, Mr Quartershaft."

"Father, this is why it's good that you have me by your side; you may be all-knowing in the matters of spirit, but you are like a child beyond your monastery, naïve of the natural world's cruelties."

Quartershaft, confident that the monk's gaze was elsewhere, took a swig of brandy from his hip flask.

"Why, the last time I sailed these waters, I lost two dozen men from my expedition, grabbed by the waves that writhe beneath us like a tuppenny whore earning her change."

The monk scowled at that and Quartershaft reminded himself that his lewder metaphors were best saved for the country set. "I had to bring the vessel to dock myself, lashed to the wheel by rags from the dead men's clothing."

"How fortunate that, though their bodies were lost to the ocean, their shirts were not."

Quartershaft stared at the young novice who had joined them with a look that he hoped, brandy or not, created the striking profile that appealed to magazine editors the publishing world over. The look that said: intrepid, brooding and authoritative. A man to be reckoned with (or, at the very least, read about). It was a look that he practiced often in the mirror, trying to emulate the sketches that had graced the cover of many a worthy periodical. It was a lot harder to achieve without pen and ink.

"Fortunate indeed, Brother William. Now, if you will excuse me, I must prepare for our landing, peruse the maps, maybe take an hour's rest. I shall be in my cabin, Father, should you or any of your order find yourselves in deathly peril."

Quartershaft sauntered below deck, leaving the two monks looking over the prow.

"You really must mind yourself with Mr Quartershaft, Brother William. He seems a sensitive man."

"He is, begging your pardon Father, an idiot and a liar. A sham, cultivated to sell lurid publications, and nothing more. I cannot begin to understand why you insist on his joining us in our quest."

Father Martin sighed.

"Money, Brother William; money. Without the financial support of his publisher, we would have been penniless halfway to Plymouth, let alone the Americas."

"Ah."

"Indeed, and while he may be prone to embroidering the accounts of his previous expeditions, you have no reason to doubt his abilities."

"He got lost belowdecks twice, yesterday. I found him relieving himself in one of the galley cupboards. Claimed it was an ancient mariner's trick to waterproof the timbers. Then there is the persistent sound of vomiting from within his cabin, as well as sundry other noises... I dread to think what he does in there away from prying eyes."

"Nonetheless, William, he may have some use in the journey ahead. And do not forget, without the documents he retrieved during his recent journey to India, we would know a lot less about our sacred destination."

"If it even exists."

Father Martin looked disapprovingly at the novice.

"Oh, Wormwood exists, my boy, never doubt it for a moment."

He gazed back out to sea, where the slim shadow of land grew closer.

"Although there may be times during our journey when we all wish it didn't."

2. TWENTY DAYS AGO...

THEY MOVED AS tight as pack animals, hugging the ground as they ran. Four in all, wrapped in dull cloth to cheat lazy eyes. Shadow clothes.

Los Redo Prison sat within a bowl of open land, surrounded by mountains. They ran towards it, virtually invisible against the ill-lit landscape.

MANCO SNORTED AND spat a wad of phlegm onto the ground. The dust filled his head. He'd worked here six months and his lungs hurt. He wished he could work somewhere where the air was clear.

Shifting position, he wedged the butt of his rifle against his gut and ferreted in his shirt pocket for tobacco. He slowly rolled a smoke in one hand, tamping down the tobacco and folding the paper around it with deft movements of his fingers. He gummed the paper down with a streak of spit and shoved the cigarette in the corner of his mouth, then flicked a match alight against the crumbling wall at his back, cupped the flame in his palm and lit up. He took a deep lungful and flicked the spent match to the ground, staring into the mountains.

The blade came from the left, sliding across his throat; the flesh parted, releasing blood and smoke. Manco slid, twitching, to the floor.

THEY CAME TOGETHER silently and vaulted one of their number onto the prison wall. Small and stunted, barely more than three foot from toe to topknot, the figure scampered along the edge of the wall before tumbling to the other side.

The wall backed onto a small courtyard in front of the prison buildings, with their corridors and poky cells. There were three guards, shuffling around the gate. The night was silent but for the distant persistence of cicadas.

Three shots rang out and the guards went down.

The midget dropped to the courtyard and, kicking at the bodies as he passed, pulled back the bolts of the gate and let his companions enter.

HENRY JONES ROLLED off his bunk and got to his feet. He pulled his belt tight and adjusted the fit of his trousers around the crotch, then ran his finger around the waistband, making sure his cotton shirt was fully tucked. Slipping his maroon silk waistcoat over his shoulders, he cleared his throat gently, testing his vocal chords. Buttoned up, silver watch chain evenly slung, he reached for his black jacket and pulled it on, rolling his shoulders to get them snug and flicking his cuffs forward. He just had time to run a careful hand over his oiled hair, checking for runaways, before the door exploded.

When the dust settled, Jones twitched his head at the sound of the small feet scuffling into his cell.

"Evenin' Knee High,"

"Evenin' Mr Jones, sir," the midget shouted over the considerable noise of gunfire.

Jones strolled out of the cell and towards the courtyard.

The gunfire had ceased now, the dirt damp with the guts of prison guards.

"Henry!" One of the figures moved forward, pulling the grey cowl from its head to reveal beautiful red hair. A tanned face, inset with sparkling emerald eyes and rich full lips, surrounded by the bushiest and most luxuriant of beards.

"Evenin' darlin'," said Jones, giving her a tongue-filled kiss and a firm grab between the thighs, romantic as he was wont to be.

"We've got you, baby," she murmured, stroking the smooth, eyeless skin that made up the top half of his face, and pulling him closer to her. "We can find it together."

He twitched his head momentarily, grabbed the gun she had slung in her left thigh holster and snapped off a shot to his rear. A wounded guard, who had nursed thoughts of being a hero, recoiled against the bullet and died.

"Sorry, darlin'," said Jones, "you were sayin'?"

"Wormwood, honey," she said, "let's find Wormwood."

3. TEN DAYS AGO...

"CAN I HEAR a hosanna?" Obeisance Hicks, emissary of the Lord and man of means, most surely could.

He cast a look at his fragile messiah, just to check the man's eyes were open and bowels in order. People could stand all manner of vagaries in their Gods, he had discovered, but a lack of toilet training was frowned upon, ecclesiastically. People wanted their Christ to smell sweet.

"I had a vision this morning," he went on to explain. "A message from God." Here he put his hand on the war veteran's shoulder, stroking the white robes he dressed the man in.

"He was telling me that the people of this town are almost lost to His sight."

There was a predictable yell of rebellion.

"That is what He said," insisted Hicks, pointing out at the faces of those gathered around the caravan. "I am merely His messenger. He told me that the devil himself had laid claim to this place, thanks to the help of his ministers and dark priests."

Again, a roar of disapproval.

"My friends," said Hicks, a man who knew how far to push matters, "you have no need to fear. I do not abandon you. And through me, God does not abandon you either. Behold!"

And with a gentle kick the tame messiah was awoken, calling out and raising his arms to the sky according to his training. Hicks never failed to take pleasure in the response of the crowd, the gasps of holy pleasure as the stigmata begin to flow.

"See how your sins are washed away in Holy Blood, see how I have the best interests of your souls at heart."

He took a sip of whisky from his tin cup (it paid not to advertise one's choice of beverage while spreading the word of the Lord; the only spirits crowds like this wanted to see were Holy in nature). He liked to leave a long moment after the blood, just to make sure it had really sunk in.

"We are here amongst you," he continued, "to save your eternal souls. We want to protect you, oh, yes... we want to see you wrapped up in the warm and loving arms of the Lord. We do! We do!"

He reached into his waistcoat pocket and removed a small glass bottle. He held it up, letting the glass glint in the light so as to add an extra hint of the heavenly. Then he placed the neck of the glass against the false messiah's wrist and let some of the blood drip inside. Just a little, a couple of drops; nothing robbed something of its mystery more than quantity. He corked the bottle and held it up to the light once more.

"Which is why I want to share this gift, this holiest of relics, this charm against the devil, this potent tonic for Jesus!"

He threw the bottle into the crowd, where it was caught by a young black girl. She held it close to her cheek and sang out in excitement. "Lord, how it sings!" she said. "You can feel God Himself just beyond the glass."

"Put it away, honey," said Hicks, "it's a precious gift." And she did so, amid the jealous clamour of the crowd.

"Friends!" Hicks shouted, "don't worry! I have a handful more I'm willing to donate to the holiest, most..."—he allowed a small pause here—"generous-spirited amongst you."

"I want to show my gratitude," shouted the girl, holding up a couple of coins. They glinted in the sun just the same as the bottle had done. Holy of holies, Hicks thought...

"I do not sell gifts from the Lord," he insisted. "If you wish to offer money to my ministry, then I thank you, and I swear to you that it will be used only in the furtherance of the holy message."

He took the coins from her and dropped them into a small basket at the front of his makeshift stage.

"There," he said. "In case anybody else might be so Christian in their wishes."

He brought forward a wooden chest and began to

unload pre-filled glass bottles from it, stepping back slightly as the line began to form. Praise be, he thought; God helps those who help themselves.

"CAN WE PLEASE get moving?"

Hicks looked up at the black face of his first 'customer' and smiled. "Just as soon as I've had a short nap," he announced, taking another sip of his whisky (from the bottle this time, he had given up on the tin mug now he was out of the public eye).

"It's alright for you," she said, despairing of the man who had never quite got the difference between 'owner' and 'employer.' "You might escape a lynching, if they catch you out as a con artist. They'd hang me up just to pass the time."

By now Hicks was snoring and there was very little that Hope Lane could do to rouse him.

She gathered up her skirts and shuffled across the caravan to where her beloved Soldier Joe lay. Hicks stored him as you would an animal, boxed away in a straw-lined cage.

Hope unlocked the door and shuffled in next to the man, pulling him up so that his head rested on her lap.

"Never you mind, Soldier Joe," she said, "we'll soon be moving on, and then you'll be able to get a little sun on your face."

He grunted, dead to the world, and rolled his face against her thigh. Hicks kept him sedated most of the time, fed him on powders meant for cattle, as far as she could tell. Better that than let him cry out, as he was wont to do. Soldier Joe had seen some bad things in his time, she was sure of that. If only the bullet that had taken out a good-sized piece of his brain and most of his sense could have taken the fear away too. When the powders wore off, he screamed like a beaten baby, and nobody did that unless they had something terrible rattling on them.

Soldier Joe tensed up and mumbled to himself. *Wumweh* he seemed to say, over and over again.

"I'm sorry, honey," said Hope, stroking his hair, "I can't understand you."

"Wormwood," said Soldier Joe, opening his eyes and speaking as clear as you like. "We need to go to Wormwood."

Then he closed his eyes and fell back to sleep.

4. NOW...

THE UNION PACIFIC got you as far as Omaha, but no further. In a few years the Central Pacific line, cutting its way east from Sacramento, would come to meet the western line, and travelling the length of the country would be possible from the relative comfort of a rail carriage. Until then, the long-distance traveller had little option but to decamp from the luxury of iron tracks and make way under his own steam.

"Come along, my dear," said Lord Forset, raising a wrinkled hand towards the sun as much to keep the dust from his eyes as the light. "They must be around here somewhere."

"How can one lose a pack of monks?" his daughter wondered, clambering down from the carriage. "They hardly dress to blend in."

"Quite," agreed Forset. He pulled a pair of goggles from his pocket and put them on, making him look even more bizarre than he had already.

Elisabeth looked at him fondly. His crumpled suit and mismatched waistcoat. His hair, which appeared to have achieved autonomy from his scalp, writhing in the hot wind and snatching at the occasional piece of litter that flew by. He was quite at odds with his surroundings, but as this could be said of absolutely anywhere in the world, he achieved a universal quality. The only country in which he felt utterly at home was that strange and complex region found between his left ear and its corresponding fellow on the right. Lord Forset was a full-time resident of his own mind; elsewhere, he was only a visitor.

"Lord Forset?" came a call from further up the platform. "Lord Forset?"

It was a young porter. The loser, had they but known, of a bet between himself and his superior as to who would have to deal with the English pair.

"Yes, my lad," replied the peer, offering a big-toothed grin that made the kid think of sand-blown marker posts.

"Where do you want your equipment, sir... I mean, my lord..."

"Never mind the manner of address, young man. After all, I can hardly be described as any lord of yours, now, can I? We're many miles away from my country seat."

"Thank God," said his daughter.

"Thank God, indeed," her father agreed, "considering who's paying. Speaking of which..." He offered a little bow towards Father Martin, who was walking towards them, the rest of his order hanging back.

"Excuse me!" shouted the immediately recognisable voice of Roderick Quartershaft, pushing his way through his religious-minded travelling companions. "Can a man not set one foot out without tripping over a cassock?"

"This young lad wants to know where to put my equipment," said Lord Forset, turning back to the porter. "Our transport is scheduled to meet us outside. Load everything up and ferry it to the street, there's a good chap."

"The driver should be here to meet us," said Father Martin. "Perhaps he's running late?"

"Taken your money and absconded for the hills, more like," announced Roderick Quartershaft, on the back of breath so alcoholic it would have made a Baptist weep.

"I don't think there's any need to assume that yet," said Father Martin. "Has anyone enquired after our arrival?" He turned to ask the porter, but the young lad had already run back to his superior.

"Can't wait to be shot of us," said Quartershaft. "No sense of service in the colonies."

"Not colonies any more, old chap," Forset reminded him.

"Not for a long time," sighed his daughter. "Your knowledge of political geography is astoundingly limited, given your reputation as an explorer," she added. "It sometimes seems startling that you've been anywhere. They say travel broadens the mind, after all."

"It's a weak man that lets the opinions and beliefs of others affect his own. I can proudly say there's not a single continent I've set my boots on that has altered my perspective on life."

"Yes," Elisabeth replied. "You can say that proudly, can't you?"

Quartershaft smiled dreamily and Elisabeth wondered if he might actually fall over. "I'm glad I impress, my lady."

"I say," Forset shouted, watching as one of his crates swung precariously from a luggage pulley, "careful with that! It contains equipment of a most fragile and temperamental nature."

The young porter waved his acknowledgement just as one of the ropes came loose and the crate plummeted to the ground.

* * *

HENRY JONES MOVED unerringly through the crowds of people on the platform. The dark glasses and cane he carried served to discourage undue attention; he certainly had no need of them. Along with the dark suit and wide-brimmed hat, they helped offer a degree of anonymity. By now, a lot of lawmen would be on the lookout for him. It was better for the life expectancy of those lawmen, and casual passers-by, that they not find him. Even had he not been wishing to keep a low profile, he frequently wore a disguise. Henry Jones had the sort of countenance that drew attention. Unfortunately, uppermost in the list of things he hated—a prodigious and changeable list—was people staring at him. Nobody, not even the beautiful Mrs Harmonium Jones, had the slightest idea how he could tell. His mood was so perpetually sore on the subject that nobody saw fit to ask.

Mrs Jones was also attempting to disguise her appearance, something only really achieved by using a derby hat and a particularly relentless girdle. Her facial hair was a source of great pride, and it would take more than a fear of law officers to get her near a razor, foam and strop.

They also had a crate to negotiate, the contents of which were a little harder to disguise in public and were therefore forced to travel freight.

"There something alive in there, sir?" asked the conductor as he admired the beautifully painted crate on the platform. DR BLISS'S KARNIVAL OF DELIGHTS, it said in curling, scarlet letters, the words sharing space with pictures of roaring lions, chuckling clowns and the snarling face of a top-hatted ringmaster. "Only some of the boys swear they heard something move when they were getting it off the train."

"It's just equipment, pal," said Harmonium in a passable, throaty tone. "Otherwise we'd have filled out the requisite paperwork."

"Good," the conductor smiled, "good. Only... we're supposed to check on all livestock; just for safety, you understand. I mean, I have my passengers to think of."

"Sure you do," Harmonium replied, tucking a dollar into his jacket pocket, "and you've looked after these two just fine."

"Oh, well, thank you, sir. Most kind."

"We particularly appreciated how you left us to our own devices," added Henry, tilting his thick black lenses towards the man.

The penny dropped. "Oh, naturally. Well, be seeing you, then." And away went the conductor.

"Rest easy, boys," whispered Harmonium into one of the discreetly drilled air holes. "We'll soon have you out of there."

But before she could receive a reply, everyone on the platform turned towards the air-rending crash of a large packing crate falling to earth and splitting open.

"What the hell was that?" asked Henry. "Someone hurt?"

"I sure hope so, honey," his wife replied. "What say we go and find out?

"CAN I HEAR a hosanna?" Obeisance Hicks was, as always, inclined to wonder.

On this particular afternoon, his timing was not ideal; the answer was a resounding 'no.' The only thing most people within preaching distance could hear was the sound of an almighty crash, followed by considerable panic.

"What in the name of Christ is that?" wondered the not-so-reverent Hicks. He decided that, since his congregation was inclined to abandon the word of God in the hope of finding out, so was he.

"Keep an eye on the messiah," he muttered to Hope Lane, before wandering into the train station.

She sighed, horribly conscious that he had now drawn attention to her, and nodded.

Inside, Hicks wasn't the only one wanting to catch a glimpse of catastrophe. He noted, not for the first time, that if there was a way for him to market gawping at the dead and dying, he could pack in the God game for ever. People flocked to blood as surely as flies.

Today they were to be disappointed. As far as Hicks could tell, the crashing sound had been a collection of ironmongery dropped from a height. If it had fallen on anyone, then they were so deeply buried that the gathered crowd had little interest in attempting to save them. There was a good deal of standing around and shaking of heads. That's the other thing with a crowd, Hicks decided; they all have an opinion and it's usually the same one. People were dumb as sheep.

"I dread to think what you've broken!" cried out one man, with an accent so strongly British that a number of the gathered crowd automatically reached for their guns. There was not a great deal of good feeling towards that particular country; Hicks, being of Dutch stock, couldn't honestly say he gave a brace of shits on the subject.

"Some of that equipment was irreplaceable," the man was saying. "Simply irreplaceable!"

As if in agreement, a loud hissing noise erupted from the centre of the piled metal, and the crowd darted back as far as the limited space would allow. Metal *clanged* and rang out like a church bell under gunfire as a large, crab-like device appeared from underneath the fragments. It sat at the centre of the heap for a few moments, as if content in its nest, and then jumped for the sky.

"Somebody stop it!" the Englishman shouted, and with no further ado, the young woman standing by him began scaling the stationary train.

Hicks decided he may well have fallen in love as he watched her run across the roof of the train in pursuit of the metal creature as it hovered along, like a vulture scanning the ground for carrion.

"Do be careful, darling," the Englishman suggested—stupidly, in Hick's opinion, and in that of many there gathered—before turning away in shock as the young woman made a leap for the escaped device. She grabbed it in its midsection and proceeded to fly over the crowd, in a manner that pleased the gathered gentlemen greatly. Showing a consistent lack of regard for feminine decorum, she swung her legs up and grasped the device between them so as to hang from it more securely.

She initially appeared to be fighting it, but after a few moments, Hicks changed his mind, having been reminded of a business acquaintance who he had often watched buttoning up her corsets post-congress.

"Well, I'll be..." he muttered. "If she ain't planning on *wearing* the thing."

With a final, triumphant *click* and a whoop from the crowd, the young woman did just that. She righted herself so that she was now stood upright, albeit several feet above the ground, then grasped a pair of handles, pushed forward and swooped gracefully back to earth.

There was a round of applause and, having disengaged whatever engine the thing possessed, she unclasped the legs and took a small bow.

"The Forset Thunderpack," announced the Englishman with considerable pride. "In full working order!"

The device in question gave an almighty *bang* and fell silent.

"And thank God I got it back before it had been

operational for more than sixty seconds," said the young girl.

"Why might that be?" asked an impressed observer.

"It has a bad habit of blowing up if ignited for longer than that," she replied, "and would have likely taken most of this train station up with it."

The crowd dispersed quickly after that, but Hicks lingered. He'd seen something that had excited that essential heart of him, the black pulsing mass of his pocketbook. He had seen *money*.

Eventually he turned around and headed back out to his caravan, disinclined to continue in his never-ending mission to save souls and accrue dollars. He might even stay off the whisky a little, give his brain time to think.

Looking up, he wondered why there was a crowd gathered around his caravan. Then he heard the sound of the dopey-minded motherfucker he offered up for the nation's prayers. The old soldier was shouting his goddamned face off about something. He couldn't leave the wet-brain alone for a minute.

"Mind out, now," he shouted, pulling at the shoulders of the idiots that had clustered around. "Nothing to see here. Man of God... coming through..."

They refused to move, fascinated by the sight of the hirsute figure, his white robes stained bloody as his stigmata gushed forth. And what in hell was that he was shouting?

"God damn you," Hicks shouted, his temper frail at the best of times. He pulled out his gun and shot a couple of bullets into the air. "Shift your sinful asses, you worthless cocksuckers, or I'll smite each and every one of you with the righteousness of a Colt .45!"

That had more success, and the crowd slowly dissipated while he clambered up onto the makeshift stage he preached from, wondering how to make the idiot shut up without shooting him.

"Wormwood! Wormwood! Wormwood!" the simpleton shouted.

"What the hell's Wormwood?" Hicks wondered aloud. "Some kind of tequila?"

"It's the name of a town," said someone behind him. He turned to see two gentlemen, one with a long and bushy beard, the other blind. The blind man pulled off his dark glasses to reveal a smooth patch of skin where the eyes should be. "And I'd very much like to hear what else he has to say on the subject."

5.

SUN-SHATTERED AND SCORCHED, the dust fields whipped tails at the sky.

The landscape roasted. A world suited only to the dead and to the reptiles and flies that scurry impatiently through the ribcage cathedrals of carrion. They, in turn, are picked off in hit and run assaults by birds, dipping in and out of this wilderness like pearl divers before returning to the skies where the winds blow fresh and clear.

The air was as thick as cooling cooking grease.

It was a quiet world. The feather-light brushstrokes of a sidewinder's body seemed loud across the dunes; the occasional screeches of a hawk pierced the silence like a railroad spike. The delicate crunch of a horse's hooves was almost unknown, an intrusive and unwelcome sound. Yet here it was, startling the snakes and lizards into the shadows of their rocks.

The horse moved gracefully, a ballet dancer moving through the inferno.

Its rider was suited to this world. His flesh dry as parchment. Old, tight eyes looked out over the trail and refused to betray a single thought. The pale overcoat he wore fluttered around the horse, the hem ragged and torn. The leather of his boots creaked like coffin lids.

On he rode. On towards Wormwood.

THE ROAD
TO WORMWOOD

THE OLD MAN
AND THE BANKER

CHAPTER ONE
A STRANGER IN TOWN

I CONSIDERED PRAYING, I'll admit that much. This account will be difficult without a degree of honesty between us, so, yes, prayer had its charm. Thing is, I'd never had much time for religion, and back then, I couldn't quite find the hypocrisy needed for a hasty 'Our Father.' Convictions are dangerous things. Believe anything too hard and life will bite you on the ass for it. Having a little extra experience, these days, I'll pass some of it on: put me in that situation now and I'd dance buck-naked in a mound of mule shit if I thought it would give me a fighting chance. Pride is the sure and safe province of the idiot.

That said, remembering the look of those three: men made from stubble, cigar smoke, ancient sweat and anger. Skin like jerky, eyes like bullet holes in a dead man's back... Remembering all of that, it occurs to me that it would have taken a hell of a hosanna to placate them.

Their leader laughed. I remember that, more clearly than anything else. It was a shock. I was about to die (to my mind a very serious and solemn affair) and this son of a bitch was full of cheer.

I made the decision not to beg. To die with some dignity. Sometimes the best you can hope for is that your last moments are not filled with screaming and the smell of your own shit.

I held a brave face right up until the first shot.

IT HAD TAKEN me three days to cross from the small township of Dashett to Haskell. One day the railways would make this journey; until then, it had to be endured the old fashioned way.

My mount was old and unsteady, a mule I had picked up from a sadist in Kansas. I was convinced the beast would die rather than see journey's end. Lying on my blanket at night, I strained to hear its laboured breathing, monitoring its health like an anxious parent hearkens to a child. Frequently it would fall silent, and I clutched my blanket tight, certain I was stranded in the middle of this wilderness with no transport. Eventually, a sneeze or fart would break the silence and I'd fall into nervous sleep.

Once in Haskell, I found that I was better disposed towards him, regretful of the harsh words and curses I'd heaped on his narrow, scabby shoulders. I tethered him at a stables, gave him an affectionate rub on the nose, and agreed a price for his safekeeping with the unsanitary creature I took to be in charge (on account of the fact that he was the only one not tied up). With the small saddle and bag I had thus far carried halfway across the country, I set off into town.

Haskell was like many of the small towns I had visited on that long trek. I had left the security of home and family for the uncertainty of the West Coast and a job that I hoped to hell would still be there when I arrived. The trip had been full of these unambitious townships: untidy gatherings of houses and stores constructed around a 'main street,' a wide dirt avenue that offered all the traveller could need (providing he wasn't fussy about hygiene or longevity). There were a couple of saloons, a hotel that I would later discover doubled as a whorehouse, a general store and stables. Around these perpetual fixtures, a littering of homes shuffled self-consciously in side streets. I assume they had taste and were as ashamed to be seen there as I was. At the head of the main street, the twin gods of Western life presided over the town, represented by their respective owners, well-heeled and conversing pleasantly on the boardwalk adjoining the two properties. To the left was Mr Joshua Forrest (Banker), and to the right was Isaac Crutchins (Undertaker). May they forever rule.

I walked towards the hotel, enjoying the feel of the ground beneath my boots, my thighs curiously light with nothing between them. My plan was simple: food in my belly and sleep in a bed.

I knew the hotel was unlikely to be up to much, having spent enough time in shabby hostels to be relieved at the sight of a mattress in a room. Even so, the filth that peppered the foyer took my breath away. New life forms mingled with the tobacco stains. I swear I could feel the carpet moving beneath my feet. Here it wasn't just outlaws that you had to be careful with; treat 'em wrong and the roaches were likely to beat the shit out of you.

Skulking in the shadows to the left of the entrance, an old man was being pumped impatiently by an ageing hooker. She showed more interest in the dirt wedged beneath the nails of her free hand than the stunted dick that was, even now, helping to pay her bar bill.

Several men were sleeping off a night of whisky (or had got bored, waiting on the hooker's affections). They were littered around or beneath the chairs and benches that lined the walls. Perhaps there was an economy drive running, and the owner was trying to cut down on excessive wear of the beds.

Coughing self-consciously, bag in my hand, saddle slung over my left shoulder, I made my way to the small counter at the end of the hall. I felt sorry for it. Old and splintered, it struggled to keep upright beneath the combined weight of a small check-in ledger and brass bell. Thinking back, maybe I should have just given the thing a firm kick and put it out of its misery. Checking around, there was no sign of a manager, so I slapped the bell as gently as I could without breaking the desk's back.

"Wha' you wan'?" grunted a voice from behind me. It was the man being jerked off. The hooker didn't stop; presumably she was disinclined to get him all fired up a second time.

"Just a room for the night," I replied. "A meal, if you can?"

For a moment I thought the man hadn't heard me. Maybe he was trying to figure out some of the longer words. Then he grunted fitfully and slapped the hooker away, having spent himself with all the passionate energy of a man hawking phlegm into his handkerchief. He got to his feet and loped over to the counter, tucking himself in as he walked.

"Cash up front. No food." He sniffed, turning the ledger towards me so that I could sign it. I did so, he looked at it (maybe the shapes pleased him; I refuse to believe he could read), then threw me a key.

"Up the stairs, third on the right."

He waddled through a threadbare curtain behind the counter, presumably feeling the need for some time alone. Perhaps to read a little poetry, press some flowers. Either that or there were still some acts he considered should be performed in privacy, like eating children or fucking a horse. Maybe he got bashful about such things.

I went upstairs and along to the third door on the right. Looking at the lock, a good sneeze would probably have opened it. Stickler for tradition, I used the key.

Inside, there was nothing but a small bed frame, featuring a mattress with attractive body-fluid decoration. Looking closely, I figured that that there were enough mixed deposits on its surface to give birth all on their own in a few months. I needed to take a leak, and there was nothing so luxurious as a pan in sight. I checked out the window and saw precious little except a horse tethered below. I tried my best, but a slight breeze made aiming tricky; when I finished, I apologised to the horse and closed the window.

I lay on the bed, trying to keep to the edges as far as possible. The damn thing curved towards the middle, and in the end I was just too damn tired to be coy. I rolled with it, and fell asleep.

IN MY DREAMS I pictured the dirt road that I had travelled, the train tracks that might soon replace it bursting from the rock and pouring forth like a river. With the tracks came the train, a hulking steel behemoth that roared and screamed in the desert night. It was terrifying, this creature: the cries of the dead that fuelled its cavernous engine billowed forth from its stack, caught in the grip of the smoke and ash that danced across the moon. The embers were fat and burned brighter than suns.

I was laying the track, running through the clouds of dust, hurling sleeper and line in its path, desperate to feed its hunger. I screamed as the razor teeth of its dirt plough chattered and devoured the sustenance I gave it, ravenous and insatiable. The muscles in my arms and back threatened to tear under the weight of the endless supply of iron, swearing that each foot of track I laid (instant and impossible as a spider's web) would be their last. But I couldn't stop. I knew this, sure and certain. If I ran out of track, those plough teeth would strip my flesh and run their last on peeled wet bone.

I woke up after that, the dream shaking me conscious as bad dreams do when a man's still young. Now, older than most would credit, I sleep right through to dawn without fail. I still have the dreams, but they don't shock me as they did. It gets so that you can live with fear.

I swung my legs off the mattress and peered out of the window. There was still little to see, except for a horse that had good reason to hate me. From the main street around the other side of the hotel I could hear the sound of a beaten piano hammering out a tune I almost recognised.

I reached for my bag, dug out a thin pouch of tobacco and began to roll a cigarette. As I rolled it, smoothly, methodically and, above all, awkwardly (this was a habit I had not long taken up, feeling that if I was adult enough for the road I should look like it), I began to hear a separate piano from my right. There were two saloons in town, I remembered. It appeared that they were in competition. The second player was no more talented than the first, but he made a lot more noise. After a few moments, the original pianist kicked up the tempo a little and began to fight back, the notes becoming rougher and more painful but loud enough to give number two a run for his money. I struck a match and put it to my cigarette, awaiting the inevitable. Sure enough, as I exhaled, number two cranked it up. I figured that was his limit, surely he couldn't get any more volume without resorting to dynamite. Piano number one took a deep breath and gave it one last shot. Tearing the night in half with their godawful racket, both pianos played together for a few moments before a pair of gunshots rang out, one from either direction. Both pianos stopped instantly. Figuring now was as good a time as any to get some more sleep, I stubbed my cigarette out, removed my glasses and lay back down on the bed.

MORNING SURPRISED ME in its usual way. I've never been good at them. They sneak up on a man.

I shifted my weight, fighting against the dip in the mattress, and tried to get my feet on the floor. After a few minutes I found myself lying across the bed with my heels skimming the floorboards. Good enough, I thought, so I went for the vertical.

I shuffled to the window, unbuttoning my fly, and, forehead resting against the wall, I pissed out of the window as I had the night before.

I guess that was the point at which I truly woke up. Language the kind of which I heard has a way of doing that.

I grabbed my spectacles and looked down at the street below.

There were three in total, all the weathered outlaw types I had seen in great numbers since leaving home. There was a certain breed of gunslinger back then, a breed entirely divorced from the dapper, silk-vested creations people talk of these days. This was the true gunslinger: uglier than a fly blown dog that's been left in the sun for a few days. They looked for all the world as if they had been rolled in shit by their mothers directly after birth and sent out with a Colt on the hip.

Having made this distinction clear, you will understand my concern when I realised that the horse beneath my window was owned by one of them. What is more, not only had I pissed on the horse but, judging by the sagging brim of his hat and the damp patches on his shirt shoulders, I had pissed on the owner as well.

I stood there for a moment, pecker in my hand and

gormless look on my face, while he stared right back, unable to believe what I had just done. I think it was basic shock on his part; being mistaken for a latrine obviously didn't happen to him often. Which is a surprise, looking the way he did.

What happened next is going to be difficult to describe without giving the boys names, and as our relationship never got on such terms, I guess I'm just going to have to christen them myself, something apt and charming. Rat Shit, Tinkerbell and Horse Ass should do them justice. Fine upstanding gentlemen as they were, these may have been their mothers' first choices too, I really couldn't swear on it either way.

Rat Shit, whose attention I had drawn by emptying my bladder on him, replied by drawing his gun and shooting at the window. As much as I would like to claim lightning quick instincts, I think it was utter terror that sent my legs out from under me. I dropped out of harm's way even as the frame splintered with the impact of the bullet.

After that, a degree of instinct did take over, as I crawled back from the window, climbed to my feet once out of immediate harm's way and ran out the door to my room.

One of the other doors in the corridor had been opened by an associate of the hooker downstairs. She looked me up and down for a moment before rolling her eyes and stepping back inside.

Downstairs I could hear the sound of shouting as my new friends burst into the foyer. There was no escape that way.

I went back into my room and worked my way around to the window. I peered outside; it was clear that all three had come inside to find me, leaving this the only route out. I clambered onto the frame and tried to judge the distance between the window and the horse beneath me. I'd seen a couple of hustlers perform this trick back home, escaping from the lodging house at the end of my street in order to avoid paying the rent they owed. How difficult could it be?

I closed my eyes and jumped. For a second, there was a pleasing feeling of weightlessness, before my face connected with the horse's rump, dislodging a tooth, and I was thrown in the air by its startled thrashing. I came to earth in a cloud of dust, with blood in my mouth, but in a better state than had I stayed upstairs and waited to be shot.

Getting to my feet, I limped around to the front of the hotel, just in time to walk directly into Tinkerbell (named on account of his sweet-looking face and gentle nature), who had waited outside in case I was stupid enough to try and sneak past the front door.

I gave a manly scream, pushed past him and ran towards the end of the street, where I had the good fortune to be run down by a coach.

Lying on my back, with a bloody mouth and a searing pain in my left side, I did a strange thing. I laughed my head off. I mean, *really*, laughed like a loon. Even as I heard a couple of passengers getting off the coach, felt their hands in my armpits as they pulled me upright, I couldn't stop.

"Jesus, fella!" someone said. "You're damned lucky."

"Not the way I see it," came another voice. "Figure he's just takin' a breather before I put this bullet in his face."

That would be Rat Shit.

"Hey, now," replied the first voice. "You'd better have a damn good reason to go talkin' that kinda talk, what did this man do?"

Things were looking up, I had a casual bystander willing to fight my corner.

"Bastard pissed on my horse."

"Son of a bitch."

The hands let go of me, and I fell back to the ground.

"Guess you've got due cause, then. I'll leave you boys to it."

Nice town. Under other circumstances, I would have considered settling down there.

I heard the sound of a pistol cocking. Its owner laughed with the pleasure of what lay ahead.

"Tell you what, boy," he said, "I'm going to do you a kindness."

For a second there, I hoped. He crouched down in front of me and I winced at breath that reminded me of my old mule's gas.

"I'm gonna let you tuck your dick in your pants 'fore I kill you."

Glancing down, I realised that, what with everything else on my mind over the last few minutes, I'd forgotten to 'stable the stallion.' So much for a dignified end.

Seconds passed.

Then a gunshot rang out.

I COULD CREDIT Rat Shit with many qualities: he was clearly able-bodied, had a force of personality stronger than most and breath that would embarrass a skunk with a yeast infection.

The one thing I would never have credited him with was possessing brains.

Shows how wrong you can be. The man had lots of brains. I knew this beyond all doubt a fraction of a second after I heard the gunshot, because most of them were now plastered in my hair and dripping off the end of my nose.

That boy had brains aplenty.

About a bucketful.

Tinkerbell followed quickly after, left twitching in the dust bare seconds behind his friend.

Horse Ass fared better. Quicker to react, he ran in the direction of the coach, hoping for cover. Nearly made it, too, before there was another loud report and his legs were cut from beneath him.

It takes longer to tell than it did to happen. *Bang. Bang. Bang.* Three sounds that left me bewildered, terrified and—fuck me, who would have thought it—*alive*.

I squinted at the shape walking towards me. A solid rectangle, tattered dustcoat whipping at his ankles. A rock of a man. He drew level with me, slipping his gun into its holster. I was surprised to see how old he was: seventy if he was a day.

"Do as the man said, boy. Put your pecker away. 'Tain't seemly."

I did as I was told and got to my feet.

"What's your name, son?" His voice sounded as if it had been cured, left out in the sun for a few days and then put back in his throat. Somewhere between a whisper and a cough.

"Wallace, sir," I replied, just as soon as I'd remembered, "Elwyn Wallace. You saved my life."

"That I did. You gonna give me cause to regret it?"

"No! I don't know how to thank you."

There was a pause at this, as if he was thinking of options. He scratched at his face with a sound as rough as a gang of armadillos fucking.

"Mayhap you can ride with me for awhile, keep a man company on his journey."

I had more than enough reasons as to why this wasn't a good idea—I had a journey of my own to get on with—but all I managed to say was:

"Where are we heading?"

"Small town over that way a stretch," he gestured meaninglessly behind me. "Place by the name of Wormwood."

CHAPTER TWO
FACE TO FACE

MY TRAVELLING COMPANION had claimed to hanker for company on the trail. After half an hour I was at a loss as to why. Trying to start a conversation with him was as productive as debating with a tombstone. Maybe he hoped I'd help keep the flies off.

He rode in silence, and I did my best to keep up. This was a battle lost within a few minutes. To begin with, my old mule—no doubt stirred to impress, somewhere within its ancient lustful heart—had made a good show in front of my companion's horse, but it couldn't keep the pace. Either that or it enjoyed the view from the rear. That's certainly where we stayed, with me gritting my teeth against the dust kicked up from the dry trail we followed out of Haskell and on towards Wormwood. Wherever and whatever the hell that might be. The old man hadn't seen fit to tell me. All I knew was that, for now, it lay in the same direction I meant to go. What the hell, I thought, I might as well ride with someone that could keep my sorry ass out of trouble for awhile.

The morning's journey passed in near silence, the only

slight noise being my skin cooking under the heat of the sun. I never did have the hide for bright skies. My companion was quite the opposite: his dust-coat, stiffened to the texture of wood after years of weathering, still looked softer than his skin, which had a cured, reptilian look. He was a man who had been exposed to the most extreme of environments, and they had left their mark. If you pounded at him with a sledgehammer I could imagine he would crumble like rock, revealing not a drop of juice in his entire body. Watching, as we descended into the narrow pass that wound its way through the lower portion of the Southern Rockies, I was put in mind of an animal rather than a man. He controlled his horse so naturally, so instinctively, that the two of them moved as one, navigating the uneven ground like a serpent. I'll admit I found myself aspiring to the old bastard's composure. He was the man I wanted to be, someone who moved across the world as if he was in control, rather than—as I was—someone who bounced from one event to another, entirely at the mercy of whatever life threw at him. A leaf on a river, frantic and directionless.

I did my best to copy him, squeezing that dumb mule between my thighs and yanking at the reins in an attempt to guide him between the rocks and trees as we descended. My skills were not up to the task, and neither was my ride. At one point the animal drew to a halt and looked over his wizened shoulder at me, for all the world wondering what I wanted from him. 'I've been on this earth long enough to know how to put one hoof in front of the other,' he seemed to say, 'and you yanking the hell out of me while I'm getting on with it is a distraction, not a help. So sit back, shut up, and let me get on with my job.' In the end, I did just that.

*　　*　　*

WE TOOK A rest at noon, having found a perfect spot by
the side of a narrow river where we could fetch water,
wash and take a bite to eat.

Sat in the shade of a tree, chewing my way through the
dried meat of an animal I couldn't place, I tried again to
get the old man talking.

"So," I said, "Wormwood. What's there that's dragging
you halfway across the country?"

"Home," he replied, in his usual talkative manner. He
turned his eyes towards the trail we had been following,
eyes narrowing, like a lizard sunbathing on a rock. "We've
got company."

I turned to look, but couldn't see anyone.

"There, a ways back," he said, "six or seven miles,
maybe."

"You can see that far?"

He chose to ignore the question, just gathered his stuff
together and gestured for me to do the same. It was no
hardship; chewing that goddamned meat was as much
effort as if the animal were still alive.

"You think they're following us?" I asked as we climbed
onto our respective mounts.

"No reason to guess so," he said.

"So why are we running?"

He stared at me, and I felt bowels that had been tighter
than a clenched fist loosen.

"We're not running," he said, "I don't run. But I don't
like company, either."

"I can tell that much."

He turned his horse and began to trot deeper into the
mountains, ignoring the comment, just as I knew he would.

THE AFTERNOON'S RIDE saw the old man pick up the pace,
always with an eye to the trail behind us.

I spent the time imagining who or what he might be. I had plenty of territory to guess at, as he'd told me not one word about himself, not even his name. I kept meaning to ask, but he was such a mean old bastard, I felt scared to. I'd talked about myself, yes, because that felt like it was allowed. Asking about him, *anything* about him; that felt out of bounds.

My Ma always said I was meeker than a first-time whore. She was a woman of words.

To hear her talk, I spent most of my childhood leaping from one fear to the next. As a babe I would curl in my cot at the sound of a storm. As a toddler I would hide from the pigs we kept, twitching with every snort and squeal. As an infant I would run from the snakes in the yard. Everywhere I turned, there was something to be afeared of. I guess she hoped I'd grow out of it. Find myself a backbone once my balls dropped. 'Course, I never did; I just found bigger things to be scared of.

The biggest of them all was my father. A man who changed his mood with the wind. Never have I known someone so fond of liquor to be so bad at drinking it. Every day he'd go at the sour mash, and every night he'd lose the battle as that sweet fire burned him up inside. Most mornings we'd find him on the porch, looking for all the world like he'd come off worse in a brawl. I guess he had, at that.

Not that he ever laid a hand on me. He would threaten as much, shout and promise 'a hellish whuppin' on either of us if we didn't do as we were told. He didn't have it in him, though. He was faulty dynamite, all fire and no force. Ma just ignored him. She'd live her life around him like he was a misplaced piece of furniture, a sideboard that nobody had seen the good sense to shove into a corner. It weren't no imposition once you'd got used to it. It got under your feet when you were sweeping. Sometimes it would scream at you for being an 'unholy, worthless cunt,' but after a while you just ignored that cumbersome old sideboard and got on with your life.

'So that's what you're running away from,' a woman told me after she'd got talking to me in a bar in Indiana.

I'd not been so long on my journey, then. A train ride across Kentucky and three days down on a twelve day coach ride to Illinois. I'd been tired and lonely, and despite the fact that I don't drink, I'd found myself in the bar, as there weren't nothing else to do and I missed the sound of people. She'd soon pulled up a chair, initially to sound me out as a potential client (she made it quite clear that a dollar would have her drawers down with the speed of a Texan sunset) but when it was obvious I had little interest and less money she settled for conversation. I was only too happy to oblige. She told me about her youth in Connecticut, her first husband who had died choking on a chicken bone, her decision to becoming a sporting woman because, 'when a gal can earn a dollar a dip doing something she enjoys, why the hell would she wait tables?' All of which was just fine, and listening to it beat the silence. When I told her something of my own life, though, she seemed to feel it all needed cross-examining. She was of the opinion that everything was due to some deep-seated problem or another. Maybe it was the fault of a book. Or maybe one of her regulars was a philosopher who talked when he should be poking. Maybe she was even right. Though I told her clear that sometimes a man does a thing just because it occurs to him to do so. We're not all the deep thinkers she pegged us out to be.

I guess I could understand why someone might wonder with regard to my trek across the country in the name of a bank job. Surely there were easier stations in life? Certainly there were closer ones. Still, the opportunity was there and I took it. My conviction wavered en route, but the idea of a long journey across land I had never seen to a home I could barely imagine seemed like a worthwhile idea. I guess it was an adventure, though I don't believe I ever viewed it in such terms. It was simply something to do that I had never done. Sometimes that's reason enough.

Maybe that was why my nameless friend had his heart set on Wormwood? Because it was there?

Even knowing nothing about him, I soon decided that wasn't the truth of it. He was not a man to do things on a whim. Whatever lay at Wormwood (and I never really imagined I'd find out, sure that I'd leave him to it after a couple of days together on the road), it was important as all hell.

WE SETTLED FOR the evening at a sheltered spot behind a rocky outcrop. I guess a practical man might guess this was to cut down on the wind, but I know he was thinking about whoever was behind us on the trail.

He sent me to look for firewood, which I did, only too happy to appear to be of some use. It also kept the two of us apart for a little longer, the unnatural lack of conversation getting more awkward with every moment in the man's company.

By the time I returned, he seemed to have mellowed a little.

"Not much for conversation," he admitted as I built the fire. "Too long on my own, I guess."

I shrugged, pretending not to have given it mind. "It gets lonely on the trail," I said, "once you're off the beaten track, anyways."

He nodded. "I don't mind that. Travel is a time for thought."

"I guess, though I think I'd managed to do plenty of

that by the time I got as far as Kentucky. Now I just want to get where I'm heading and get on with my life."

"What's the rush?"

"I don't know how long they'll keep the job open, for one thing," I said. "But it ain't just that. I don't mind travelling, I've enjoyed some of it for sure, but I guess I'm impatient to start afresh."

"You did that the day you left home."

"I guess I did. Still, until I get myself behind that desk, find a roof for my head, it feels like everything's up in the air. Is that what I'm going to be? A teller in a bank? What will my home be like? Who will be my new friends? It's all just life waiting to happen."

"You might not even get there. Which means you'll have spent all this time waiting, when you could have been living."

"There's a cheerful thought."

"Maybe it is. It all depends on your perspective."

"So you're not impatient to get where you're going? Whatever lies in Wormwood doesn't pull you along the trail?"

He paused at that, no doubt wondering how much he should say. "That it does. Though it's an unusual situation. The thing I'm riding towards won't be there forever. If I'm slow, I'll miss it. But I've lived most of my life just travelling, and there ain't nothing wrong with it. Happiness ain't at the end of the road; happiness *is* the road…"

"Said like a poet."

"It's a profession I've had in my time. Along with many others."

"And what are you now?"

"Hungry. Let's get that fire lit."

*　　*　　*

THE COMPANY HE had been expecting arrived just as the pan of beans began to bubble.

He heard them long before me, my attention fixed as it was on that popping, spitting stew. After days on the road with only my own cooking skills to count on (of which I had none), the idea of a stew that might not need to be snapped into bite-sized pieces was appealing.

"They're here," he said, standing bolt upright and moving out of the light of the fire with a speed that didn't match his years.

Night had fallen, and he vanished a couple of feet from our camp. I pictured him taking up a position in the shadows, watching as they drew closer, maybe fixing them in his sights.

Which made me the lure, of course, and sat there in the fire's glow I found myself working up a sweat that was nothing to do with how close I'd gotten to the flames. Might they shoot me from a distance? Gun me down, meaning to steal our horses (well, *his* horse; they surely wouldn't even consider my mule worthy for meat, let alone riding). My only hope was that they must know I hadn't been riding alone, and you wouldn't shoot until you had both targets in sight. Would you?

"Hello, there!" came a shout from a short way off. "Would you have room for a couple more around that fire? We've a little food and whisky to share, if you're willing."

The voice had a slight Irish tinge to it which put me in mind of a man I'd known back home. A mindless ass by the name of Duggan who had offered shoe shine outside the prayer house on a Sunday. Of course, he'd turned out not to be so mindless after all, when he made off with the contents of the Eastern Savings bank. According to the papers afterwards, he hadn't been Irish, either. You never can take a fellow on trust.

"Come on over," I said, knowing that my companion wouldn't want the company, but unable to think of a polite way of saying so. I guessed if he was that opposed to breaking bread with fellow travellers, he could shoot them dead or stay out there in the dark until morning.

"Much obliged," the Irishman said. "We've been on our own for near a week and if I have to listen to Willie's conversation one more night, I'm likely to cut his throat with my pocket knife."

They appeared within the light of the fire and I relaxed a little. They were not a threatening pair.

"The name's Thomas," said the Irishman, holding out a fat hand for shaking. He was a big man, but in all the wrong ways. His gut shook along with our hands, pressed against the cotton of a light blue shirt that had seen almost as many hot meals as its owner. He was balding, but for a pair of light grey wisps that rose, like cattle horns, towards the night sky.

Willie was a black man, long grey beard and a tailcoat that made him look like he was from the circus.

"You'll have guessed I go by Willie," he said, shaking my hand.

"Elwyn," I replied, "travelling to California."

"On your own?" Thomas asked, noticing the two animals we had tied up.

"No," said the old man, looming into the light of the fire, "but I wanted to keep an eye on you for a little while, make sure you weren't something I had to worry myself about."

"Can't be too careful, I guess," said Thomas, moving to offer his hand before the heat of the fire had him snatch it right back.

"That's right," the old man agreed, nodding to them both. "That said, sit down and let's eat."

I noted that neither Thomas or Willie asked the old

man his name either. They offered their own, like any civil man would, and when his wasn't offered by return they simply carried on regardless. Maybe they hadn't even noticed. Maybe they were so put off by his attitude that they didn't like to inquire any further. Whatever the truth of it, we sat down and he set to stirring the stew one last time.

"Like I said"—Thomas began rummaging in his satchel—"we have some meat to add to the pot, if you've a mind."

"Never eat it," he replied, which seemed to strike Thomas as mighty strange.

"It's beef," he said, as if that might make the difference.

"I don't care if it's unicorn," he replied. "Beans are all I need. You got a plate?"

This question wrong-footed Thomas terribly, more because he was confused already than because he didn't know where his plate was.

Willie passed his over. "Just beans is fine by me, I've been trying to shit his dried beef out for the last five days, figure my ass could do with the break."

"You didn't complain when it was going down," Thomas replied sulkily.

Willie shrugged. "It tastes fine once you've broken it down some, but, you ask me, the spirit of the cow lives on in it. It fights back every morning."

"You sound like a goddamn Comanche."

"Too dark for an Injun, you blind fool."

They both laughed at that. I figured it was one of those jokes that built up between people on the road.

"The soul doesn't stay in the meat," the old man said. "Not unless you kill something just right."

Which put an end to polite conversation for a while.

We all focused on our beans, Thomas dropping chunks of his dried beef into it and to hell with Willie's comments. They looked like pieces of wood: as hard as oak and half as tasty. Thomas ate enough of them, though.

Willie lost half of his in his beard. The damn thing looked like a bloodied scalp by the time he was done, great streaks of dark red matting the grey hair.

They were good beans, I'll give the old man that. Spicy. I had no doubt I'd have cause to regret as much as the night wound on.

"So," said Thomas, not one to give up on conversation for long. "Where are you headed?"

I looked towards the old man, but he didn't seem to plan on replying. He had finished his food and was rolling himself a smoke.

"I'm heading to California," I told them. "Been offered a job in my cousin's bank."

"It must be one hell of a job to be worth the miles."

I shrugged. "I fancied a change anyway. He's heading for a town called Wormwood."

"Can't say as I've heard of it," admitted Thomas.

"I have," said Willie. "Well, no... it can't be the same place; the town I heard about was just a story."

"Stories are good!" said Thomas. "Food's been ate, time for drinking and stories." He rummaged around in his satchel and pulled out a bottle. This boy was a regular grocer on the trail.

Willie shrugged. "Don't mind tellin' it, though it'll take me a minute to get it straight in my head. Been some years since I heard it."

"And if that ain't an excuse for first go on my whisky I don't know what it is," said Thomas with a smile, offering his friend the bottle. Willie didn't argue, just took a mouthful and looked contemplative. He offered me the bottle, but I shook my head.

"I don't drink," I explained.

"No meat, no drink... Willie, my boy, I think we've found ourselves a pair of monks!"

"I didn't say nothing about not drinking," the old man said, holding his tin mug out rather than just taking a swig. "That doesn't kill anything except yourself."

"Well, that's the way to get the party spirit going," laughed Thomas, pouring the old man a good sized measure and then taking a mouthful from the bottle himself.

"Wormwood," said Willie. "This is how I remember it..."

"I DON'T KNOW how much faith you should put in this. I heard it from an old sideshow performer called Alonzo, and he always was one for drink and lies. The more of one he had, the more the other came out of his mouth. Still, it was a good story and that's all that really matters.

"He told me that Wormwood doesn't really exist. It's a dream of a town. A ghost. Not like the godforsaken wastes of wood and sand you see now, towns that ran out of people and money before the last board was nailed. Nobody abandoned Wormwood. It just ain't quite part of the world.

"It's had lots of different names. Appeared in lots of different places. Once it was a bunch of huts in Tibet. Then a tribal gathering in Africa—and you can shut your goddamned mouth, Thomas, I ain't never set foot there, my skin may be black but I was born in Texas, as well you know. Wherever it appears, it's a small place, empty and as a solid as a dream. It appears for a day then it's gone. Every hundred years, so Alonzo said. Lots of people have heard of it. Lots of people want to find it, because Wormwood is more than just a town. The buildings are just a disguise, something it wears so it

fits in. What Wormwood really is a doorway. Right at
its heart there's a place where you can step through and
walk right into Heaven.

"Yeah, well, bullshit that might be, but that's the story
and stories are always built of bullshit.

"They say you can walk right into Heaven, take a look
around and then walk back out again. No need to die
first. Though, hell, if you could really walk into paradise,
who would come back? And maybe that's what happens,
because there ain't nobody who has ever been there and
returned.

"Yeah, Thomas, most likely it *is* because it's a crock of
shit. Keep that fat mouth of yours closed.

"Thing is, while there ain't none who have been there
and come back, there are plenty of folks who say they've
seen the town itself. Not only that, but they've seen some
of the crazy shit that's come out of it. You don't just dump
a door to the afterlife in the middle of the world and think
that nothing's going to leak. They say that Wormwood
infects everywhere around it. They say that the world
goes mad just to have such a thing in it. People say they've
seen people they know to be dead, creatures that ain't
never been alive, fires that burn and burn and there ain't
no way of putting them out. Things just go wild the closer
you get to Wormwood."

THAT'S AS CLOSE as I remember it. And of course, like
Thomas, I thought it was a crock of shit at the time. It
was only later, once I'd seen Wormwood for myself, that I
knew the story didn't exaggerate. The opposite, in fact: it
didn't come close to the truth. Wormwood was a hell of a
lot wilder than anyone could begin to guess at.

"That the place you're looking for?" Thomas asked the
old man with a laugh.

"I look like someone who would go chasing fairy stories?" he replied. He got up from the fire, drained his whisky and tossed the cup back into his pack. "I'm going to get some sleep."

I took that to be a sign that he had no more interest in conversation. Not that he had really taken part in the first place.

"Well," said Willie, "that's what I heard. Ain't saying I believe it."

"Where are you two going?" I asked, wanting to take the conversation away from my travelling companion and where he might or might not be heading.

"Bought ourselves a ranch in Nevada," said Thomas. "I ain't one for riding, but I know a good horse when I sell one."

"And I can climb on one without breaking its back," said Willie. "We make the perfect team."

"I guess you do at that," I agreed.

We talked for a little longer, Thomas only too happy to tell stories wilder and less believable than the one he'd sneered at from Willie. Most of them came from his time fighting for the North in the war. He painted himself as every hero you ever imagined. I took it all with a few grains of salt. Rightly so, as it happened, Willie telling me the truth while Thomas took a piss break.

"Damn fool makes it all up," he said, "to cover the fact that he marched with the South. He thinks I'll shoot him in his bed if I figure it out. Like I care; what's done is done."

Eventually we all decided to turn in.

I WOKE TO noises in the night.

As a rule I'm a heavy sleeper, but the last couple of days must have got to me because, as hard as they tried to stay quiet, Thomas and Willie woke me as easily as had they started banging on the cooking pot.

"I'm telling you that's what I saw!" This was Thomas, panicking, though he was fighting to keep his voice to a whisper. "It was glowing!"

"Sounds like the drink to me," Willie replied.

"Like I give a damn what you think."

"You were dreaming."

"We're getting out of here. Just shut your mouth and grab your pack."

Willie sighed, but I heard them picking up their things and then the sound of their boots as they ran away from the fire and into the darkness.

I sat up, looking over to the old man. He must be awake; if I'd heard them, there was no way he'd slept through it.

"Let them go," he whispered, "and go back to sleep."

And, like a child at the sound of his father's voice, that's exactly what I did.

CHAPTER THREE
RUN, MAN, RUN!

IT WAS MORNING soon enough, and I unpacked my aching bones from where they'd spilled over the bumpy ground and tried to fit them back together. I will never understand those men who were able to spend their lives sleeping in the open. The dirt ground is there for one reason and one reason only: to be walked across in search of a bed or chair.

Naturally my companion showed no ill signs of the night; he was impervious to everything.

"Coffee?" he asked, having stoked enough life back into the fire to get some water on the boil.

"Absolutely."

I could only imagine how this man made his coffee: aggressive, surly and likely to kick me in the stomach. After the night I'd had, that sounded just about right.

I wasn't disappointed. The black soup I set my lips to a few minutes later was assertive enough it almost counted as a third person sat around the fire.

"What scared them last night?" I asked, deciding that it was a subject best faced head on.

"Who knows?" he replied, as evasive as ever. "They weren't men used to the open trail. I don't imagine it took much to have them running."

"I heard Thomas say that something was glowing."

He shrugged, drained his coffee and began to kick dust into the fire.

IN A FEW more minutes, we were back on our mounts and heading further into the rocky pass.

My mule seemed improved from its night's sleep, moving along the narrow trail with more confidence than ever before. Maybe my companion had slipped it some of the coffee.

While we were close together I decided I would finally ask his name, but, no matter how hard I tried, the words just wouldn't come out. No doubt that sounds foolish to you, but I'm telling it like it is. It wasn't that I didn't dare to ask—though I admit I was still in awe of the man—it was just that I couldn't make the question form in my mouth. I would imagine the question in my head, open my mouth and end up exhaling nothing but air.

When I was growing up, there had been a woman by the name of Hawthorne, who lived a short distance away. She had worked as a nurse, making up medicines and handling the sort of bumps and scrapes that were beneath the attention of the doctor, an angry little Swede called Skarrsen. Skarrsen acted like every single ailment was an insult, one of those medical men who responded to enquiries with a mixture of fury and despair, as if every patient was there to spite him. It got so Mrs Hawthorne took most of his business.

She had problems of her own, however. Around her throat was a livid, pink scar. People were full of stories as to how she got it, some saying she'd fallen foul of a hangman's noose, escaping before the rope choked her off for good. Others suggested Indians—the root of all evil in those days—had set upon her during her youth and slit open her throat.

The rumours grew and Mrs Hawthorne would never set them right, because whatever the cause, the result had struck her dumb. She communicated with a combination of mime and written notes, the only sound she could make being a dry cough. That cough would bubble up out of her when she got frustrated, either through the ignorance of her patients or irritation at wanting to make herself understood and failing. When the anger settled on her, she would shake slightly, her skin reddening, open her mouth and issue that short cough. A woman desperate to force a word out, but left without the tools to do so.

That's what it felt like.

In the end I stopped trying and rode in silence, scared at what it was that robbed me of my voice.

MID-MORNING BROUGHT US an open canyon and a view that seemed to offer up the whole of Colorado.

"What a sight," I said, speaking for the first time in a couple of hours.

The old man wasn't as impressed, more concerned with the route directly ahead than the landscape.

"The going's steep," he said, jumping off his horse and gazing down over the edge of the trail. "There's just room if we go single file."

He scratched at his face, his eyes working their way along the route and anticipating dangers. "Your mule is about to come into its own," he said. "Slow and steady will be the way."

"Slow and steady we can do," I agreed, patting said mule's head.

He climbed back in the saddle and began to make his way down into the canyon.

He hadn't exaggerated the width of the track. My left shoulder brushed against the stone walls and my right hand dangled over nothing but air. Sometimes I had to lie flat against the mule's back, ducking beneath jagged outcrops that stabbed out over the trail. It seemed to me that there had to be a better way to continue on our planned route.

My mule had the advantage, the old man had been right about that. The extra height of my companion on his horse caused him problems. Eventually, he was forced to slide off the back of the animal and push it ahead of him.

After twenty minutes or so, the path widened briefly and he suggested we both dismount and continue on foot, leading our animals behind us.

"They're going to find the next stretch hard enough without having our weight to bear too," he explained. "It's only a mile or so; the walk will do us no harm."

I agreed readily enough. I'd been so tense on the back of the mule that my thighs were shaking from where I had been gripping it so tightly.

He continued to lead as the trail dropped to an even steeper angle, boots and hooves frequently skidding in the loose grit of the narrow path.

I looked over the edge and felt that welcome coffee threaten to return for a spell as the scale of the drop sank in.

"Next time we come upon something like this," I said, "we go round."

"No journey worth making is ever easy," he replied. "We'd have lost an extra day or so if we'd tried to go round, and that's time I can't spare."

I had been avoiding the subject of Wormwood after Willie's story of the night before. It was obvious the old man had no interest in talking about it—like everything else—but my curiosity was too big to ignore.

"The town you're heading for," I said, "it's the same Wormwood Willie was talking about, isn't it? A place that only exists for a short time."

"It is."

"And does it really contain the doorway to Heaven?"

"I'm not sure Heaven is really the name for the place that stands on the other side of it."

"So what is the name?"

"It has so many," he sighed, obviously wishing the subject would just go away, but aware that, having chosen company for the journey, it couldn't be avoided forever. "It's the world that comes after."

"After you die?"

"For some people."

It was like digging for water in the desert.

"You called it home."

"I did."

"So... what? That's where you grew up?"

At that moment, he paused and held up his hand. At the time I thought he was just trying to avoid any more talk, but as I came up close, I looked over his shoulder and saw what lay ahead.

The trail was turning in towards the canyon, giving us a view of the way ahead before it wound back against the outcrop and vanished again from view. Just a few feet away, something was obstructing the path; it took me a little time to figure what it was. It looked like a bonfire, a pile of white branches gleaming in the sun. The branches had strips of something wet and glistening hanging from them, thin red banners like skinned snakes.

"I guess our dinner guests didn't get far," the old man said. That was what it took for me to puzzle out the obstruction: the two men and their horses, all folded in together, the meat from their bones tugged away until all that was left of them was a jumble of bone and skin.

"What happened to them?" I asked. "Did they fall?"

"No," he replied, moving closer. "Something attacked them."

"Something?" I looked around, suddenly terrified.

The old man stooped down to examine the pile of bones. I did my best to see past the back of his horse, but the trail was too narrow for me to get a clear look.

"Something stripped the meat from them," he said.

He stood up and began kicking at the pile, sending the remains toppling over the edge of the trail to fall down into the canyon itself.

"You can't just do that!" I shouted.

He turned to me, a stern gaze in those ancient eyes of his. "Keep your voice down," he said. "We don't want to attract whatever it was that did this."

He turned back to the bones and carried on clearing them. "We need to get past, and quickly. It ain't doing them no favours to leave their remains where they are. They're gone. The fate of their bones don't matter."

I watched as he kicked a skull out into the air, a ragged pink and white ball dragging a long beard behind it. Willie's head.

Once the way was clear, he continued to walk, moving quicker now.

"We need to be faster," he said, his voice quiet and controlled. "Stuck here we're at a disadvantage. Whatever attacked them could strike at any minute, and we haven't room to fight."

As if I hadn't been terrified enough.

The mule fought my attempts to drag it along the track; it knew its own pace, one foot placed carefully after another. At one point it drew to a halt, determined to stop my yanking on its reins.

"Come on!" I told it, trying to coax where brute force had failed. "It's in your own best interests, you dumb ass!"

Eventually it began to move again, the old man now several feet ahead. I watched him turn around the next outcrop and vanish from sight. The idea that I was now alone was even more terrifying and I broke into a slow run.

That was nearly the death of me, when my feet slipped in the loose rock. I dropped to my knees, one leg slipping out over the edge of the canyon, my hands scratching at the dirt so I could get a grip and keep myself on the trail.

It was the mule that helped, yanking back on the reins I still held in one hand and giving me enough of a lift to regain my balance and get back to my feet.

"I owe you," I told it, patting it on the head again before continuing on our way, more carefully than before.

I worked my way around the outcrop, and once more the old man was in sight. Even better, I could see that the narrow trail we were on began to widen about half a mile ahead, turning into a dirt track more than big enough to let us ride again.

"Nearly there!" I shouted and the old man turned to stare at me, a look of real anger on his face. He held his finger to his lips and I remembered what he had said about keeping quiet. In my relief I had clean forgotten about it.

"Sorry," I whispered, so quiet now I doubted he heard me.

It was clear that he heard *something*, mind, his head cocking to one side like a raven's.

It took me a few moments to catch the noise myself, a low ticking sound like that of a pocket-watch. It got louder, and the old man waved at me to keep moving, turning back to the trail and breaking into a run, pulling his horse behind him.

Wary of how close I had just come to tipping myself over the edge, I tried to match his pace. To my relief, the mule didn't fight me this time. Perhaps it was aware that something was heading towards us, its animal senses more finely tuned than mine.

I fought the urge to look over my shoulder. Desperate as I was to know what might be bearing down on us, it took all of my concentration on the trail ahead to ensure I didn't miss my footing.

The ticking noise was getting louder and louder.

"Move!" the old man shouted, having nearly reached the point where the pass widened. "They're nearly on top of you!"

They? I just couldn't help it. I had to see what it was. I turned slightly and it seemed as if the entire wall of the canyon was on the move, great waves of creatures charging towards us. My feet skidded and I snapped my eyes back forward, head filled with childhood memories of ant hills. We had one out back of the house one summer and it terrified me (naturally). A volcano of vicious, biting insects. Ma had poured steaming hot water into it, thinking that would make me feel better. It didn't. For weeks I dreamed of those hundreds of insects, washed around the banks of their nest, some still wriggling as they boiled in their own shells. The fuckers were back to haunt me.

The old man had reached the wider trail, mounting his horse and turning to watch me as I ran the last few steps.

"Quickly, damn you!" he shouted. "Or you'll be the death of both of us."

No need to blame me, I thought, nobody's stopping you riding off as soon as you like.

There was a sudden loud clacking noise from right by my head and I saw one of the insects, a fat beetle the size of my forearm, its carapace glistening like oil. Its mouth parts clashed together and I now understood the cause of the clicking sound.

A gunshot rang out and the evil-looking bastard exploded in a cloud of shell and ichor the colour of rotten apple flesh.

I saw the old man shifting his aim and firing again and again over my shoulder as I finally reached the wider stretch and climbed on the back of my mule.

There's no way the damn thing will run fast enough, I thought; I was probably quicker on my feet.

Then one of the beetles leapt on the animal's ass. It bucked, kicked, and began to sprint down the path at a speed I suspect it had not known since its youth, many centuries ago. It was all I could do to hang on as we bolted down the track, the old man just ahead of us. He held up his gun, shook the spent shells from it and reloaded. I'd seen the sheer number of these things. If he thought we were going to shoot our way out of the situation he'd lost his mind.

My thoughts on the matter became more focused as a loud clicking set up just behind my head and I felt sharp legs poke into my ribs. One of the things had jumped me.

"Fall forward!" the old man shouted, and I did so without even thinking, only realising as I pressed my face into the mule's hair that he planned on shooting it.

The gunshot rang out and I screamed as the bug dug in with its pointed feet. There was a cool splash of its guts on the back of my neck and I tried not to throw up over my poor, terrified ride.

"It's dead," he shouted.

"It's still holding on!"

"That's as may be, but it has no head. It's beyond doing you any harm, boy."

I sat back up and tried to shrug the thing off, but it seemed to have securely latched on, its feet wedged into the material of my jacket (and no little amount of my skin).

We continued to ride, the old man naturally pulling away, however hard my mule tried to match them.

The clicking remained constant. Every moment I expected to feel another of the creatures leap on me.

Then, as we turned out of the canyon and continued on towards open ground, the noise grew softer. It faded away until, eventually, all we could hear was the sound of our own hoofbeats.

The old man stopped and turned, gazing back towards the canyon.

He held up his hand. "You can stop, boy," he said. "They ain't following."

I did so, that poor ancient mule of mine actually sinking to the ground in exhaustion. I clambered off and looked back the way we had come.

"Seems they don't leave the canyon," he said. "I guess that's their territory."

"They're welcome to it." I began fighting to shed the remains of the bug off my back. In the end, I had to pull off my jacket and throw the lot to the ground. I touched the back of my neck, still thick with the insect's guts.

"Look at the thing," I said, prodding at it with my foot. "Did you ever see the like?"

He dismounted and walked over, stooping down and unhooking the remains from my jacket. He handed the jacket back, though I was in no mood to wear it, and examined what was left of the creature.

"It ain't natural," he said, "something this big."

"Damn right," I agreed. I may not know much about nature and the like, but I am fully aware beetles don't come the size of dogs.

"We're going to see more of this sort of thing," he explained, getting up from his examination. "The closer we get to Wormwood, the more nature takes a pounding."

"Then I guess it's time I carried on towards my nice safe job," I told him. "If this is the sort of thing I can expect in Wormwood, I sure as hell don't want to go there."

He fixed me with a stare at that, as stern and disapproving as a church statue. "Boy," he said, "what makes you think you've got a choice?"

CHAPTER FOUR
FIND A PLACE TO DIE

NOW, I'LL ADMIT, I hadn't seen that one coming. I'd wondered whether he'd truly wanted my company on the road, given how damned uncommunicative and secretive he'd been. Now it seemed that there was a reason, and one important enough that he wouldn't let me leave.

"And what's to stop me just riding off?" I asked, my anger giving me a little steel.

"You'd be lost within the hour," he said, "and likely dead within a couple of days."

"I managed to get along just fine before I met you," I insisted.

"That's as may be, but you're on the trail to Wormwood now. It's marked you. It knows you're coming."

"To hell with that!" I shouted. Weeks of frustration on the road flooded out. "I ain't even going to Wormwood! If the place even exists... which I doubt. I'm heading to California, remember? To take up a good job in a nice town, miles away from giant beetles and mad bastards like you."

"Said like a man who's never been to California," he replied, and for the first time he actually split his face into a half-smile. "But that's not where you're going. Your road ends at Wormwood, it always did."

"We'll just see about that!" I turned my mule and tapped at its sides with my heels. The damn thing refused to move. "Get going, you lousy ass!" I shouted, hot with anger now. The mule wouldn't take a single step.

"See?" said the old man. "He knows." He shook his reins and began to continue on the way we had been riding. "Come on," he said, and, damn the rebellious bastard, that mule turned and followed.

I tugged and kicked, but it paid me no heed whatsoever, trailing behind the old man as if it was the most natural thing in the world.

I hated that mule.

I wondered how far I would get if I just jumped off the thing and walked away. We had been following the route I had planned to take before we cut through the canyon, but now I wasn't sure where we were. Maybe with my map, I could get back on track. I reached down and pulled the map from my saddle bag, holding it carefully in case he turned around and guessed what I was doing, not that he would have cared.

We were miles from any town. I could end up walking for days out here and never find my way. Besides, without my mule, how far would I get? I didn't have the money to buy another, and I could hardly walk all the way to the coast. But if I stayed with the old man, I wouldn't get to the coast anyway.

I tucked the map away again. I felt desperate. I wished I'd never met the crazy idiot (conveniently forgetting that if I hadn't, I would have died back in Haskell). Most of all, right then, I wished I'd never left home.

He kept far enough ahead that I couldn't talk to him.

The pair of us trotted along in silence. I figured we'd stop for lunch, but he just kept on riding. The sun rose to the middle of the sky and then began to sink down again. I ate a little dried meat as I rode; whatever my problems, they didn't stop me being hungry.

As the afternoon stretched on, the rocky landscape began to flatten and I could see a small town in the distance. I started to question my map. There certainly hadn't been a town marked on it there.

As we drew closer, a plan began to grow in my mind. If I could convince someone there to help me, tell them that the old man was forcing me to ride with him at gunpoint... I bet I could shake him loose there. I still didn't know the first thing about him, but it was obvious he was wary of company. Maybe he had a history with the law. If I could call on the town's sheriff, I was sure the old man would soon be a cloud of dust on the horizon. The idea made me feel better.

We were maybe a mile away when he stopped his horse. The sky was getting darker, and it seemed obvious to me that we would spend the night in the town. Why camp out under the stars if you didn't have to?

He stared at the town, watching tiny figures move around its streets. I wondered if one of them was the sheriff.

"No," he said, turning his horse away. "That place ain't right, we'll ride on by."

"What do you mean, it ain't right?" I asked, furious at the thought that my plan was crumbling around me. He must have guessed what I'd planned to do.

"Just that," he replied. "I can sense it from here. That's no natural town."

That said, he picked up the pace and began to ride off at an angle, skirting it by a mile or so.

The mule trailed on like before and I followed the town

with my eyes, trying to decide what to do. If I made a run for it, would he just chase me down before I got there? It seemed more than likely.

Night was beginning to fall and we would camp soon. If I stuck with him, waited for him to go to sleep and then made a break for it, I might just get there before he noticed I was gone.

By the time we stopped we were probably five miles or so past the place: no great journey, even in the dark. My plan of action decided, I didn't kick up a fuss as we prepared a fire. I'd be away from him soon enough.

That didn't mean I didn't want the answers to some of my questions, though.

"You talk about Wormwood as if it's alive," I said. "Saying it knows I'm coming."

"I don't know as I'd call it *alive*, exactly," he replied, working over the stew, "but it knows, right enough."

"That don't even *begin* to make sense."

"Only because you don't know about the place. You'll learn."

We'd see about that, I thought.

"Why's it so all-fired important I go there anyway?"

He thought about that for a moment. "I don't know," he admitted, "but it's what you're supposed to do."

"That don't make sense either."

"We live in a world of choice," he said. "The Almighty was good enough to give His creations that. Still, there are times when a thing just must be done. Lines converge, destinies are created and fulfilled. You're meant to go to Wormwood; probably were from the moment you were born."

"You know how crazy you sound when you talk like that?"

"You mistake me for someone who cares. Never live your life worrying about what others think of you."

He tapped his head. "Worry about what you think of yourself."

"You're a regular philosopher."

"Just old. You don't get to my age without learning the important things."

I had nothing to say to that. I was so desperate to be out of the man's company that I had ceased to care what he thought or said. He was mad, that much I had decided. All I had to do was get through the evening alive, and then I'd be on my way.

We ate in silence. The night dragged on as he sat and looked at the stars. We both smoked. The fire crackled. When would the bastard just go to sleep?

"Time to turn in," he said finally. "Tomorrow always brings another long road."

Only for you, I thought.

He stared at me for a moment and I suddenly had the weirdest impression that he was reading my mind, looking right in there with those old, pale eyes of his. It scared the hell out of me.

"'Night, then," I said, turning away from him and bundling myself up in my blanket.

I lay there for a couple of hours, occasionally checking the time on my pocket watch in the fading glow of the fire. I listened out, hoping for the sound of snoring, something that would show he was asleep. Every now and then I thought about turning over and looking at him, but the idea terrified me. I imagined he would be looking right back at me, those piercing eyes of his staring right inside me.

Eventually I couldn't help myself. I had to know if he was asleep or not.

I moved as quietly as I could, lifting my blanket and turning as slowly as possible.

He was facing away from me. I couldn't decide if this

was a good thing or not. On the one hand, he couldn't see me as I carefully got to my feet; on the other, I couldn't tell if he was asleep or not.

I could stand there all night wondering about it. The only thing to do was try.

I had left my pack on the mule. I figured I'd lead the animal away a short distance and then climb on. Assuming the stupid thing would move at all.

I walked around the fire, careful to try and avoid casting a shadow across where the old man lay. If he did have his eyes open, I didn't want to make it too obvious I was moving around.

The mule was tethered to a tree a few feet away. I would have tied it up further off, but I didn't want to cause suspicion.

I stroked its head, mentally begging it not to make a noise as I untied the reins.

I turned to check on the old man, and it was all I could do not to shout out in panic.

'*It was glowing!*' That's what Thomas had said only the night before, explaining to his friend what it was that had so scared him he refused to stay in the camp a minute longer. *It was glowing.*

The old man's mouth was open and light poured from it, light that was the same flickering hue as the flames behind him. It was as if someone had set a fire in his throat.

At that moment, his eyes opened and they were on fire too. To hell with the mule; I turned and ran, panicked, into the darkness.

At that point I wasn't even aware of direction. I just wanted to put as much space as I could between myself and the demon I had been sharing the trail with.

"Come back," I heard him whisper, and even though I knew it was coming from some distance behind me, it was as if he was whispering right over my shoulder. "Come back and I'll explain."

Explanations could just go and fuck themselves, I decided. All this time I had been travelling with something as inhuman and monstrous as those giant beetles.

He would be on my trail, I decided. There was no way he would just lie there. Now I was away from the fire, my eyes were adjusting to the moonlight. I moved between the cover of trees, wishing for the rocky terrain of yesterday. Once I had put a bit of distance between us, I hid behind the thick trunk of an acacia and tried to spot him. There! I must have got just enough of a head start; he was some way away, scanning the horizon, trying to see which way I had run.

I waited until his back was turned and then ran again, aiming for a line of bushes dead ahead. If I could keep the cover between us, I stood a chance of getting away, though I had no doubt he'd probably spend the night hunting for me if he had to.

At the bushes I stopped again and turned to look for him. There was no sign at all, and I could only hope he had headed off in the wrong direction. I took a minute to try and get a sense of my bearings. Which way was the town from here? It was no good. In my panic I'd got myself all turned around.

A few hundred yards away stood another large acacia. If I climbed up it, I should be able to see where I was, and it would also make a good hiding place.

Checking around again first, just in case the wily bastard had been sneaking up on me, I made a run for the tree. During those long moments in the open I kept expecting him to appear, that ancient body pounding through the dust towards me, mouth and eyes on fire. Those eyes had seemed terrifying enough when they had appeared human, boring into me like drill bits. What would he do when he caught up with me? I imagined him lowering that blazing mouth towards me. One laugh and my face would be a blackened mask of burned meat and crisp bone. Hadn't he said that he'd come from Wormwood? The more I thought about this mythical town, the more I began to believe in it. In the last day, I had seen giant bugs and a man with fire burning inside of him. My sense of what was impossible or not had taken a pounding. Either that or someone had been spiking the beans and I was out of my head.

A few weeks ago, I had seen a guy in Illinois running around the street screaming at demons. A shopkeeper had told me they'd all just got used to it. 'Smokes some weird Injun shit,' he had said. 'At his best he's fighting thin air, and at his worst he's face down in the dirt smelling of his own kaka.'

It might explain things, but I knew in my gut that what I had seen wasn't a hallucination. If I'd been given a dose of something, *everything* would have seemed weird. The tree I was climbing was solid, there was an ache in my ass from spending so long on the mule, I had a badly-timed need to piss. These were real, earthy sensations. Life was as solid as it had ever been; it just had some weird shit in it that I couldn't even begin to explain.

I was never one to climb trees as a kid (of course not, I would always be put off by imagining the split head caused by falling out of one), but I scaled that acacia easily enough. Fear puts a spring in your step.

I lodged myself as high as I dared, the branches above me looking too thin to support my weight. Lying back against the trunk, I was covered by the leaves enough that I figured I was as hidden as I could hope for. I tried to get comfortable, not wanting to thrash around too much and give away my position.

From up there, I could see the old man. If he even *was*

a man, which I was beginning to doubt. I mean, Christ, I didn't know his name and now I didn't even know what kind of creature he was. He was walking in a wide circle around the camp, staring out into the darkness trying to catch a sight of me. The moon wasn't full, but it was big enough to turn the world into a photograph, a world made of thick blacks, washed-out whites and bland greys.

He clearly hadn't seen me get this far, which was a relief. Hiding up a tree was one thing, being cornered up one something else.

His face must have returned to normal. He was climbing up a ridge some distance away, nothing but a black outline, moving against the stars.

I tried to relax. I was going to be stuck up that tree for some time, and I'd like not to be crippled by the time I climbed back down.

He began to walk towards me, and for a moment I thought he must have seen me. Maybe those eyes of his worked better in the dark than mine. Maybe he could smell me. Who knows?

Then I heard him talking, and I realised he was just working his way around, hoping I would hear him.

"I ain't a danger to you, son," he said. "I know it must seem that way, but I'm not. I understand you got scared. I know all of this seems too much. But sometimes a man has to face his destiny head on, and yours is by my side, taking the walk to Wormwood. Wherever you go, however far you run, you'll always end up back on that path. And you don't want to walk it alone, believe me. I can't promise I'll keep you safe, but I sure will try, and that's the best offer a man can get in this world. So why don't you come out and we can talk about it?"

It was the most I'd ever heard him say. Part of me wanted nothing more than to believe it, too. He had saved my life a couple of times, hadn't he? Why would he do that if he meant to harm me? But I did not climb down.

He passed right beneath me, still talking, repeating the same kind of words, coaxing talk like you'd give to a child.

"Fearing the unknown is pointless," he insisted. "There's enough to be scared of in this world without being frightened of something that may never come to pass. Or something that ain't what it appears to be. Let go of it, boy. Come out here and we can go on together..."

He moved away and I stopped listening, his words eventually lost in the faint wind that had begun to blow.

Once he was out of sight again, I shifted a little, trying to see if I could spot the town. Either it was further away than I thought or they had no lights burning, because there was nothing but open land and shadow. I'd have to stay up here until first light; hopefully then I'd be able to find my way.

Finally the urge to piss got so it was more than I could bear. There was still no sign of him, so I unbuttoned myself and let go of my bladder, the stream worryingly loud as it rained down on the dirt below. Once done, I was a lot more comfortable and I managed to wedge myself tightly enough I was able to close my eyes and nod off a little. The fear had kept me awake that long, but it had been a long day and night and my head wanted to close up for a while.

I woke to daylight. I checked my watch. A quarter of eight.

I looked around for the old man, but there was no sign of him. More importantly, the town was now clear, over to my left. It was closer than I imagined. If only I could have seen it the night before, I could have run there in less than half an hour and saved myself a night up a tree.

As my wise old mother had used to say: 'If wishes were horses, we'd all be buried in horse-shit.'

I checked again for the old man. I couldn't see the camp, but I hoped he might have moved on anyway. Having not found me, he must have guessed that I was long gone.

I climbed down and began to run towards the town. I did my best to stick to cover where there was some, constantly checking all around me in case the old man had been lying in wait.

There was no sign of him and I was soon at the edge of the town.

'Wentworth Falls,' a sign announced, hanging neatly from a wooden frame. 'Population 403.' Underneath someone had added an extra note: 'No outlaws, gunmen or sporting ladies.'

Maybe that was why he hadn't wanted to stop here the day before. If those eyes of his had been able to read the sign at a distance, he would have known that he fit two of the criteria for being unwelcome. Personally, I decided he could keep Wormwood. Wentworth Falls sounded like my kind of heaven.

I walked under the sign and down the main street. You would have thought that out of four hundred and three law-abiding men and women, I'd have heard at least one of them, but the place was utterly silent. The buildings were in good order. In fact, the town was one of the nicest I'd seen on my journey. Everything was fresh and brightly painted, the timbered homes showing no sign of wear. It was as if everything had only just been built, made as pretty as a picture book, and then nobody turned up.

I figured it was late enough that there had to be some people up and about, so I began to shout as I walked along. "Hello?" I called. "Anyone around?"

To my left was a general store. Its sign claimed it to be

the property of James Hodgkins, and that it offered The Best Prices in the State.

That might be true, but it seemed to me that Hodgkins had slept late, as the doors were firmly closed.

I climbed up onto the boardwalk and peered through the window. It was too dark to see a thing.

I knocked on the door, in case the owner was inside. "Hello?"

There was no reply. Beneath my feet the boardwalk shifted slightly, and I had to lean on the closed doors to steady myself. Hodgkins may offer the best prices, I decided, but he should fix his damn planking before one of his customers broke their neck.

I stepped back down onto the street, walking on to a junction between a bank on one side and a dressmaker on the other. I looked both ways and felt a huge weight of relief when I could see someone standing on the boardwalk a little up to the left. I had begun to think the whole place must be empty.

"Hi, there!" I shouted, heading towards him. "Am I glad to finally see another face. I've had a couple of days like you wouldn't believe."

He had his back to me and I expected him to turn around as I was talking to him, but he just stood there, staring towards the far end of the street. Maybe he didn't realise I was addressing him, though there sure wasn't anyone else to talk to.

"Hey, feller," I called again, "could you help a man out?"

He was wearing a plaid shirt and loose grey flannels. A derby was pulled down low on his head.

Still he wouldn't turn to face me.

By now I was right behind him and all I had to do was reach out and touch his shoulder. It felt strangely cold and hard.

"Feller?" I asked.

Finally he turned to reveal a face of rough wood, the same heavy grain as the boardwalk we were stood on. There were small knots for his eyes and a larger one for his mouth, open in a lopsided 'O' that widened as he moved. He creaked like a fence in high wind, the wooden hole in his face groaning as it opened wide enough to let out a sharp, snapping noise like you'd get if you trod on a branch.

I took all this in in a matter of moments, so shocked at the sight of it that I hadn't even thought to be frightened of him. It was so unbelievable I just stared, my jaw dropping as wide as his.

He reached out an arm and the fingers were long carpenter's nails, slightly bent. They glistened a little in the sun. He was like a bad sculpture made from offcuts, an approximation of a man knocked up with saw, hammer and chisel.

My legs finally moved and I took a couple of steps back as those sharp, nail fingers flexed and tried to get a grip on me. That open mouth issued another loud snap and I turned to run, stumbled off the boardwalk and rolled into the dirt street.

Getting to my feet, I looked over my shoulder to see the pretend man was following slowly, his wooden legs bending and creaking as he shifted first one and then the other. If nothing else, I should be able to outrun the thing, whatever the hell it was.

I saw movement across the street. The dressmaker's doors burst open and another strange figure stepped out into the light. Swathed in gingham, it had wicker arms and legs and a face cut from a pane of glass. The glass flashed reflected sunlight into my eyes before it shifted slightly, tilting its head as if curious. There was a cracking sound and a pair of eyes appeared like bullet holes. Another and there was the sketch of a smile, a sharp crescent curving from one edge of the glass to another.

I ran around the corner. The boardwalk on either side of me was coming to life with a bunch of similar figures. There was a man made from stretched leather and straw, creaking and crunching his way towards me. Another was made entirely from bread, a hot wave of air from the baker's oven pushing him out onto the street. Yet another had been built from vegetables, leeks like bones, potatoes at the joints, a soft pumpkin head that oozed juice from its split smile. Finally, a lumbering giant with the belly of an oil drum clanged and boomed his way out of the General Store. His head was an oil lamp, burning with excited flame and smoke to see me.

I kept moving, desperate to get across the town line and out of the madness of Wentworth Falls. What had the old man said about the place? *That's no natural town.* It would seem he'd been right. I began to wish I had just listened to him. Of all the mad, freakish things to have walked into my life in the last couple of days he was the only one that seemed to have my best interests at heart.

As I got closer to the arched town sign, it suddenly flipped around to face me. *Wentworth Falls*, it said, but where before it had counted its population as 403 the numbers faded and then reappeared, as if being burned into the wood by an invisible finger. Now it said 404.

The town name vanished and new letters appeared. STAY, it said. I was not inclined to follow its advice, but the town wasn't in the mood for argument. The buildings on either side of the street suddenly splintered, breaking down into planks, glass and felt. It was as if the place had been hit by a hurricane, with time slowed to a point that you could watch the destruction stretch out in front of you.

The two buildings met in the middle, forming a barrier beneath the sign.

The word STAY vanished, to be replaced with the word FOREVER.

Not a natural town. No. Not a natural town at all.

I veered off to the left, running between a pair of buildings that groaned and shifted on either side. There was a shattering of glass and I ducked as one of the windows exploded out towards me. The glass shards rained into the wood on the other side of the street, any one of them sharp enough to cut me to the quick.

The narrow street opened out into a small square. At the centre of the square was a chapel, from which soft organ music was playing. I could take no comfort from it. The doors swung open and I was close enough to see inside. Lit by the red and blue beams of sunlight passing through the stained glass, I could see a mound of skeletons, piled high like a bonfire. I guessed I had found the remains of the previous four hundred and three visitors to Wentworth Falls.

The large double doors banged open and closed, like snapping jaws. The organ music got louder and louder, the notes distorting. I could imagine the metal pipes inflating and bulging as the air flowed through them, like a rat working its way down inside of a python.

I ran out of the square, only to find myself in the main street again. The boardwalk was rippling, its planks flapping up and down as if excited.

I ran in the opposite direction. The slow procession of pretend people followed me as I tried to get out of the other side of town.

Again there was the tantalising promise of open country ahead of me, but I knew what was going to happen before

I even got close. I was ten feet from the end of the street and again the buildings uprooted themselves and fell to block my path.

Across the flat planking more words appeared: WHY RUN? and, THERE'S NO PLACE LIKE HOME.

This was no home of mine, and though I could see no way of ever leaving it, I would collapse with exhaustion before I gave up trying.

Now I was running past the pretend townsfolk. They reached out their strangely-shaped arms, trying to grab hold of me. I felt fingers of broken glass scratch at my arm. A woman with a head carved from a brightly-painted shop sign coughed a shower of splinters at me as I ran past; they bristled on the side of my face like cactus spikes.

I turned off the main street again, once more aiming for the open. I was sure the blockade would be repeated again. What I hadn't counted for was to come face to face with someone else.

It was the old man, stood on the town line, his gun in his hand.

"Maybe next time," he said, as I fell at his feet, "you won't be such a dumb fool and you'll listen to my advice."

I was relieved to see him, which goes to show: all you need to embrace something that scares you is to find something that scares you more.

"I'm sorry," I said, "but you didn't seem to exactly have my best interests at heart."

"Shows what you know," he replied. "Now get behind me."

I did so gladly.

"What are you going to do against a whole town?" I asked. "I can't imagine shooting it is going to make much difference."

"That all depends on what I shoot," he replied, walking towards the gathering crowd. He raised his gun and took a single shot. There was the *clang* of metal and I saw the figure that had come from the General Store, the man made from an oil drum and a lamp.

The old man nodded gently to himself and then fired repeatedly.

I could see the holes appearing in the oil drum, thin spurts squirting out like blood from a wound.

The other figures were grabbing at the old man as he kept pushing forward, marching towards his target.

He holstered his gun and shoved his hand in his pocket.

I saw his hat fly off his head as someone swung for him, and then he vanished under a mob of them.

I could only imagine the damage they were doing. Those fingers of nails, those teeth of glass.

Then there was a soft explosion and the crowd erupted into flame.

The effect was instant, all of the figures dropping away, spiralling around in panic. At the centre I could see the old man, his body ablaze. The flames didn't seem to slow him down as he grabbed at the figures on either side of him, hurling them towards the boardwalk and the buildings. He grabbed at a blazing straw head, tearing it from its shoulders and tossing it through an open doorway.

The buildings all began to move, shrinking back from the flames, folding in on themselves and trying to keep their timbers away from the fire.

The old man turned and walked back towards me, the fire still flickering around him, trailing from the hem of his coat and coming off his head in a fat plume that made him look like a walking candle.

"Doesn't that hurt?" I asked as he came up to me.

"Fire can't burn me, boy," he said. "Haven't you guessed that much yet?"

He stooped to pick up his hat and dropped it on his flaming head, snuffing it out. "Now, let's get out of here while the town has more important things on its mind."

CHAPTER FIVE
TAKE A HARD RIDE

WE WERE MAYBE half a mile away from Wentworth Falls before I risked taking a look over my shoulder.

The whole town was shifting and writhing, buildings losing their shape and reforming. It was like a snake, I thought, camouflaged until its prey got close enough for it to break cover and strike.

"How did you know?" I asked. "You could tell the town was unnatural."

"I have a sense for these things," he said. "One you should listen to next time; it would have saved us a hell of a lot of trouble."

He was still smouldering, thin wisps of smoke rising from his clothes and skin. The fire seemed to have had no effect on either. He should have been black and raw, and yet he looked just as he always did: a tombstone in a dust coat.

"I guess it takes one unnatural thing to know another," I said.

"That's about the size of it. Now are you going to keep running off or can we finally get on?"

I had no more fight left in me. "I ain't going nowhere."

He nodded and kept walking, rising towards where he had tethered his horse and my mule to the low branch of a ponderosa. "Good, because things are about to get difficult."

I looked at his face, hoping this was an example of his rare humour, but it wasn't. The lunatic seemed to think everything up to this point had been easy.

We climbed onto our respective mounts and began back on the trail.

"So," I said after a short while, forcing the mule to do its best to keep up. I wanted explanations from the old man. I accepted that he had taken to saving my life with regularity, and was grateful for it. I'd even go so far as to say I was beginning to trust him. I'm not an idiot; you can only pull my ass out of trouble so many times before I settle on the fact that maybe you're not the enemy. That was all well and good, but it didn't change the fact that I was riding to Heaven alongside a man that held a fire in his throat and seemed as invulnerable as the Rocky Mountains. "You going to tell me what you are?"

"Someone you can trust," he said. "That not enough?"

"Not really. You're telling me that I have no choice but to follow you to Wormwood. You say it's my destiny. Fine. I'm not sure how I feel about that, but I'm not so stupid as to keep fighting it right now. That's not to say I don't deserve an explanation."

He thought about that for a while.

"That is fair," he admitted. "But you have to understand there are some things I just can't tell you. Not because I don't want to, but because there are laws that I can't break."

"Like what?"

"You want an example of something I can't tell you?" He gave one of those dry laughs. "And how is that supposed to work? Actually... maybe there is an example. There's a question you've never asked me, something simple. The kind of thing you would ask anyone you had just met. Can you think what that is?"

His name. I could never ask his damned name. Even then I tried to say it out loud, not even as a question, but the words wouldn't come. In the end, as frustrated as ever, I just had to nod. "Yeah. However much I try and say the question, it won't come out."

"Even if you could, I wouldn't be able to answer it. That's one of the laws. Most of the time people don't even notice. Maybe afterwards they'd realise it was something they hadn't asked. You and I have spent more time together; the idea's crept into your head, made worse when you realised you couldn't do anything about it."

"But why? What's so important about your...?" I gave one of those dry coughs, like old Mrs Hawthorne, the word lost in my mouth like water boiled away in the sun.

"It's part of who I am, and that's what I can't talk about."

"So you're saying you can't tell me a thing about you?"

"Pretty much. I can tell you where I'm going and I can tell you that I mean you no harm. That'll just have to do."

"Can you tell me about Wormwood?"

"Some. Not as much as you'd like, and most of it will have to wait for nightfall." He stopped his horse and nodded ahead. "One thing I can tell you for now: we'll find it at the end of that."

In front of us the landscape had changed, the rocks and greenery swamped by sand. As far as you could see, there was nothing ahead but desert.

"That's not right," I said, pulling my map from my saddlebag. "Since when has there been a desert here, for Christ's sake?"

"Since we wanted to find Wormwood," he replied. He nodded at my map. "You can put that away, it's of no use to you. The road we travel, like all in life, is a personal one, and you won't find it on any map."

"But how far does it stretch?" I pushed the mule forward a little, its hooves crossing from the trail and onto the sand. I was suddenly hit by a wave of heat. Crossing that line was like sticking your head in a kiln.

"Hot?" he asked.

I loosened my collar. "Like Hell."

He shook his head. "No, it ain't." He rode over and joined me. "But hot enough."

He looked at my saddle. "How much water you got?"

We'd filled our canteens a couple of days ago. Of the four I carried, two were still full, with maybe half gone from the third. I'm not a big drinker, and the coffee and cooking had come from his supply.

"I guess that'll just have to be enough," he said.

"And if it isn't?"

"Then of all the ways to die, thirst ain't the worst."

And with that happy thought, we entered the desert.

I'D KNOWN SOME hard environments in my journey from the East Coast, but none like this. The old man claimed Hell to be hotter, and maybe that was so, but I couldn't imagine it. The heat roared around us, a baking fist that had me leaning over the saddle within a couple of hours riding.

I was scared to drink, now suddenly aware of how precious the water could be. I had heard there were stretches like this in Arizona, had planned my route so as to avoid them. This was no real desert. This was another impossibility, on a journey that had become marked by them. Who could tell how many miles the sand would stretch on for? Who knew how hot it might get? We were riding into the unknown, and I couldn't help but feel it would be the death of us.

The old man had said that Wormwood would lie on the other side. I guessed if anyone knew, it was him, so that was what I held on to. He hadn't seen me dead yet; if he thought we could survive this, then likely we would.

That comfort lasted me through until late afternoon, by which point, my skin red and as sore to touch as if my fingers were knives, I was a long way from hope.

We hadn't stopped; there was no shelter, and you could sip at your water just as easily from the back of your horse as stood next to it. By the time night began to fall, a welcome darkness that smothered the sun, we must have been riding for ten hours straight.

"Let's rest," he said, climbing down from his horse and sitting down on the ground. There was no cover, no break in the rise and fall of dunes, so we made our camp right there in the sand.

"Nothing to build a fire," he said. "We're going to have to eat dried food."

"I don't think I could stand having a fire anywhere near me," I admitted. "Not with my skin so burned."

"You say that now, but you just wait until the night settles in."

And he was right. The temperature dropped through the floor, and I was soon wrapped in my blanket, shivering and wondering if I'd be solid ice by the time the sun rose to bake me again.

"It's just impossible," I said between chattering teeth. "Too hot or too cold. How can anything survive this place?"

"That's the point," he replied. "The challenge. Wormwood calls to you, but it makes it difficult. It wants only the strong."

"You're making it sound like a living thing again."

"I guess I am. It's hard to talk about the place without granting it a sense of life." He fell silent again, but I didn't interrupt. It was clear he was planning on speaking, just trying to get his thoughts in order. Eventually he continued:

"Wormwood, or the place that lies beyond it, has always drawn people to it. It needs more than the dead. But it only wants the best. The way that things change, the closer you get, that ain't just an accident. It's a way of filtering out the weak from the strong."

"I'm not strong."

"You'll be alright. I'll make sure of that."

It seemed to me that that was a promise he couldn't be sure he could keep.

"But I wasn't drawn to it," I said. "Not like you. I wasn't heading that way. This is all by accident."

He shrugged. "Maybe if we hadn't met, you would have carried straight on to California. Maybe. But we did meet and it felt right. I believe in my instincts, and when I saw you I thought this was your road."

"Well, if I die halfway, then you'll know you were wrong. I'll do my best to spit on you when I'm breathing my last."

"You're stronger than you give yourself credit for. Maybe that's why you needed to make this journey. To prove as much to yourself."

"Now you're reminding me of that whore in Indiana," I said, "trying to understand why a man does what he does. It seems everybody thinks they know me better than I know myself."

"Of course they do," he replied, "that's always the way."

I decided I wasn't in the mood for that sort of head talk. I wanted facts or I wanted sleep. Having had no more than a couple of hours rest in the last two days, the idea of sleep won.

I WOKE TO find the sun beating down on me again and the prospect of another full day's ride ahead.

I had emptied what water was left in the third bottle and made a dent in the contents of the second. I figured that meant I had to drink less, or we had to reach the end of the desert in the next day and a half. But what was the point of trying to predict how far we would have to ride? For all I knew this desert could stretch on forever; we could ride and ride and never get anywhere. The old man was using the sun to get his bearings, but even then, could we trust it? I asked him as much once we'd been going for another couple of hours.

"I can feel the right way," he said. "It's not just a case of north or west. Wormwood pulls at me here." He tapped at his belly. "I could no more lose it than I could forget which way was up or down."

Of course, by noon, even up and down was fast slipping away from me.

I had read about people who became delirious in the heat. Their brains boiling away in their skulls until they couldn't tell dreams from reality. That was a distinction that had been hard for me to make even before we set foot in the desert.

I began to see things out there. The never-changing landscape began to take on new colours and shapes, the sand shifting from a pale yellow to a deep red, the white sky darkening to a sickly blue.

"My eyes," I told him, voice dry in my throat, lips beginning to blister. "Everything looks wrong."

"It's not just your eyes," he replied. "The world is slipping, we're riding right out to the edge of things."

This made not a spit of sense to me, but I didn't care. So little did.

At one point I heard a roar above me and I looked up to see a dark triangle cut its way through the sky. My eyes struggled to focus on it. At first I thought it was a bird, and then I saw its lines were too perfect, the dark structure man-made, black iron. Fans whirred within the frame of its wings and the sound it made as it passed overheard threatened to split my head wide open. My mule began to panic, shifting from side to side, not knowing which way to turn as the sand blew up in clouds around us.

"What is it?" I shouted.

"Echoes," the old man replied. "Something from one of the other worlds leaking in to ours. Pay it no mind, it'll soon be gone."

And he was right. Just as its shadow seemed so deep and heavy we'd never see the light again, there was a grinding sound and it was gone. The sky as empty as before.

"A flying machine," I said. "Is that what it was?"

"Doesn't matter," he insisted, "keep yourself grounded in the here and now, in this world."

This was easier said than done, with the desert constantly changing colour and shapes rearing in and out of the dunes.

At one point we passed a statue that reached right up into the sky. A grotesque representation of an eagle, its beak wide as if it was crying out towards the sun. At its base there was a sign and, despite being warned away by the old man, I couldn't resist riding close enough to read what it said:

"23rd June 1890—Reformation Day. Let two worlds become one, united under the great flag of the United States of America."

I repeated it to the old man, but he didn't appear in the least interested.

"That's next year," I said, "but it looks old..."

"Time stands no more still out here than anything else," he said. "Just keep riding, keep your focus."

Easy for him to say. He was carved out of rock, nothing seemed to move him.

I kept sipping at my water, desperately wanting to make it last, but so thirsty beneath that blazing sun that it was all I could do not to drink the bottle dry. I never saw him drink at all, he seemed to give all the water he had to the animals.

After noon we began to see others out there with us. Some on horseback, some on foot.

"Don't talk to them," he said. "Don't even look at them."

More advice that was all but impossible to follow.

I couldn't help but glance from time to time. There was a party of about ten or twelve, all wearing suits like they had just stepped off a riverboat. "Who knows where you find it?" the man at the head of the procession said, addressing his fellows. "Death is gone now."

I wished I could believe him, it felt close enough to me. I had tried to eat, but the food dried my mouth out even further and I couldn't bear feeling even more thirsty than I had before.

That night, at the old man's insistence, I tried again.

"You need the sustenance," he insisted. "The energy. You won't make it through otherwise."

I believed him well enough, but still it was like swallowing bullets, the food burning all the way down my throat.

"I don't think we'll ever leave," I said to him just before falling asleep. "I think this is the world now. All there is."

* * *

THE THIRD DAY started with the roar of those flying machines. I opened my eyes to see the sky full of them. They were moving across us in a diagonal, like migrating birds.

In the distance there was a crack like thunder and I watched as flames blossomed on the underside of a machine.

"They're fighting," I said, "shooting at one another."

"War is a constant," the old man agreed.

"Just like this fucking journey."

By late morning I had run out of water. I had been doing my best to conserve it, but the heat was too much. My body shook with it, my mouth cracked and bleeding. In some ways it was a relief; as long as there had been water the journey could continue, but now there was none there seemed little point.

I told the old man this. I think I was even smiling, my lips splitting in tiny cracks all along their length.

"We carry on," he insisted. "You're not dying out here."

"We'll see about that," I told him. "We'll just see."

Still we rode on.

My sense of time was getting as confused as everything else. I kept falling asleep on the back of the mule, experiencing the journey in broken sections like a road seen through the window of a speeding train. I think it was the afternoon when we passed the naked man. His skin was bright red, a bandana tied around his head. Next to him was something that looked an over-developed bicycle, its wheels too thick and its frame packed with machinery and motors.

"You got any gas?" he asked us as we passed.

"Ignore him," the old man reminded me, though I couldn't help but look at the man briefly.

"Just some gas!" he shouted. "The bitch has packed up and I'll never get out of here on foot."

He continued to shout as we rode on, and I resisted the

urge to look over my shoulder as his voice echoed across the dunes. "Gas!" he kept screaming. "Just some gas!"

He was the last thing I remember clearly for awhile. My next memory was of lying on my back on the sand, gazing up at a night sky that swirled with colour, great bands of red and purple and green, shooting over my head.

I think I tried to speak to the old man about it. Maybe to ask him what he thought it was, or just to share the experience. My voice was gone, though; trying to make words was like swallowing glass.

I closed my eyes, so very tired, comforted by the fact that it was unlikely I'd ever wake up.

But I did.

To begin with, I thought the flying machines had returned. Then I realised the thunder was exactly that, a storm raging above us. Lightning scratched white lines between the stars, trying to cut the darkness into sheets like a tailor sketching out material for a suit.

Then it began to rain, and the water hitting my face was the most miraculous thing I had ever experienced.

Every single raindrop that hit my dry, blistered skin felt wonderful.

We're trying to find Heaven, I thought. I reckon it's here.

The old man opened the canteens so they could catch some of the rain, warning me to be careful. I was so dehydrated that drinking too much could do me more harm than good. It was hard to resist, but I let the rainwater fall in my mouth, then sloshed it around and spit it back out onto the sand.

Eventually he let me take a few sips. It tasted sweet and clean. Heaven indeed.

It continued until dawn. When the sun rose, it brought clouds of steam from the water-soaked sand as we continued on our way.

The canteens weren't full, but they held enough to keep us going for a little longer. Yesterday I had lost the will to move another step, but life clings, and while I was still weak and sore, I began to hope we might see the end of the desert. The humidity nearly robbed me of that hope. It was like riding through a Turkish bath, our clothes soaked and clinging to us like hot towels.

The sun continued to rise higher in a sky that had turned the colour of an infected wound. The old man still showed no sign of suffering, the same unstoppable bastard he had always been. Occasionally he offered words of comfort, assurances that we would soon be through, that Wormwood was close. I chose to believe him, he wasn't a man to lie for the sake of another's comfort. By mid-afternoon on that third day I began to wonder. The thought of spending another night in the desert, wet clothes freezing around me as the darkness fell, was almost more than I could stand.

Ahead of us the sky suddenly filled with what, at first, I took to be birds. Black shapes fluttering towards us in the air. As they came closer I saw they were bits of paper caught on a wind that I couldn't even feel. I snatched one as it passed me and tried to force my eyes to focus on what was written on it.

"It's a picture of you," I told my companion, holding the sheet up.

He was wearing a suit, which seemed as misplaced as putting a necktie on an iguana. Above the picture, it said VOTE: REFORMATION; beneath, FOR A UNITED WORLD.

"I don't want to know," he said, refusing to look. "What will be will be."

I let the poster loose and it soared away above me, vanishing into the brightness of the sun.

Just as night began to fall, we saw the edge of the desert.

Mountains rose ahead of us, the first sign of a break in the sand since we had entered days ago.

"We'll keep going," he said. "I'd rather sleep under real stars."

When I had entered the desert, the air had changed the moment I set foot on the sand, and leaving was the same in reverse. A wall of fresh air suddenly passed over me and the sky cleared. The mule pulled us onto solid ground again and a strong wind whipped across us.

"Now we can rest," he said.

THE ROAD TO WORMWOOD

THE INVENTOR
AND THE MONKS

CHAPTER SIX
A GENIUS, TWO PARTNERS AND A DUPE

ELISABETH FORSET WAS getting more than a little tired of the attentions of Roderick Quartershaft, Adventurer and Darling of the Popular Press.

They had spent their first night in a hotel in Omaha, the pre-arranged transport having failed to arrive as promised. After an hour of standing outside the train station, they had given in to the obvious and resigned themselves to a delay in their schedule. Her father had spent a couple of hours in the local telegraph office, shouting at the operator at such volume it was a wonder his voice hadn't carried out over the wires. Of course, none of it was the operator's fault, something he made clear time and again when the mad Englishman seemed inclined to visit physical violence on him.

"I can only send the message, sir," he had insisted. "The fiery vengeance you can visit on them yourself, should you ever meet face to face."

Retiring to a suite of rooms at the Cozzens House Hotel, news had finally reached them that the expected transport would arrive first thing in the morning.

After an acceptable evening meal, Elisabeth had retired to her room, as much to avoid the constant talking of Quartershaft as the tedious company of the monks. The move successfully achieved the latter, but the former proved more tenacious. This was helped no end by the hotel having provided him with the room next to hers, complete with an adjoining door.

"My lady!" he announced, bursting in for the fourth time in half an hour. "It occurs to me that you may benefit from some advice on local customs."

"I'm sure," she replied, setting down her book with an irritated slap, "that in Omaha, as with everywhere else in the Western world, the customs are fairly similar. For example: a gentleman would not simply burst into a stranger's bedroom without first having the courtesy to knock."

"Ah! But you're no stranger."

"And you're no gentleman, but one would hope the rule still stands."

"Forgive me, but it was open..."

"It was not. It was locked. I ensured as much myself."

"Damned cheap locks, a lady must feel secure while travelling. Perhaps you will allow me to take a look at it and see if it cannot be set to good order?"

"As you're the person I most wish to keep out, that hardly seems necessary. Go to your room and we'll forget all about it."

"Well..." Quartershaft made to sit on the corner of her bed, lost his balance and tumbled to the floor.

"I see you've been drinking again?" said Elisabeth. "Though in truth I can't say I have noticed a time when you haven't."

"Nonsense," came Quartershaft's muffled voice. "Beyond the occasional medicinal draft, I never touch a drop. It dulls the nerves, and that is something that I, as a hunter and adventurer, can ill afford. I was merely taking the opportunity to surprise anyone that might be hiding beneath your bed."

"And is there?"

"Is there what, my lady?"

"Anyone hiding under there?"

"Careful inspection proves that all is safe." He pulled himself up and sat down, more carefully this time. "Are there any other tasks I can perform for my most beautiful companion?"

"Certainly. You can leave the room and make a concerted effort to stay out of it this time."

"Are you sure? It can be terribly lonely while travelling; it's a shame not to make the most of each other. There is such an abject lack of civilised company in this country."

"I certainly haven't found any," she countered.

She looked at him and worked hard to be objective. She knew that many ladies considered him the very height of attractiveness. He cut an assertive profile and would certainly have been handsome in his day. Now, with years of poor diet and alcohol abuse, he was a puffy, bloodshot mess; a shadow of the man he used to be, who still stood bold on the covers of his books. He was, in her opinion, repulsive, inside and out.

"Mr Quartershaft," she said, "I shall say this only once more. You are a member of our party purely because of financial expediency. I tolerate you as I tolerate a number of practical limitations that encumber our progress. I do not, however, *like* you very much."

"You barely know me!" he retorted.

"I know enough. You're a fool and a pest, a lecher and a drunk. I may not be able to ban you from the expedition, but I can most certainly ban you from my room. So get out before I call reception and demand they have you removed."

"Only trying to be a help," he said, his voice quiet. "If you wish to be alone, you need but ask."

He made his way out of the room. Once he was gone, she took the precaution of slipping a chair beneath the handle of the door. Feeling more secure, she prepared for bed.

She was not well-travelled, as Quartershaft frequently reminded her. But then, neither was he, whatever claims he made to the contrary. This did not make her a fool, nor someone that needed constant supervision.

She was sure that Quartershaft's motives were far more basic than that. He hoped to get her into bed. He was certainly not the first to try, nor was he the only man to fail. Society demanded that a lady of her standing be the height of purity. This was not altogether the case, for her, but even so, she was not inclined to let him get close enough to breathe on her, let alone gain access to her undergarments.

Next door she heard a thundering crash and guessed that drink had finally got the better of him.

Truth be told, he would be the very least of her discomforts on the road ahead.

When her father had first suggested this expedition, her thoughts had been entirely negative. She had known all about Wormwood and her father's obsession with it. He was a man who infected his home with the contents of his head. Walking into his study was like taking a stroll across the contours of his cerebellum, the room littered with research papers, schematic drawings, maps, stuffed animals and more ironwork than would be found in a modestly-sized blacksmith's. It was precisely because her father was quite incapable of running a household without it eventually collapsing under its own weight that she still lived with him and did her best to manage the affairs of the estate. Many daughters would resent such a station, hankering after marriage and families of their own. Elisabeth was not that sort of woman.

"But how could I live with myself if I didn't at least try to find it?" her father had announced over dinner. "I should never forgive myself."

She understood that, of course. Just as she understood that she could not allow him to travel alone, any more than she could expect him not to blow up the house if she gave up her residence.

Wormwood had been a subject of conversation since she had been very young. Her mother, passed these thirteen years, had possessed no patience for the subject, so her father, always a man who needed to talk an idea out rather than let it stew inside his own brain, had looked to her.

"Just imagine," he would say as she lay in her bed. "To set your eyes on Heaven. To walk its streets or corridors, to breathe its air. To think Paradise could be within the reach of anyone clever enough and brave enough to track it down."

She had never believed it was. Even as a child, she had viewed her father's stories as fictions.

He would tell her of the time it had been sighted in the Cotswolds, a tiny village appearing overnight, its stone houses immaculate and yet empty, its lush square and pond beautiful but free of fish or fowl. A picture of a village. A model in fact.

Folk from nearby had descended into its streets, exploring every nook and cranny of the impossible place, trying all the doors, peering through all the windows.

The work of the devil, some said; the work of God, claimed others.

"Nobody ever seems quite sure who is responsible for what," her father had laughed, "in that most complex of spiritual relationships."

And then, as swiftly as it had appeared, it had vanished, but not without taking several of the curious explorers with it. Anyone still left walking the paths between the houses when it dissipated into air had disappeared with it, victims of an infernal impossibility that was the talk of the area centuries later.

Not that anyone ever had evidence. The tales of Wormwood were never more than that. Eyewitness reports—and scant few of those—passed on down the generations, twisted no doubt, their facts irrevocably altered, until it existed as nothing more than an outdated and unpopular myth.

Precisely the sort of thing her father loved.

The two halves of Lord Jeremy Forset. On one hand, the inventor and engineer, a man who worked iron, oil and steam, beat the solid into shapes that pleased him and created new—and frequently lethal—contraptions. On the other, the dreamer, the man with his head in the clouds, susceptible to every passing fad and notion.

She had once spent six weeks trying to stop him building a replica of Noah's great ark in the grounds after a chance comment from the local vicar convinced him they were heading for another flood.

On another occasion it had been his determination to reach the stars. A few hours in the company of an HG Wells novel had convinced him of life on other planets, and filled him with bloody-minded plans to set out and find them.

Most of these convictions passed as quickly as they had come. Wormwood was at least a constant.

Perhaps that's why the trip worried her more than usual. She knew that her father's beliefs were as slippery as the grease that frequently stained his hands and trousers; when the balloon burst, it was rarely a great loss. But when he discovered—as she honestly believed—

that Wormwood was not real, she worried that it would destroy him. How then could she let him travel alone? Even if she could rely on him to stay safe during the trek—which she most certainly could not—she could hardly abandon him to the ultimate disappointment she believed lay at its conclusion.

QUARTERSHAFT CLOSED THE adjoining door behind himself and buried his head in his hands.

He was not a stupid man, though he knew others thought so. He despaired at his own weak behaviour just as much as—if not frequently more than—the people subjected to it. He simply couldn't help himself.

He knew that Elisabeth Forset assumed he simply had designs on her sex (and he would be lying if he didn't admit to a sizeable lust in that regard) but his desire to be in her company was driven by something even simpler than that. Quartershaft was that rare and untenable thing: an explorer that couldn't abide being alone.

His room was dark, the lamps unlit, and he felt the blackness swell around him, thick with the weight of absence. He moved forward, tripped over the rug, and found himself, even more pitifully, lying next to his own bed like a child cowering from imaginary monsters.

He had always been a man that found terror easy to conjure. The world seemed to him to be nothing but a minefield of fears and dangers. In fact, that had been his first motivation to write, a belief that setting the very worst life might have to offer on paper might box those nightmares away at arm's length.

He had begun with ghost stories, written under his real name of Patrick Irish, but they had been limited, unsuccessful affairs, the spooks too tame, the heroes too weak.

Then he had tried crime stories, but he knew nothing of their mechanics, and his plots were so transparent it was a dim child indeed that couldn't finger the murderer within the first couple of pages.

So, finally, he had written adventures, catalogues of faraway lands and the perils and monsters they contained. He had written of cannibal tribes, savage reptiles, terrors beneath the sea. They were good. But still he struggled to sell them.

"Readers prefer something real," the editor of *Fireside Quarterly* explained. "I like the stories a great deal, but they seem a little too absurd, too unbelievable. Our readers love journals, essays written about real expeditions, real monsters. Of course, they're often terribly dull; who gives a tinker's topknot about a bunch of fellows hunting for rare orchids and such? Well... my readers do, God bless them, but I'm damned if I can see why."

"Well," Irish had said, "it seems to me that we don't know half of the terrible things that might be found out in the wild."

"Oh, your average London reader gets a cold sweat on when he thinks about visiting Nottingham," his editor had agreed. "That's why the jungles and mountains of far off lands have such an appeal."

"In that case, would there be any real reason why we couldn't pretend...?"

And that day, Roderick Quartershaft was born.

The stories gained traction. Everybody loved a good monster, especially if it was located an ocean away and unlikely to trouble the reader with any more tangibility than the sketches that accompanied the stories. As far as most people were concerned, Roderick Quartershaft was the most thrilling, brave and wise gentleman in the Empire.

Of course, most of his readers had never met him.

He pulled himself up on the bed, ferreted in his waistcoat pocket for a box of matches and reached for the bedside lamp. Let there be light before he despaired entirely.

The soft orange glow matched the brandy in his system, and he regained some of his composure, swallowing the panic and disgust as he sat staring at the wall of his room.

There was a terrible oil painting hung there, a ship in a storm, tilting its way through grey waves tinted with titanium white froth. The damned thing made him feel sick just looking at it.

He got up and read the title: "The Settler's Journey— Sailing to a New Life."

"Well bully for you," he said, unhooking the picture and placing it on the floor, face to the wall.

The journey across the Atlantic had been the most terrifying experience of his life. Every night he had fallen asleep only by drinking sufficient alcohol to knock him out. Even then, barely able to latch on to a cohesive thought, his brain so pickled, the one thing he had never doubted was that he would be dead by morning. Every new day he had proven himself wrong; and every new day he had found himself slightly disappointed.

Now, with feet finally on dry land, he faced yet another journey his nerves could barely cope with. Travelling away from civilisation and into the unsettled, dusty terrain that lay to the west. He had read enough stories (usually those either side of his, in *Fireside Quarterly*) to know that it was a world of poisonous snakes, vicious bears, mountain lions and—terror of terrors—rampaging Indians. The red devils were violence incarnate, remorseless killers who sought out the white man, filled him with arrows and then held him down to cut the scalp from his head.

He shivered and removed his wig, running his hand over the bald head beneath. How the Indians would roar when they discovered he had cheated them. How he wished he could just stay here in the hotel and write his piece from the safety of the letter desk.

He got up, removed the wig stand from his case and set it on the other side of the bed, giving the hairpiece a drunken comb with his fingers.

Perhaps he could engineer an accident? Something noble yet tragic, brave yet inarguable? He looked out of the window in the hope of spotting someone that might have the decency to shoot him in the foot.

The street outside was busy enough, full of gentlemen and ladies making their way between the saloons and dance halls. These Americans seemed a jolly lot, he thought. Which proved how terribly stupid they must be. He had been in their country for only a few days and he had already discovered that there was absolutely nothing to be happy about.

In his head he began to formulate a plan whereby he might anger a passer-by sufficiently to cause a ruckus. Said passer-by would then pull his gun and... Yes. There was no way of guaranteeing the stranger would only shoot him in the foot, was there? And, as much as he would love to get out of the journey ahead, if he had to risk a bullet in the brain to achieve it, then he would let the idea pass.

That was another thing that concerned him: all those guns! That showed you how dangerous the place must be; what sort of civilisation was it, where everyone needed to carry a murder weapon in order to feel secure?

He wished he had more guns of his own. A rifle and two revolvers might not be quite enough.

It was no good, he was getting himself agitated again.

He dug out his hip flask, drained the little that was left and then searched for another bottle of brandy in his luggage. Finding it, he topped the hip flask back up, sealed it and proceeded to drink from the bottle.

* * *

FATHER MARTIN WAS troubled.

This was not unusual. For all he maintained a calm exterior with the rest of the brothers, presenting a man of peace, rich in happiness and spiritual enlightenment, this was as much of a sham as the character of Roderick Quartershaft. Perhaps that was why he found he had some small measure of sympathy for the man; he knew how difficult it could be to maintain a character so completely at odds with oneself.

Father Martin worried about a great deal of things. This was not unexpected, given his position of authority. The Order of Ruth were a dedicated, devout lot, only twelve in number. They were philosophical, studiously inclined and terribly clever. They could also not be relied upon to do up their own shoelaces—were they to have any, which thankfully they did not—and it took a good deal of Father Martin's time and energy keeping them all on the straight and narrow.

This in itself was not currently troubling him. The brothers were all secured away in their rooms, lost amongst the decadence and soft furnishings—Brother Samuel had expressed fright at the bearskin rug on his floor, concerned that the animal's spirit might begrudge him standing on its shed fur.

What troubled Father Martin was the future. What troubled him was Wormwood.

He stood looking out of his window, watching the people in the street below. They seemed especially carefree, he thought. Revelling in sin, of course, decadents to their core, but he didn't judge them. The Order of Ruth was easygoing on that score, a group of likeminded believers dedicated to philosophical expansion rather than silent hermits hiding away from the world. A part of him most certainly envied the Americans their relaxed, happy nature. There was nothing he would like more than to be able to walk up this wide street, the sound of music and laughter in his ears and nothing but light carelessness in his heart. But that was not his place in life. He was a man who worried. A man who discovered problems and then fixed them.

His eyes were caught by a flash of red in the crowd. A woman's bonnet, perhaps? Or a gaily coloured cap?

He pressed his face against the glass and stared at the figure that had caught his eye, the sudden revelation of what it was sinking deep into his belly like the sensation of falling into ice water.

The man was dressed in the robes of his order, light grey habit and black belt. The red that Father Martin had mistaken for a hat was in fact the man's face, a glistening, peeled head of muscle and teeth, even its eyes lost, become empty black pits that appeared to gaze right up at him.

Who was it? Which member of the order?

And why did nobody else on the street seem to notice them?

The monk extended an arm out towards Father Martin, reaching up through the lamplight to extend a raw, bloody finger that pointed right at him.

"Dear God," Father Martin exclaimed, "what are you telling me?"

He put his face in his hands, desperate not to meet the gaze of the monk below.

When he looked again, the vision was gone.

THE BRIGHT OMAHA morning was torn in half by the sound of pistons.

The residents had never seen a machine of the sort that made its way through the city's streets, a behemoth of black metal and clouds of steam. By the time it came to rest on Harney Street, it had gathered a considerable crowd.

"What the hell is it?" one bystander demanded to know, staring at the long convoy with open distrust.

"That, sir," announced Lord Jeremy Forset, "is the Forset Land Carriage, a marvel of engineering and science the likes of which you will likely never see again."

"I damn well hope not," the man replied. "It stinks like hellfire and is as ugly as a buffalo's ass."

While both of these observations were unquestionably accurate, Lord Forset ignored them. This was a proud moment. It was the first time he had seen the machine as anything beyond pencil lines on paper. The product of his own design, the Forset Land Carriage was, on the surface, a set of three rail carriages pulled by a traction engine. Beneath that surface there were many modifications, all designed to make the journey ahead easier. The wheels were large and heavily sprung so as to handle rough terrain; the base was heavily weighted in order to provide stability. Most revolutionary of all, the steam boiler was connected to a set of batteries, so that electric supply was maintained even at a standstill, a network of water pipes also providing hot water. It was designed for practicality and comfort, the latter being something that he imagined would be in short supply outside of its carriages.

Forset felt his daughter's hands on his shoulders, and at that moment he couldn't have been happier, surrounded by his creations.

"It's wonderful, father," she said. "Whatever the residents of Omaha might think."

"It'll soon be beyond their consideration," he replied. "We load up immediately, and set a course for adventure!"

Father Martin, clearly the worse for a sleepless night, led a number of his brothers down the steps.

"It's an infernal-looking thing," remarked Brother Samuel. Nobody responded, or indeed seemed in the least surprised at this.

"It's certainly impressive," said Brother William and, despite his troubled head, Father Martin was pleased to note enthusiasm from the novice.

Brother William was a good boy, but the fact that he was a clear thirty years younger than the rest of the order, and had had a youth that could charitably be described as 'chequered' meant that he was often an outsider. Father Martin had done his best to limit that, making time for the boy and encouraging him as much as he could. "It's a feat of science," he agreed. "Proof that the rational and spiritual can work side by side."

The novice nodded. "And it must have cost him a fortune."

Father Martin sighed at the speed with which the novice's thoughts had descended to the earthly.

"Thankfully it has been funded by the noble chaps at the National Motor Company," Forset explained, "since my worldly standing is not quite as proud as it once was. I designed it, they built it. Should it prove successful on this, its maiden voyage, they will begin mass production, and soon this entire country will be filled with such engines!"

"Time will tell on that one," said a young man climbing down from the engine's cabin. "It's been the devil's job getting it here on schedule, that's for sure."

He lifted a pair of goggles up onto his head, displacing a violent shock of ginger curls so they resembled a pair of spiralling ram's horns.

"Billy Herbert," he said, holding out a coal-smeared hand towards Forset. "Driver, engineer and representative of the National Motor Company."

Forset shook the lad's hand with enthusiasm. "I'm pleased they sent someone who knows what he's talking about," he said. "I had terrible visions of sharing our journey with an accountant."

"Oh, they thought about it," Billy admitted, "but not a single one of the suits was willing to make the trip, so I got lumbered with the job." Noticing the look of disappointment on the inventor's face, he tried to backpedal slightly. "Not that I'm not happy to be here. Beats being stuck in the factory, for sure."

"That it does, my lad," said Forset. "I can promise you a wild time on the road ahead."

"Aye, well, not too wild, I hope." Billy looked at the monks. "Here to bless us before we head on our way?" he joked.

"This is Father Martin and the members of the Order of Ruth," Forset explained. "They will be accompanying us on our journey and have, in point of fact, also helped finance the whole endeavour."

"Well, that's wonderful," Billy replied. "Even better if one of you knows how to shovel coal."

"If they don't, I do," said Elisabeth, stepping forward.

Billy was clearly flustered at the thought of that.

"My daughter, Elisabeth," explained Forset. "There is nothing she won't do when it comes to engineering, I can assure you."

"Great," Billy replied, unsure what else to say.

"Don't worry," Elisabeth said with a smile, "it always takes men a good few days to learn how to handle a woman who is their equal." She turned to her father. "Someone should rouse Quartershaft, the only guest at the hotel who seems to have managed to sleep through Mr Herbert's arrival."

"By all means wake the fellow up, my dear," said her father. "I shall oversee the loading of our cargo."

That was the last thing Elisabeth had on her mind.

"I'll help," she insisted. She turned to the monks. "I'm

sure Brother William would be only too happy to hunt out our erstwhile adventurer?"

The novice nodded. "I shall simply follow my nose," he said, walking back into the hotel.

"Quartershaft?" said Billy. "He's the famous explorer, right?"

"In his own mind, Mr Herbert," Elisabeth replied, "but scarcely anywhere else."

QUARTERSHAFT HAD NOT, in fact, slept through the arrival of the traction engine. He had been on his feet and considering a hiding place in the wardrobe when it had first made its noisy way down the street.

"God's teeth," he said, staring down at it through his window. "Someone's built a train line in the street while I slept."

By the time Brother William knocked on his door, the adventurer was halfway decent, needing nothing more than a pair of trousers and a cigarette to face the day in earnest.

"We're preparing to leave," the novice explained when Quartershaft opened the door, not bothering to disguise his disgust at the sight of Quartershaft's bare knees.

"I am moments away from readiness," the adventurer assured him. "Sally forth, lad, and I will meet you down there."

"How gratifying," Brother William replied, walking off to rejoin the rest of his order as they prepared themselves for the journey ahead.

THE MONKS GATHERED in Father Martin's room, kneeling in whatever space they could find.

"We have been travelling for so long," the Father began,

"and yet, in many ways, our journey starts now. The road ahead will be perilous. At times, it will seem quite beyond our capabilities."

He looked at Brother Clarence at this point, the most aged of them all and already suffering after having been on his knees for a minute or so.

"Yet we will prevail; have no doubt about that. Our mission is holy and our intent is pure."

The image of the monk he had seen outside his window the night before flashed into his mind. That slick, bloody head, that accusing finger. He fought to push the thought away.

"However often we might feel the journey is beyond us, I ask you to remember that. God would not have set us on this path unless He knew we were capable of walking it. We will find our goal and we will achieve our mission. That is God's will."

There was a ripple of 'amens,' and Father Martin bid them all to stand

"Let the journey begin," he said, the smile on his face a lie as bright and pretty as a shop sign hung outside a burned out building.

CHAPTER SEVEN
AND FOR A ROOF, A SKY FULL OF STARS

THE FORSET LAND Carriage made its way out of Omaha, much to the relief of both its passengers and the residents of said city. While some of its more forward-thinking citizens could admit that the behemoth was of engineering interest, that didn't alter the fact that it was loud, smelly and liable to crush anything else trying to use the roads.

The rear carriage was loaded with coal and their equipment—crates that all but the Forsets treated with fearful suspicion—and the fore and central carriages contained living space for the party. Up front, growling and hissing like a rabid dog, was the engine that pulled it forward.

However much Lord Forset tried to negotiate otherwise, the engine was Billy's domain. He had a bunk set up there and was of a mind to never leave the place.

"It's like rolling a small town across the world," he said. "Only a lunatic would take his eyes off that."

Forset could see this was good sense but, as the machine's inventor, he still insisted on a turn at the controls. Billy indulged him once they were in open country. He figured you could roll a small town around out there without killing too many innocents.

"It's everything I hoped it would be," admitted Forset, goggles and grin in place, both covered in soot. "A miracle of the modern age, and one that will revolutionise travel forever."

"I don't know about that," Billy had to say. "It's hungry as all hell, the coal it takes to keep us moving could fuel a whole town in the winter."

"Mere details," Forset insisted. "Wrinkles to be ironed out in the fullness of time."

"And the boiler has a habit of creeping up to a lethal pressure. A lazy driver would have the whole lot blow up from underneath him if he forgot to vent it regularly."

"I don't build machines for lazy people! Just look at how fast we're going!"

"It's a fair old lick, I'll give you that. Though I've had to plot our course carefully: the wheels compensate for a lot, but if we went over any major obstacles at this speed we'd be shaken to pieces."

Forset would not be swayed from his childish enthusiasm. "I couldn't be happier."

"That's nice," said Billy with a sigh. "Why don't you make sure the rest of our passengers feel the same?"

Forset was reluctant to leave, but he could see the engineer wanted to resume control. Maybe if he worked on the lad in stages, he'd let him drive the machine for a longer stretch.

"Very well! The controls are yours, I'll see how our venerable monks are taking to a life of steam."

NOT ALL OF them were taking to it well. Brother Samuel had retired to his bed, making noises about 'infernal engines,' and the aged Brother Clarence had begun to complain of a deathly ringing in his ears.

"It's a warning!" he had claimed.

"It's the water pipes," Elisabeth had replied.

At least some of the holy men had taken to their new vehicle with enthusiasm. William had led a party to the windows, where they now hung their heads out, squinting against the plumes of steam.

Father Martin had done his best to affect a casual air, and was currently busying himself with the preparation of lunch.

Naturally, Quartershaft was not altogether at rest. It seemed to him that they were now travelling inside a giant stick of dynamite and, as much as he worked at relaxing himself, every bump and whistle had him clenching his teeth and stiffening his arms and legs. As a result he looked like a happy corpse, sat in the dining area. All did their best to avoid him.

Forset made another tour of the carriages, taking in the large communal area in the first carriage, a dining room and lounge with a small kitchen tacked to the front. He examined the provisions therein and helped himself to a mouthful of Father Martin's soup, under the pretence of checking if it needed more salt.

The second carriage was entirely laid out as sleeping compartments, with a washroom at either end. There were eight compartments in all, the gentlemen sharing two to a berth, with Elisabeth afforded room of her own. Perhaps not quite to the standard of the finer trains he had travelled on in his time, but certainly more comfortable than they would have been as part of a horse caravan.

"I think," he said to his daughter, who was going over the maps of their journey in her compartment, "that we are having a splendid adventure!"

"For now," she replied with a smile. "You wait until we've been stuck on this thing for a few days."

"I couldn't be more comfortable. Side by side with you, travelling through new lands in a miracle of engineering. This is the sort of life a man needs! To hell with England and its social dinners, pompous old soldiers and dusty maids who sew and gossip."

That, at least, Elisabeth could agree on. While Quartershaft was hardly ideal company, she missed the local gentry around their estate not one jot. Elisabeth Forset was not the sort of woman who came alive at tea parties.

"It seems to me," she said, "that if Quartershaft's information is right, we should be at Wormwood within a couple of days. Depending, of course, on what sort of speed we can maintain."

"Billy tells me that we'll have to slow down when we hit more uneven territory. He's quite right, of course; as much as I love the great beast, she'll fly off into a thousand pieces if she hits a rock at this speed."

"Assuming we can maintain an average of, say, thirty miles per hour and travel for at least twelve hours per day, we can make it in three days."

"Which gives us a four days' grace, according to both Quartershaft and Father Martin."

"Then we have a journey ahead that can be described as leisurely."

"Well, that rather depends on what we meet on the way. The monks claim that we're likely to brush up against trouble."

"No surprise there."

"The closer we get to Wormwood, the more the local environment is affected."

"Affected?"

"Yes, well, he was rather vague about the details. I've heard stories of strange animal attacks, visions in the night sky... you know... omens and portents, all the usual sort of ballyhoo."

"How I shall look forward to that, father."

"Oh, I'm sure it'll be alright. After all, in a whopping great thing like this it'll take one hell of an animal to make a dent, what?"

As THE FIRST night fell on the passengers of the Land Carriage, Billy slowly let the speed slacken off until they came to a gradual stop in a gathering cloud of dust. Lord Forset and Elisabeth had joined him in the engine's cabin, the former rather hoping he might have been allowed to help.

Billy, far too concerned with anything going wrong, had insisted the peer kept his hands to himself.

"God help us if we ever have to stop quickly," Billy said once they were completely still. He stepped down onto solid ground, resisting the urge to drop to his hands and knees and kiss it. "We'd be likely to concertina like an accordion. You just don't move this weight of wood and iron through the world without complications."

"All the more reason not to travel at night," Forset agreed. "At least during the day we can keep a steady eye on the road ahead."

"I've vented the boiler into the water system," said Billy, "so we can all have a hot bath tonight."

He found himself looking at Elisabeth and suddenly got himself flustered. "Not together, obviously," he added, only making his awkwardness more profound.

"Of course not," said Elisabeth with a smile. "You'd only make the water all sooty."

Billy had no idea what to say to that, torn between an urge to laugh, cry or just scream in panic. Forset took pity on him.

"What say you come back with us and see if you can't find some well-earned rest? Dinner will be ready shortly."

"Then if you don't mind," Billy replied, "I'm going to head straight to the washroom. The last thing I want to do is stain your dinner table looking like this." He smiled, white teeth shining bright from a dirty moon of a face.

BILLY WAS NOT a man used to refinement. He lived in oil, steam and smoke, not bleached cuffs and collars.

This had been of some concern for his boss in New York. Caspar Diogenes felt an English peer needed to be surrounded by people that glittered like diamonds.

"You mind your language," he had insisted, nervously chewing on the tip of a cigar, "and take a decent suit. Do you even own a decent suit?"

"One that I wore to my father's funeral," Billy had replied, irritated. "If it's good enough for my dead dad, it's good enough for anyone."

Even Diogenes, as insensitive as he was, knew better than to argue with that.

"Of course," he said, "we should really be sending someone along from the executive level."

"I don't imagine you'll find anyone willing to make the journey, sir. Unless you fancy taking the trip yourself?"

Diogenes shifted awkwardly in his chair, as if the very thought of those miles on the road were enough to make him ache.

"I've never been a great traveller," he admitted, "and you have to play to your strengths in business."

"Absolutely, sir. So you'll just have to trust me to do the job well, won't you?"

And they had, given little in the way of choice.

For Billy, travel was no great hardship. Admittedly this expedition carried extra complications, but he was a man without ties, and that meant the road held few problems he couldn't handle.

He ran a little of the hot water he had boasted of and scrubbed hard at his skin, trying to remove the day's grime. After a few minutes, he was pink and sore, but presentable.

Having no carriage of his own, he struggled to change his clothes in the compact washroom, banging his elbows against the walls as he fought his way into a clean shirt and jacket. As far as he could tell, tilting the small shaving mirror fixed to the basin, he looked good enough for polite company.

Dumping his dirty work clothes on his bunk in the engine, he returned to the dining car.

The monks were all gathered around the table. He was relieved that they seemed much more out of place, presented behind white linen and silver cutlery, than he did.

"Good evening," he said, loitering to one side, unsure as to where he should sit.

"Good evening," Father Martin replied, appearing from out of the kitchen, a towel draped across one shoulder. "I hope my meagre cooking will be enough reward for a hard day working the boiler."

"I don't take much pleasing, as far as food's concerned," Billy assured him. "It's all just coal for the fire."

"Indeed," the holy man agreed with a smile.

The door opened and Quartershaft entered, walking as if the carriage was still in motion, frequently taking a hold of fixtures in order to guide him to the table.

"Brothers," he announced, taking them all in with a sweep of his arm and dropping into one of the seats. He looked at Billy and gestured towards the seat next to him. "Stop cluttering up the place and sit down," he said. "You can tell me all about this thing we're riding in and how incredibly safe it is."

"I'll do my best," Billy replied, sitting down and wondering whether he should put the napkin on his lap or not. Quartershaft was using his to wipe at his sweating brow, so he supposed it didn't really matter.

"Though," Billy continued, "the whole point of this trip is to see how safe the Land Carriage is, so maybe you'll have to ask me again when we're done."

"I thought the trip was to find Wormwood," said one of the monks, looking towards the fellow sat next to him in confusion. "Wasn't that rather the point?"

"The trip has a number of uses," said Father Martin, "though our destination is certainly the primary goal."

"Can't say I know anything about that," Billy admitted. "I was just given the map and told to keep shovelling coal. So what's so important about Wormwood?"

Quartershaft laughed and began the hunt for a bottle of wine.

The monks looked to one another, unsure as to who should do the explaining. Luckily for them, Lord Forset and his daughter entered and the subject of conversation shifted to how lovely the young woman looked. Billy had to agree, though he did his best to push the thoughts from his head. He was fairly sure that lusting after the client's daughter was not something Caspar Diogenes would approve of.

"Now we're all here," said Father Martin, "I shall serve!"

The first course was the soup Forset had tested earlier, and all present declared it to be good. Billy watched the monks sip their noisy way through it with some amusement. They seemed to move as one, synchronised after years of shared dinners.

"I'm never quite sure if soup is a food or a drink," announced Quartershaft. Silence met the observation, so he bowed his head and continued eating.

Billy decided that if he didn't try and start a conversation, nobody would.

"So," he said, finishing his soup with an appreciative sigh, "what's the deal with Wormwood, then? Nice place is it?"

Of course, Lord Forset was only too happy to tell him the story, at great length. He told him the historical accounts, the rumours and the supposed eyewitness reports. He barely paused for breath as Father Martin brought the next course, a rather insipid stew that, in Quartershaft's opinion, was merely another soup with bigger lumps in it. Finally, the peer sat back and looked at the young man with open amusement.

"I dare say it all sounds rather far-fetched?"

Billy wasn't quite sure of the politic way to reply, but couldn't quite manage a lie.

"It does at that," he admitted. "Does the company know that's what you're hunting for?"

"I saw no need to tell them. As far as they're concerned, I'm simply on an expedition to explore the wilder parts of your country."

Probably just as well, thought Billy. He had little doubt that Caspar Diogenes would have treated the whole enterprise with scorn.

"From your point of view," the peer continued, "might I suggest that it scarcely matters. My daughter doesn't believe a word of it either..."

At this Elisabeth made to speak, but her father held her hand and smiled. "Don't worry, my dear, I'm only too aware that you consider it little more than a fairy tale. But the point is: does it matter? Either it exists, as I believe it does, and you are about to see the most miraculous place on Earth. Or it doesn't, and we genuinely are on nothing more than an exploratory trip to see new sights and test the limits of the Forset Land Carriage."

"If I may," interrupted Father Martin, "there is a slight difference. Our friend here is about to be plunged into potentially life-threatening situations; we all know that Wormwood fights back. I'm not sure that he should have been brought here under false pretences."

"Wormwood 'fights back'?" Billy repeated.

"It is said that the town has an effect on its environment," Forset explained. "Which is natural enough, one would hardly expect such a miracle to intrude on our reality without there being consequences. If Wormwood is real, then the sight of it will not be the only thing to stretch your preconceived view of natural law."

Only too aware that he was inviting the peer to offer yet another long winded speech, Billy asked for examples.

Forset gave them: animal attacks, supernatural creatures, the dead revived... it was a list of fantasies that Billy couldn't begin to take seriously. The fact that the rest of the party did, however, unnerved him a great deal. Was he in the company of a band of lunatics? The Englishman seemed sane enough; eccentric, sure, but not a man prone to delusions. He looked to Elisabeth, who met his gaze with a sympathetic smile.

"And how do you know where this place is going to be?" he asked.

"That is where our colleague Mr Quartershaft comes in," Forset explained. "He discovered a set of papers on one of his recent expeditions. Calculations, in fact, purporting to predict the precise date and time of the town's next appearance, as well as map co-ordinates of the spot in which it will appear."

"And we can rely on that information, can we?"

Quartershaft blustered a little at that. "I can assure you the papers are quite genuine, sir. They were found in a hut in Delhi. The work of a man renowned within his village as being a man of great learning and wisdom.

Naturally it was only when I presented the papers to my publisher—"

"A friend of mine," Forset chipped in.

"Indeed," said Quartershaft, momentarily derailed, "as you say, a friend and... well, he put two and two together and proposed this trip."

"I had already made plans along these lines," Forset admitted, "but without the sponsorship of *Fireside Quarterly*, the Order of Ruth and, naturally, the fine chaps of the National Motor Company, I would have lacked the wherewithal to carry them through. Of course, the fact that Mr Quartershaft was able to provide such precise data made the whole trip a much more viable concern."

Billy was far from sure how much he agreed with that.

"And you?" he asked Father Martin, "how does your order come into this?"

"We have religious obligations," the monk explained. "We are a philosophical order. We consider it our purpose to explore and question such possibilities as Wormwood. For many years, I have also been convinced of its existence. I have conducted similar investigations to my learned friend"—he nodded towards Forset—"and had come to the same conclusion that the town would appear again on the date Mr Quartershaft confirms."

"So it's not just his papers?" Billy asked. "You have your own calculations?"

"Indeed."

Which was something of a relief. Roderick Quartershaft was not a man that Billy would choose to put so much faith in.

"That given," continued Father Martin, "we see it as our duty to try and find the town, to understand the religious implications and spread what we learn."

"I thought you just operated on faith?" said Billy. "Aren't you supposed to accept miracles?"

"We are. But we are also supposed to question, to prove the faith that our God has placed in *us*. Why has He created Wormwood? What is it for? To understand that, we must first see it."

Billy's opinion was divided. They were discussing something that he could scarcely conceive of as real. Yet they were doing so in a way that was more reasoned and balanced than he could ever have imagined. Perhaps, as Forset had said, the goal of their expedition really didn't matter. Either he would be proven wrong in his doubts, or he wouldn't.

"I guess our destination makes no odds to me," he said. "I'm just the driver. I go where I'm told. You say there may be dangers ahead; that's fine. Aren't there always?"

"Perhaps you'll change your mind when you experience them first hand," said Father Martin. "Though I still think it would have been better had you been told."

"If I have endangered you under false pretences," Forset said, "then I apologise. I can be rather self-centred, I'm afraid. My determination to see this expedition through outweighs almost everything else in my mind. I dare say Father Martin is right, I should have given you the choice."

Billy shrugged. "If you had told me all this before we set off, I don't think it would have made me stay away." He wondered how honest he should be. His determination to be polite was one thing, but in the open spirit of the room, he felt he should speak his mind. "Perhaps I would have viewed you all slightly differently," he admitted, "but that's neither here nor there. We're together now, and I'm a man that believes it's important to stand by his companions, so consider me a willing—if skeptical—member of the expedition."

Forset clapped his hands. "Excellent! And if that doesn't

call for the brandy bottle to be opened, I don't know what does."

"One thing, sir," said Billy, holding up his hand, "and I would have said this whatever the goal of this trip. I am the engineer here, I am the man responsible for keeping this locomotive running safely. If I say that we can't go on, or that we have to alter our route, then my voice is the last you will hear on the subject. I will not put us all at danger over what may just be a myth. I intend us all to get back to Omaha alive and well."

"Accepted," Forset agreed. "Though there are bound to be some risks, yes?"

"Some risks are fine," Billy replied, "but I will be the one who decides if they are worth taking, as far as this engine is concerned. Once you're off it, I can't stop you, but while onboard, my word is the law."

Elisabeth looked to her father, suspecting he would argue. He did not.

"I have wanted to find Wormwood for many years," he said, "and were it my life to risk, and mine alone, I cannot promise to what lengths I would or would not go. But we are a big party"—he reached out and took his daughter's hand—"and one of us is a woman so precious to me that her safety overrides all other concerns. I agree to your terms, young man. In fact, I insist on them."

"Then I guess we're all good," Billy said. "Where's that brandy?"

AFTER A NUMBER of the monks had made their discomfort clear, it was agreed that those who wanted to smoke cigars could do so outside.

Quartershaft was first out of the carriage, Billy following and Forset with Elisabeth bringing up the rear.

They each held a sizeable measure of brandy, and Billy

had to admit a real liking for the stuff. In his world, you drank beer or whisky, but he could see himself developing a taste for the liquor and the smooth fire it set off in his belly.

He smiled to see Elisabeth help herself to a serving just as large as the gentlemen. She was not a woman who believed in separate rules for women, clearly. He half expected her to take a cigar, but she just passed the case on to him, staring up at the wide-open sky above them.

"It's an amazing country you have," she said. "I can't pretend to like everything about it, but sat here looking up at all that space, I find I have to admire it."

"It does us well enough," Billy agreed. "There's everything a man could want in it, from the snow and mountains, to the greenery, to the desert. We are a hundred different worlds in one."

"That you are," she agreed with a smile.

"Shame it's filled with such idiots," said Quartershaft, before suddenly thinking what he had said through. "Present company excepted, naturally."

"Naturally," Billy replied, taking no insult. He had found the measure of the man and knew to dismiss most of what he said.

"So," he said after a quiet moment, "if you do find this place, what then?"

"Well," said Forset, "then we will have the greatest opportunity a man could hope for. A chance to explore Heaven."

"Is that the greatest opportunity?" Billy wondered. "I'm not sure it would interest me much."

Elisabeth looked sideways at him. "I find that hard to believe."

"Really? I just can't see the point. It seems to me that one of the main problems with people is that they refuse to make the best of what they have." He stamped his foot in the earth. "This is our world, and we spend our entire lives upon it. What's the point in always looking to what comes after?" He took a sip of his drink.

"My Ma was the same," he continued. "A real religious lady. And whatever happened to her, she would always think of it in terms of the hereafter. Say a man was rude to her. 'He'll get his comeuppance at the time of judgement,' she would say. Or she was in pain after a day working in the fields. 'That's fine,' she'd say, 'I can rest when I'm dead.'

"Now, to me that just seems foolish, though I would never have told her so. I know that life can't always be one long holiday, but if you hate your job, find one that suits you better. If someone hurts you, then you tell 'em. You don't wait for God to do it. What's the point in deferring the important stuff? That's nothing but a great way to stop living your life."

"I can see that," said Forset. "And you're quite right. But wouldn't you want to see what Heaven was actually like?"

"No. If it's going to be there for me when I die, then I'll see it then. If it's so all-fired wonderful, then it's only going to make me see the real world in a lesser light, and why would I want to do that? Would I end up wanting to stay there and never come back? Think of all the things down here I haven't seen. What a waste that would be. Much better to get the most out of Earth before you start hankering over Heaven. I'd rather see Europe any day..."

Forset laughed. "You talk a lot of sense, lad. I only wish I could be so grounded. I often forget to look at where am because I'm too busy looking at where I might be. I just can't resist the pull of the unknown. I want to *understand*."

"You'll never understand everything," Billy suggested.

"No," Forset agreed. "And that is the saddest thing I can imagine."

"What about you?" Billy asked Quartershaft. "Is it just another continent for you to set your eyes on? Another landscape to map?"

The explorer shuffled his feet in the dust, clearly uncomfortable at the question. "I'm here at the behest of my publisher."

"Fine, but you must feel a certain way about it."

Quartershaft drained his brandy. "Frankly, it terrifies me," he admitted.

Elisabeth felt sorry for him then. He'd finally offered a truthful answer. Though the sudden surge of sympathy was soon replaced by a fear of her own.

"What's happening over there?" she said, pointing to the sky ahead of them. "All the stars are just... vanishing."

The rest of them followed her pointed finger. It was just as she had said; a black mass seemed to be spreading across the sky, widening ever further and blotting out the light of the stars as it went.

"Clouds?" Quartershaft wondered. "Perhaps there's a storm on the way?"

"If so, it's moving damned quick," said Forset. "We should get back inside."

Quartershaft needed no more encouragement, pushing his way past them and climbing up the steps into the carriage. Forset and Elisabeth followed, Billy loitering to watch the darkness creep ever closer.

"I don't think it's a storm," he said, turning to join the rest of them inside. "Get the doors shut and the windows closed!" he shouted.

"You think it's a swarm of something?" Forset asked, having wondered the same thing himself.

"You want to take the risk of assuming it's not?"

The peer nodded and moved into the dining carriage.

"Gentlemen," he announced, "I need you to move as quickly as you can along the length of the transport. We need to make sure everything is sealed, all doors and windows firmly closed."

"What's wrong?" asked Brother Michael.

"Probably nothing, we're just being careful, but please do it quickly."

As the monks spread out, Forset unlocked a cabinet above one of the bookcases, revealing three rifles. "Better to be safe than sorry," he said. He turned to Quartershaft. "I would fetch your rifle if I were you, Roderick."

"Right," Quartershaft replied, nodding. "Yes..." He ran towards the sleeping quarters, the panic cutting through his drunkenness.

"If it is a swarm," said Billy, "I can't see that shooting at it is likely to be much help."

"Indeed not," Forset agreed, handing Billy and Elisabeth rifles, "but it might make us feel a little safer."

Billy shrugged, took the rifle, cracked it open to check it was loaded and then moved over to the window. "Whatever it is, it's nearly on top of us," he said. "It's too dark to know what we're facing until it hits."

"We could do worse for cover," said Forset. "I'd rather be inside here than a tent or a caravan."

Billy nodded. "We should be able to weather most things as long as the glass holds."

"Might it not be an idea to turn off the lights?" Elisabeth suggested. "We could be attracting whatever it is."

"Excellent idea," her father agreed.

"Everything's secure," announced Brother Clarence, shuffling back into the dining carriage, the rest of the order filing in behind him.

"Then might I suggest you retire to your compartments?" suggested Forset. "We're going to turn off all the lights, and you'll be safer there than here."

"Safer or less of an obstruction?" Brother William asked, smiling.

"Both," said Billy. "Now go, quickly, and make sure the doors are closed behind you."

As the monks departed, he moved to the far end of the carriage, pulling back a heavy rug to expose a panel beneath. "I'm going to disconnect the batteries," he explained. "The corridor lights stay lit as long as the charge lasts, so it's the only way to get complete darkness."

Forset moved to the door between them and the sleeping carriage. "Going dark now!" he shouted.

Billy unscrewed the wire connectors and the train went black.

A few moments later the entire transport shook, as whatever it was that had been heading towards them hit.

The carriage tilted a few degrees backwards and for a moment Billy was quite sure they were going to topple. Then they fell back again, the air filling with the sound of falling crockery and glass.

QUARTERSHAFT HAD RETRIEVED his rifle just as the lights went out. When the carriage rocked, he fell back against the far wall, tumbling to the floor.

His panic broke; he was quite convinced in that moment that he was facing the death he had always known was forthcoming. The carriage righted itself and he curled on the floor, hyper-ventilating. The fact that he was still breathing took a moment to register. The idea that he might continue to do so for some time was slower to develop.

I am a pathetic man, he thought. Barely a bloody man at all.

That surge of self loathing was what pushed him forward, reaching out into the darkness for the rifle he

had dropped. If he was going to die, then at least he should make a pretence of doing so bravely.

He felt his way out of the compartment and into the adjoining corridor.

"What's happening?" asked a frail voice from an open compartment next to his. One of the monks; he had given up trying to remember who was who.

"I haven't the foggiest notion, old chap," he replied, "but I'm on my way to try and find out."

While the carriage now seemed to be stable, the narrow corridor was filled with the sound of pounding as whatever it was outside beat against them. It was too dark to discern a thing, but he kept his back toward the compartment doors and inched his way along, fearful that the glass windows could shatter at any moment and let their attackers in.

The carriage had become a drum, playing a fast, staccato rhythm that accompanied him all the way along the corridor.

His shoulder bumped against the end of the sleeping carriage. It was only as he half-turned the handle that he realised he would be opening the door to the outside.

"If you open that, you might let them in," said Father Martin from behind him.

Quartershaft found himself irritated by the comment, entirely because it had only just occurred to him.

"Naturally," he replied. "I was just making sure it was secure."

There was a loud cracking noise from the far end of the corridor.

"The glass," said Father Martin. "It isn't going to hold!"

"Get inside and stay inside!" Quartershaft shouted, reaching out blindly to shove the monk back inside his cabin. He groped for the door and tugged it shut, just as the corridor filled with the sound of shattering glass and the thrashing of wings.

"Oh, God," Quartershaft whispered as he realised the sensible thing to have done would have been to jump into the monk's compartment after him.

There was a high-pitched screeching and he raised his rifle, panic consuming him as he pressed the trigger. Light flared as the rifle fired, and he saw a glimpse of countless dark shapes thrashing around in the confined space. In a moment they were on him, beating at his body, smacking against his screaming face. He dropped the rifle and fell to his knees, covering his head with his hands.

"WHAT IN HELL is going on?" Billy shouted, on hearing the rifle shot. He ran towards the connecting door, but slipped on a fragment of a shattered plate, hitting the floor with a resounding crash.

"Careful!" Elisabeth shouted, her voice barely carrying over the pounding noise. "You won't help anyone if you break a leg just getting to the door."

Then, so suddenly that it was almost as alarming as the attack had been, the noise ceased. Light from the moon outside returned to the carriage, showing the wreckage the shaking had wrought.

"They've passed," said Forset, looking at the opposite window and tracking the dark cloud as it shrank away in the opposite direction.

"The lights," Billy said, picking himself up and working his way over to the battery panel.

In a moment the lamps glowed back into life, and Elisabeth was running towards the connecting door.

"Wait," Billy said. "It may not be safe."

"Of course not," Elisabeth replied, opening the door anyway. "That's precisely why we need to check."

The cool of the outside air hit them as the door opened, and she and Billy dashed across the gangway and opened the door to the sleeping carriage.

They were in time to see a small cloud of bats vanishing through the smashed window. Quartershaft was lying on the floor, arms over his head, the bodies of more stunned bats littering the corridor all around him.

"It's alright now," said Billy, patting the explorer on the back. "They've gone."

Quartershaft slowly lifted his head and Elisabeth was embarrassed to see he'd been crying.

"I thought I was done for," he said. "There were hundreds of them."

"Just bats," Billy said. "Probably as scared of you as you were of them." He looked at the damage on the far wall where the rifle shot had punched a hole in the wood. "Especially after you started blasting away at them."

"I didn't know what they were."

The compartment doors all began opening, the monks peering out.

Father Martin went to Quartershaft. "My dear man, I hope you're all right?" He turned to Billy and Elisabeth. "He pushed me out of the way of danger, with no thought as to himself."

Both were surprised at that, as indeed was Quartershaft. In truth, he simply hadn't been thinking straight, but it was such a rarity to have someone speak highly of him he couldn't bear to explain.

Billy began to pick up the fallen creatures, tossing them out of the open window.

"God knows what damage they've done to the outside," he said. "Never seen anything like it. There was so many of them, what could have spooked them so much that they'd flock like that?"

"Wormwood," Father Martin said. "This was our first glimpse of the unnatural."

"We're hundreds of miles away," Billy replied. "Even if it does affect its surroundings, surely we're nowhere near close enough."

The monk shrugged. "All we know are rumours. Who can say for sure? Perhaps the disturbances aren't just random."

"What do you mean?" Forset asked, having joined them.

"Maybe it's not the world that it attacks," the monk suggested. "Maybe it's the people that are trying to find it."

CHAPTER EIGHT
SHOOT THE LIVING, PRAY FOR THE DEAD

MAYBE IT'S NOT the world that it attacks. Maybe it's the people that are trying to find it.

Having hit upon this thought, Father Martin simply couldn't leave it alone. His comment had been met with a degree of skepticism amongst the party, which was not unexpected. Quartershaft dismissed everything unless it came out of his own mouth, and Billy and Elisabeth didn't believe Wormwood even existed.

Lord Forset was a believer, certainly, but only insofar as he had traced the myths and rumours and now pursued them. He held no great spiritual belief. To him Heaven was an abstract concept, something from a book. To Father Martin and the rest of the order, it was a core part of their existence, a central pillar in their faith. To Father Martin, the idea that they were approaching the home of God threatened to burst his very soul.

So what if it *was* trying to repel them? Perhaps all of this was designed to keep the inquisitive from its borders. Was he fighting against the will of God? This was not a question he could take lightly. Nor was it one he could answer.

If God did not wish people to approach Wormwood then why allow it to exist at all?

The order had endlessly discussed the passage from the Book of Revelation:

The third angel blew his trumpet, and a great star fell from Heaven, blazing like a torch, and it fell on a third of the rivers and on the springs of water. The name of the star is Wormwood.

Some of the brothers—those with a little more fire and brimstone in their bellies—were concerned that this meant the arrival of the town was, in itself, a sign of the Apocalypse. The majority (and Father Martin had been one of them) pointed out that the town was said to have many names in its time and, really, it was probably only called Wormwood now because the name had a suitably ominous tone. There was a great difference between Holy Scripture and hearsay; one did not allow the latter quite the same potency for metaphor and allusion. While there was enough truth in the myth to be worth investigation, you couldn't let it gain sufficient weight as to predict the End of Days.

Now, however, Father Martin found his conviction on the matter weaker than it had been a few days ago.

He sat in his compartment, looking out onto the plain beyond the glass. The skinless monk was there again. Father Martin had accepted the fact that the apparition was a portent of some kind, a warning of hardships to come. All of his order were safe and sound for now. Whoever that was beyond the glass, his peeled skull quite black in the white light of the moon, he had yet to manifest himself into a reality. Was it—the most obvious assumption—a prediction of the death of one of the order? Or perhaps the death of them all? Father Martin supposed this was likely. It did not altogether distress him. If you were a man of faith, then death held little to fear. What was death but a transition? A journey just like the one he was on now. One that may even have the same destination at the end of it.

But that head, that exposed bone... that spoke of great pain. It was all very well accepting death as the end of one state and the commencement of another, but that wasn't to say that one wished to make the journey in a chaos of tears and suffering. He dearly hoped that his decision to undertake this journey wasn't to result in the torment of one of the others. He was no masochist, but if the physical pain was to be his to bear, then at least his soul would bear it easier.

He watched the figure as it slowly paced the dusty plain like a caged animal. Was it that impatient for the future to be written?

QUARTERSHAFT FELT ABSURDLY pleased with himself. His actions may not have been the stuff of heroic legend— indeed, if he had written them into one of his stories, his editor would have soon insisted he 'gave it a bit more pep'—but nonetheless, as it was certainly the closest he had come to an act of bravery, he felt justified in a degree of self-congratulation.

For the first time, he began to wonder if he might not survive the trip after all.

He cast his mind back to that hazy afternoon in the snug of the Velvet Pocket. He had been on the wrong side of a couple of bottles of simply delicious champagne, courtesy of a publisher's lunch. The dark walnut and maroon leather furnishings had taken on the soft, welcoming appearance of pillows, and he had folded himself into an easy chair with the desire to nap for a few hours. It would not have been the first time he had slept in the bar; indeed, a number of the regulars had taken to calling his favoured armchair 'Quartershaft's Rest.' Usually he slipped into unconscious for a couple of hours only to wake with a voracious appetite and the renewed stamina needed to quench it.

That day he had been interrupted.

"I say," said a voice that poured itself unbidden into his ears from behind the padded armrest, "aren't you Roderick Quartershaft, the famous explorer?"

Quartershaft was always wrong-footed when a fan found him in his cups. He was quite aware that some of the more devout readers of his exploits would find the sight of him in a drunken pile something of a disappointment. It was a major concern to him, not only because of his desire to keep his popularity high, but also because he felt quite enough self-disgust without the need to see it reflected back at him from others.

"I am," he replied, desperately trying to pull himself upright and shake his head into some semblance of sobriety. This was more than mere biology could manage, but he did at least open his eyes and point his face towards the enquirer.

He was a well dressed, middle aged man with light blond hair. If he noticed the inebriated state of the explorer, he seemed content to ignore it.

"I knew it was," the man said. "Spotted you from across the way there. I've been a fan of your work for many years."

Not that many, Quartershaft thought, I've only been in print for eighteen months. This was not a new phenomenon; it constantly surprised him how many people seemed convinced he had been a mainstay of literature since they were barely weaned from the breast. 'Always the way,' his publisher assured him. 'It's the true sign of success when people can't remember a time without you on their bedside table.'

"That's extremely gratifying to hear," he replied. "I'm glad my little exploits bring you pleasure."

"They do, they do." The man sat down in the chair next to him and Quartershaft's heart sank. It was one thing managing to maintain a conversation for a minute or two, but quite another if the fellow decided to make an afternoon of it.

"In fact," the man continued, "I was discussing you this very morning with a friend of mine."

The man withdrew a pipe from his jacket pocket and proceeded to fill it. This was not a good sign, thought Quartershaft. The bugger means to play the long game.

"'If anyone knows about Wormwood,' I said to him, 'then it would be Roderick Quartershaft.'"

"Wormwood?"

The man's face fell in a theatrical frown of disappointment. "Oh, don't tell me you've never heard of the place. I was so sure you would have done that I admit I made him a small wager. 'Alonzo,' my friend said to me—my name's Alonzo, blame an Italian mother—'if you're that struck by the feller, then why not put your money where your mouth is?'"

If there was one thing liable to bring sympathy from Quartershaft it was the possibility of a failed bet. He was not a gambling man, for the simple reason that the only two horses he had ever staked money on had died before finishing the race. Luck like that puts a man off.

"Oh!" he said. "Wormwood! Well, of *course* I've heard of Wormwood, yes. Forgive me, my mind was elsewhere for a moment. Planning the next trip, you understand."

"Wonderful!" Alonzo replied, clapping his hands with excitement. "And may I be so bold as to suggest we both know the destination?"

Quartershaft had no idea if the man could be so bold, but thought a simple smile was the safest reply.

"I knew it, I knew it!" Alonzo reached into his pocket and pulled out a sheaf of papers. "You know, it's funny, but I picked these up the other day and thought of you then." He spread the papers out on the table between them. "I dare say they're forgeries, but I considered sending them to you via your publisher anyway. You never know, I said to myself, they may be of some use."

Quartershaft tried to read the scribbled notes on the paper but a combination of bad handwriting and champagne made it impossibly hard work.

"It's obviously someone's research notes," Alonzo continued. "He talks about the whole myth of Wormwood, where the town has appeared before, where it might appear again. Who has seen it, what secrets it may contain..." The man selected a specific sheet, every inch of it covered in frantic calculations and sketches. "What was particularly interesting, though, is he's actually had a stab at predicting the next location and date of the town's appearance." He shrugged, tossing the paper onto the top of the pile. "I dare say he's quite wrong. Still, makes you think, doesn't it?"

"It does, it does," muttered Quartershaft, still utterly at a loss as to what the man was talking about.

"I mean," Alonzo continued, lowering his voice as if discussing the greatest secret in the world, "if he's right, then you have everything you need to attempt the most amazing expedition of your career. There isn't a man or woman in the world who wouldn't be singing the praises of Roderick Quartershaft if you attempted this. No sir, not a man or a woman in the world..."

He leaned back in his chair, once more affecting a casual air. "Of course, if you were already planning the trip, you probably know all this. I dare say you've conducted far better research of your own. Still, I thought it was worth passing on."

Alonzo suddenly snatched at his pocket watch as if it had been burning a hole in his waistcoat pocket. "I say!" he exclaimed. "Is that the time? I'm terribly late." He leaned forward and placed his hand on Quartershaft's shoulder. "Worth it to have made the acquaintance of a hero, though, naturally."

He got to his feet. "I'll leave the papers with you, in the unlikely event they might help corroborate your research. Least I can do."

And with that, he vanished, leaving Quartershaft to stare at the papers for a moment before falling asleep to dreams of worldwide adoration.

When he woke, the notes had taken on an entirely new light. Sleep had given him enough sharpness to attempt reading them and, while it was unquestionably hogwash, the blond fellow had certainly been on the money when he had said it could provide the backbone for a new piece in *Fireside Quarterly*.

The last thing he had imagined was that his editor would manage to verify them. More than that, he had found others who had heard of the myth and were eager to mount a trip to investigate. What had begun as a dollop of inspiration for a new story had wound up dragging him across the ocean and hurling bats at him. He could safely say that the very next person to suggest an expedition to him in a bar would be given short shrift.

"How sad," said Elisabeth, looking at the pile of dead bats they had thrown from the Land Carriage.

"You wouldn't think so, had the things been assaulting you half an hour ago," Quartershaft suggested, though the look on her face immediately made him regret the sentiment. "Although they could hardly help it, I suppose," he added. "Driven wild by some other force."

"They couldn't have done much harm," Billy said, "though you weren't to know that in the dark. I'd have been as terrified as you."

Quartershaft wasn't altogether fond of the word 'terrified,' but he appreciated Billy taking his side.

"Of course," he said, "there are some species of bat that can kill a man with ease. Why, I once saw a beast that was four foot across. It drained every drop of blood from a cow in a matter of moments."

He kicked himself, as their respect for him visibly dwindled. "Well," he admitted, "I heard about it, at least. Didn't see it with my own eyes."

His moment of acceptance within the party having drawn to a close, he made his excuses and returned to his compartment. As he lay in his bed. he wondered if he would ever learn to keep his mouth shut.

THE FOLLOWING MORNING, Billy was up early and examining the outside of the Land Carriage for damage.

"How is she looking?" Forset asked, emerging from the sleeping carriage and stepping down onto the plain. The ground was still littered with dead bats, though perhaps less than there had been the night before. No doubt nocturnal predators had taken advantage of an easy meal.

"I suppose it could be worse," said Billy. "Most of the damage is only superficial, she looks a little rough but she's still in good shape."

Forset couldn't help but feel sad at the state of his proud invention. One day 'in the wild' and the paint was chipped, glass was cracked and everything had been marbled with guano. Still, as Billy said, functionality was the thing. As long as the engine wasn't impaired in any way, then they had escaped the night unscathed.

"I suppose we can hardly justify delaying the journey

for the sake of a scrub and touch up," he said. "We're not out here to impress with our appearance, after all."

Billy was far from certain they ever had, but he was sensitive to the peer's feelings. "If they're not impressed by the sight of us tearing our way across the land, then they're blind."

THEY WERE UNDER way again within the hour, Billy stoking up the boiler and slowly accelerating towards optimum speed.

Inside, everyone lent a hand to fixing the damage of the night before, sweeping up broken china, righting fixtures and fittings. By mid-morning, the Forset Land Carriage was all but restored, bar a boarded-up window in the sleeping carriage and the damage caused by Quartershaft's rifle.

If the rest of the party noticed Father Martin's discomfort, they didn't mention it. He spent much of his time on his own in his compartment, trying to reconcile the warring thoughts in his head. The rest of the order had reverted to their attitudes of the day before: Brother Samuel tutting over everything modern he could find while the rest looked out of the windows and enjoyed the view.

It was Brother Jonah who first noticed the smoke plumes on the horizon.

He was one of the meeker members of their band, a man more content inside his own head than in the company of others. Before leaving his old life behind, he had been an assistant at the British Library, happily whiling away his days in a fog of indices and translation. Like most of the order, his private reading eventually brought him to a crisis point: he had become so obsessed with his researches into apocrypha that he could no longer maintain both his job and his private reading. Something had to give, and he had taken to religious servitude like a natural. Silence and arcane papers. He had never been happier.

His reading had taken its toll on his eyesight, however, and for the first couple of minutes he was quite sure that what he saw was nothing but the tops of distant trees. It was only when the trail of smoke began to carve its way towards them that he realised his error. Trees simply did not move in procession.

Even then, his natural reluctance to draw attention to himself made it difficult for him to speak up. It was only when he considered the possibility that the smoke could be the passage of a vehicle much like theirs—perhaps one on a collision course, for it seemed to be making a bee-line for them—that he realised he had to say something.

"Excuse me," he said, raising his hand, "but can anyone else see that trail of smoke that seems to be coming towards us?"

He was joined at the window by Brother Clement, an altogether more outspoken member of the order who spared no time in raising the alarm.

"It's another train!" he shouted. "Watch out, or we'll end up crashing into it."

"We're not a train," explained Forset. "We have no track."

Brother Clement, a man only too used to nit-picking over dogma, felt relieved by that until it occurred to him that, in this context, the difference hardly mattered.

"There's something coming from this side, too!" called Brother William, peering out of the right-hand window. "But I don't think it's a train. It's a whole procession of smaller vehicles."

Forset moved through into the engine to find Billy already gazing at the twin smoke trails coming in from both directions. He had a pair of binoculars and was turning from one side to the other.

"You've seen them, then?" Forset said. "Able to tell what they are?"

"Not with any certainty," Billy admitted. "They look..." He handed the glasses to Forset. "See for yourself."

Forset did so. He understood why the engineer had found it hard to describe.

The closer the twin processions came, the more he could discern their detail, though that hardly helped him understand. "They look like people on horseback," he said. "But their heads..."

Soon the figures were close enough that they were both able to take in their surreal appearance without the binoculars.

"They're incredible," said Forset. "*Unbelievable.*"

Billy was forced to agree. The bats he could have written off as an accident of nature, but this was harder to explain. At that moment, the existence of Wormwood seemed a little less absurd.

From the waist down, the riders appeared to be a tribe of Native Americans. As the eye rose, however, they were impossible to identify. Brown skin fused into plates of iron or steel. In some places the metal appeared as if it might have been bolted on to a human torso, while in others the joining was less clear-cut, the skin growing over the metal. The metal became dominant as it rose to the head, jagged constructions of pipes, valves and pistons that towered above their shoulders like girders. The glow of hot coals emanated from each metal skull, trails of smoke flickering behind them in the wind like feathered headdresses. Their arms seemed an awkward combination of nature and engineering, glimpsed muscles and fingers poking from between hinges and panels.

"What should we do?" Forset asked. "Do you think they mean us harm?"

"They're riding in an attack formation," said Billy, "a pincer movement closing in from both sides." He hoisted himself up on the side of the cabin. "I wouldn't be surprised if there weren't more of them coming from the rear."

He couldn't get high enough to tell, and, wary of presenting himself as a target, he dropped back down again.

"Have we enough firepower to defend ourselves?" he asked.

"Not really," Forset admitted. "I'm afraid I'm an inventor, not a soldier. I didn't really think about this sort of thing."

"Well, maybe you should go back there and see what you can rustle up. I'll keep the speed as high as I can; we'll see if we can outrun them. The horses look normal enough and, carrying those guys, you'd think they'd tire easily."

Forset stepped back into the dining car, where everybody was staring out of the windows at the approaching army.

"What do you think they are, father?" asked Elisabeth. "Are they wearing armour?"

"I think it's a little more unconventional than that," the peer admitted. "We need to get ourselves armed and ready for trouble."

Quartershaft visibly paled, but said nothing. After the trouble last night, he had made the decision to keep his rifle with him at all times and he clutched it tightly now, hoping to absorb some courage from it. Hadn't he known that they were bound to fall foul of an attack by Indians? Weren't they likely to be sharpening the scalping knives even as they drew closer?

"Brothers," Forset announced, "I think I should once again ask you all to retire to the relative safety of the sleeping carriage. Please do so now, and quickly. Try not to stay exposed between the carriages for too long."

The men filed quickly towards the adjoining door, all except Brother William.

"I may be a man of God," he said, "but I am willing to fight if He wishes it."

"If He didn't, old son," said Quartershaft, "He would hardly send a whole load of ruddy Indians at us." He reached for his belt and pulled out a revolver. "Take that with my gratitude. The more of us pointing guns at the enemy, the happier I shall be."

FATHER MARTIN, LOST in his thoughts, had failed to even notice the figures outside the window. It was only as the adjoining door banged open and the sound of fretting monks filtered through that he shook himself free of his woolgathering and investigated.

"We're under attack, Father Martin," shouted Brother Clarence, the first through the door.

"From what?" He stared through the window, scarcely able to believe what his eyes were seeing.

The riders were drawing in on the Land Carriage now, twin bands of dust and smoke building on either side of them.

"Come on!" Father Martin shouted, pulling the monks through the doorway. "You're exposed out there; get through quickly."

Brother Jonah was only too aware of this, being the last in line to pass from one carriage to another and still standing in the open air.

"Do go a little faster, if you could," he said to Brother Samuel in front of him.

Brother Samuel was moving as quickly as he could, but the gangplank was shaking violently as he tried to cross it, the wind tugging at his cassock. He gripped the handrail, trying to pull himself across, but his shaking arms had little strength.

"I think I'm stuck," he admitted. "Unless you can pull me back?"

The riders were either side of them now, and Brother Jonah stared in terror at the sight of them, only feet away. "O merciful Lord," he whispered, "can these be Your creation?"

The rider to his left raised his arm, and there was a terrifying shriek as a spray of steam jetted from the pipe at the end of his wrist and engulfed Brother Samuel.

The old man didn't even cry out as he boiled, contorted and tumbled from the gangplank.

"Oh, my Lord!" Brother Jonah cried, stepping back. "*Oh, my Lord!*"

IN THE ENGINE, Billy was also under attack.

The riders on either side of him had come in as closely as possible, their hands extended towards him. Unlike the rider that had killed Brother Samuel, these wielded fire, great tongues of it lashing over the side of the engine and curling in towards the cab.

Billy forced himself up against the boiler as the flames licked around him, only too aware of how exposed he was.

The flames stopped and he took an opportunity to take a shot with his rifle. He shot to the right, with some regret aiming at the horse rather than the rider. The animal toppled and its rider flew forward. Top heavy, the thing immediately fell, hitting the ground head first with a crunch of impacting metal. There was a burst of fire from the attacker's boiler and a spray of shrapnel hit the side of the engine.

The rider on his left raised his arm once more and Billy ducked. The fire flowed over him, coming close enough to set his shirt alight. He rolled on his back, crying out in pain at his singed skin and forcing himself towards the front of the cab where the cover was greatest.

FATHER MARTIN RECOILED in shock at the sight of Brother Samuel's death. Was that it? Was that the premonition he had experienced? Certainly Brother Samuel's old white scalp had turned bright pink in the seconds before he had fallen from sight.

He shook the thought away. Now was not the time. The rest of the order were still alive and that was where his attentions should be.

"Go back!" he shouted to Brother Jonah. "Stay in the dining car."

Which was certainly sound advice, Brother Jonah decided, if only he could turn around. The door was closed behind him, with his back flat to it. It opened outwards. In order to open it again, he would have to step into the line of fire, pull the door towards him, step past it, then back inside. All of which seemed too much to accomplish without meeting the same fate as Brother Samuel.

"I can't," he said, his quiet voice barely carrying over the sound of the engine and the hooves of the horses on either side. "They'll catch me for sure."

IN THE DINING carriage, Brother Jonah's predicament was only too clear to Elisabeth, who had watched in horror as Brother Samuel had fallen to his death.

"We need to provide him with covering fire," she said. "Or he'll never get across."

Before the death of the monk, her father had been congratulating himself on having insisted on windows that opened. The—much cheaper—suggestion of the National Motor Company had been to provide fixed panels with sliding vents in the roof to allow air circulation. If that had been approved, they would have had nowhere to take a shot from. All the windows were now slightly opened so they could poke out the barrels of their rifles.

Quartershaft had fired already, but he was not the finest shot, and the challenge of hitting a moving object from inside a moving object seemed altogether too much for him.

"Easier said than done," Forset told his daughter, lining up a sight on one of the riders. "I just can't get the angle to shoot that far back." He fired once, the bullet ringing off the rider's metal torso with the resonant *clang* of a church bell, then fired again. This second shot found its mark, hitting the rider just above its waist and sending it toppling from its horse.

The wave of riders behind the stricken creature were forced to shift as their fallen comrade embedded itself in the dirt.

BROTHER JONAH SAW his opportunity as the riders to his left veered out of their fallen comrade's way. He jumped forward, eyes closed in terror, desperately hoping he could make the open doorway ahead of him.

The rider to the right flexed his wrist and a shower of shrapnel cut through the air.

Father Martin grabbed for Brother Jonah and yanked him through into the sleeping carriage as the shrapnel clanged off the gangway behind him. The monk cried out as several pieces of metal whipped through his trailing cassock, and fell on top of his superior in the passageway.

"Are you alright?" Father Martin asked. "Were you hit?"

He looked into Brother Jonah's startled face and saw no response.

He dragged himself out from under the other monk, and recoiled in horror as he saw that the back of the monk's head had been sheared clean away by a piece of metal.

Around him the other monks began to panic, shouted prayers and desperate pleas filling the confined space as the hole in Brother Jonah's skull began to fill up with blood.

THIS WAS NOT the first time Brother William had fired a gun. Unlike the rest of his order, William's background was not among book-stacks and ancient papers. William had grown up in London, a bitter, angry young man. The closest he got to books was when he had been beaten with one by an uncle who had no desire to look after a child just because the boy's parents had had the audacity to die. A member of the notorious Caine Gang by the age of sixteen, William spent his eighteenth birthday in Newgate Prison, marching in circles around the tiny exercise yard. He decided that the best gift he could allow himself was the chance of a new life; his first had not worked out as well as he might have hoped.

On release, he turned to God, and since then, God had not let him down. He very much hoped today was not to be the day.

He fired the revolver, catching a rider in the hip. A second shot entered just below the rib cage and had the desired effect, the rider toppling sideways off the horse.

"Forgive me," he muttered, "but we are on a mission from God."

He lined up another shot, this one more immediately

successful as the bullet entered in the upper stomach, appearing to ricochet before reappearing from the rider's smoking mouth.

"Good shot," said Forset from over his shoulder. "Keep it up. Our only chance is to dissuade the attack by making a sufficient dent in their numbers."

"If they don't 'dent' ours first..." said his daughter, seeing the fate of Brother Jonah through the window of the adjoining door.

"Damn them," said Quartershaft, kicking at the wall of the carriage before taking a deep breath and moving in front of the window to line up another shot. It clanged off the chest of the closest rider, as did the second.

"Aim lower," said Forset, taking a successful shot of his own. "You'll have no chance against the armour."

Quartershaft chose not to admit that he had been aiming lower. He was not what one could call a marksman.

He reloaded and aimed again.

BILLY COULD BARELY move. The constant tongues of flame lashing over the rear of the engine cab kept him pressed up against the coal store. This close to the boiler, oppressive heat was coming at him from both sides. To make matters worse, they were now driving blind, but he knew that if he stuck his head up to look at the landscape ahead, he would have it burned away in moments.

The rider he had shot on his right had been replaced by another, and it and its opposite number now took it in turns to shoot at him, keeping the flames up between them so that he never had an opportunity to move.

There was only one idea that occurred to him, and he would have acted on it already, but that it had a fair chance of destroying the Land Carriage and all its passengers. That kind of risk gave a man pause.

The longer he remained boxed in, however, the more he began to give it consideration. It was a gamble, but not one they weren't already taking, driving blind as they were. At any moment, they could hit a rock or ditch in the road that would tip them. They had deliberately been travelling through open plains, but at their current speed it wouldn't take much to throw them.

To hell with it. They weren't going to get out of this situation without taking risks.

He checked his revolver, took a deep breath and then threw himself towards the steering column.

At this speed the one thing you should never do is make a radical change of direction. While the locomotive was designed to be manoeuvrable, the carriages behind were less so. If he forced the locomotive into a sharp turn to the left, the carriages would push forward and swing out to the right. They had been weighted heavily in order to limit the chance of them toppling over, but nobody could have anticipated such a reckless piece of driving.

His back to the column, he shot at the riders on the Land Carriage's right. The locomotive engine began to shift, cutting into the path of the riders on the machine's left. There was a squeal of metal and a roar as the wheels cut into the ground, the momentum of the carriages pushing it forward. Slowly he applied the brakes; if they kept moving forward at speed, they would roll for sure. The column of riders impacted against the nose of the locomotive, two of them thrown from their horses and rolling over the top of the smoke stack, hitting the ground on the opposite side.

The last carriage began to snake sideways, a great cloud of dust flying up before it. It slammed into the riders on that side, scything through them from the rear even as all three carriages began to tilt.

Billy fired again, but the riders were ignoring him now, too panicked by the vehicle now cutting them down from both sides.

He turned back to the controls, pulling the steering column straight and keeping the speed steady. If he could ride the momentum out, he stood a chance of keeping the Land Carriage on its wheels.

THE EFFECT OF the sudden shift in the carriages was catastrophic inside.

Father Martin, still lying in the passage of the sleeping car, weathered the movement best, rolling against the wall of the carriage, the dead body of Brother Jonah slamming against him. The other brothers all fell sideways, toppling into the windows. Most held, but the damaged pane from the night before did not and Brother Clement found himself flailing out into open air as one of the nailed boards gave way.

It was Brother Clarence that prevented him falling further, grabbing hold of the old man's cassock and tugging him back inside.

IN THE DINING car, Forset and his daughter were pressed against the windows they had been shooting through, while Quartershaft and William rolled over to join them.

"What the hell is the young idiot doing?" Quartershaft shouted.

Forset, watching as the riders fell before the sliding rear carriage, guessed only too well. "Possibly saving our lives."

"He has a bloody funny way of going about it," Quartershaft moaned, crying out as a bookshelf showered him in copies of Jules Verne.

*   *   *

It took all of Billy's strength to control the steering column. Eventually the Land Carriage righted itself and, with that, the greatest danger was gone. Now all he had to do was maintain their forward momentum so as to absorb the pressure from the carriages behind. He was so focused on keeping the Land Carriage from destroying itself he had no choice but to ignore the attacking riders. He could only hope they continued to have problems of their own.

"I think we might have given them pause," said Forset, shifting now that the carriage had righted itself and taking another shot out of the window. "Keep shooting, and we may repel them yet."

Elisabeth raised her rifle and added to her father's fire. Quartershaft and William returned to the other side of the carriage and did the same.

"It's working!" said William. Both columns of riders were peeling away, abandoning their attack.

"Aye," Quartershaft agreed, "we've got the swine on the run."

"I must get Billy to stop!" said Forset.

"Stop?" his daughter asked. "Surely that's the last thing we want to do?"

Billy agreed with Elisabeth's sentiments, but Forset was adamant.

"Only for a few minutes," he insisted. "We need to turn around and gather a few of the fallen bodies."

"We have fallen bodies of our own," Elisabeth said. "If we stay here, we're likely to end up with more."

"But don't you see?" the exasperated peer insisted. "If they do attack again—and they probably will—we need to know as much about them as possible. If I had some of them to examine, I might be able to create something to defend us. We survived this time purely by the skin of our teeth."

"We won't get to pull a move like that again," Billy agreed. "They'll be wiser next time." The engineer thought about it. "Alright, we go back and we grab a couple of bodies, but we do it quickly, and then we push on as fast as we can."

CHAPTER NINE
MASSACRE TIME

THE LAND CARRIAGE wasn't designed to turn back on itself easily. Billy swept it around in a large curve, describing a circle across the plain, and paused so that they could pick up some of the fallen riders before continuing around. It was a deviation of ten minutes in total, every moment spent in the anticipation that the riders would return.

"These things are unbelievable," said Billy as they lifted one of them onto the rear carriage. Up close, the merging of metal and flesh was even more disturbing. If it was artificial, then it had been a process of many months, the human bodies fully fused with the black iron.

The monks had wanted to find the body of Brother Samuel, but Forset had refused for two reasons. The first—the one that he told them—was that they would have to travel back on themselves too far. What they were doing was dangerous enough; Samuel having fallen so early in the attack, it could easily be another few miles before they found him, time they could ill afford to risk. The second, and more truthful, reason was that he couldn't bear to think what state the body might be in. If it had fallen beneath the wheels—as it most likely had—then he had no doubt the remains would little resemble the fallen monk. It would help nobody to be presented with such a grotesque reminder of their mortality.

Forset remained on the rear carriage, working between packing crates so as to be protected against the wind. Brother William remained with him, ostensibly to provide a second pair of hands but also to keep a lookout for the return of the creatures that had attacked them. He perched on one of the packing crates, rifle in his lap, gazing out across the plain.

"You are a very unusual monk," Forset commented, while attempting to unbolt a shoulder section from the rider he was working on. "I never thought I'd see a man of the cloth fire a rifle."

"I dare say I will have a similar conversation with Father Martin once I return to the fold," William admitted. "I am by no means sure I haven't broken the rules of the order. In which case you won't have to worry, as I won't be a monk anymore."

"Well, you won't get any complaint from me. I appreciate the tenets of your fellows, but we needed all the help we could get. I am not a violent man, but I will do what needs to be done to protect the lives of those I love."

The monk nodded. "An acceptable compromise, I think, though don't take that view as doctrine. I rather think the others would be of the belief that if we die, we die."

Forset got the shoulder free, the whole left arm coming away in a splatter of blood and engine oil. He frowned in disgust at the messy wound thus revealed.

"It really is half mechanical, half natural," he said. "Even the bone contains metallic elements."

"Men or machines?" Brother William wondered aloud.

"Both, it would seem."

Brother William glanced down at the body as Forset moved on to the head. "A shame, as destroying the latter would certainly not threaten my immortal soul."

"Who is to say what state any of our souls will be in by the time this journey is over?" Forset replied.

THAT WAS A concern that was uppermost in Father Martin's mind. Two of his number had met violent deaths, and a third, the young novice he had been so determined to embrace into the fold, seemed to be following a path away from righteousness. Or was he? Father Martin was no longer sure he could even discern what path that might be. The certainty with which he had begun this journey seemed more like childish naivety with every passing hour.

It had been decided that, for now at least, they should all travel together in the dining car. Several of the monks were at the windows, keeping a watch on the land around them in case of a fresh attack.

Quartershaft was pacing, his ever-present nerves even closer to the surface than normal. Father Martin supposed this was because he wasn't drinking. The man had obviously decided that, as much as he relished the numbing effect of the alcohol, he would rather keep his wits sharp in case he needed them. Abstinence was clearly taking its toll. After a few minutes, Father Martin began to wish the man would just have a drink and calm down.

"Are you alright, Father?"

He looked up to see Elisabeth, the very epitome of the divided nature of this journey. Here was this young, unmarried woman, so aggressive and with a rifle in her hand. He really could not begin to know what he felt about that.

"Not really, my dear," he replied, "but I dare say I will find my spirits again shortly."

"It's understandable, you know," she said.

"What is?"

"Regret. You wish you had never come. You know that if you had simply stayed at home, Brothers Samuel and Jonah would still have been alive."

"Probably they would, but you don't understand me as much as you think. I don't regret coming, and that is precisely why I am feeling out of sorts. It's more important to me to pursue this journey, with a goal that I cannot even reconcile with my beliefs. A journey that has killed two men and will no doubt kill more. If we *could* turn around now, I am by no means sure I would. And I am wondering precisely what sort of man that makes me."

THE RIDERS DID not return, but that was not to say the day passed uneventfully.

Billy tried to get as much speed out of the engine as he could. This made the journey rough, but he was determined to pass through the area as quickly as possible, in the hope that the riders' territory could be put behind them.

The world seemed to fight back, the sky filling with a storm that raged throughout the middle of the day. There was no rain, but lightning strafed around them in a manner that couldn't fail to put Father Martin in mind of the wrath of God. Rocks shattered, the earth was scorched, but the Land Carriage pulled through unscathed. The air around them was filled with a static charge that forced Billy's red hair straight up from his head as he kept the engine pushing forward.

As they passed into afternoon, a fog descended that caused much greater problems, It became so thick that it was difficult to navigate more than a few feet ahead. After a while, Elisabeth took to the skies in the Forset Thunderpack, making brief trips above the fog in the hope of seeing how far it extended. It was an arduous business, always mindful of the fact that the pack might explode if allowed to ignite for too long. Throughout, goggles in place, Forset worked on.

When the fog finally cleared, it was late afternoon and they were forced to decide about how to pass the night. Some were convinced that they should keep moving, terrified of the idea of turning themselves into a stationary target. Others—Billy the most vocal among them— insisted that it would be suicidal to try and navigate in the dark. The Land Carriage had lights, but their effect was limited and, besides, wouldn't they make even more of a target as a roaring beacon that could be seen for miles around?

The latter argument won out and it was a nervous party that settled down to eat on their second night aboard.

"To think," said Forset, gazing out of the window into the growing darkness, "we are only a matter of hours away from Wormwood." He was gathering together a plate of food, having insisted on working for a few more hours by the light of oil lanterns.

"They could be long hours," Billy replied. They had fallen behind schedule due to the conditions, and he wasn't naive enough to think the rest of their journey would be any easier. What seemed like a few hours on the map could be a day's travel or more, depending on what they might face. "What have you discovered about the Indians?"

The peer sighed, looking down at his plate of cold meat and bread. "I'm an engineer, not a doctor. That said, so much of their physical make-up was machinery I probably had as much chance of understanding them as someone with medical training. I suspect it's pointless trying to decide how their modified bodies are scientifically possible; we're dealing with miracles, not biology."

"The only thing we really need to know," said Quartershaft, "is can you stop them if they attack again?"

Forset nodded. "That's what I'm working on. As fascinating as they are, now is not the time for satisfying curiosity."

Father Martin was becoming visibly uncomfortable. "I can't say I relish our discussing how to slaughter living beings."

"I think, Father," said Brother William, "they have already proven that our choice in the matter is limited. Either we kill them or they will kill us."

"And where does that leave higher concerns?" Father Martin asked. "A man can lose much more than just his life."

Nobody could answer him on that.

LATER, ELISABETH MADE her way to the rear of the Land Carriage to visit her father. He had stretched a large section of tarpaulin over the packing crates surrounding him, creating a makeshift tent.

Three of the deconstructed bodies lay before him, reduced to their component parts.

"I think Father Martin is suffering a crisis of morality," she said. Looking at the butcher's shop display in front of her, she wondered if the monk might have a point.

"I can't say I relish my current work," her father admitted, "but I have the advantage over our clerical friend in that I consider our position more clear-cut. Either we defend ourselves or we die. I am not willing to accept the latter, so I must work to ensure the former."

"And what have you come up with?"

"Something terrible," he replied.

* * *

FATHER MARTIN WAS in his compartment watching the faceless monk pacing in the moonlight beyond the window. It almost appeared like it was dancing, moving to and fro in the dust.

"Was it me that made you?" Father Martin wondered aloud. "Are you the manifestation of a diseased conscience? Or a reminder of what will become of us unless I forego some of my beliefs?"

The figure stopped moving, turned to face the window and slowly walked towards the Land Carriage.

"O God," Father Martin whispered as it pressed its wet face up against the glass. "What do You want from me?"

FATHER MARTIN'S CRISIS of conscience was not shared by either Quartershaft or Billy. The two men were stood in the cab of the engine, a large brandy each, keeping a watch on the plain. Thankfully the moon was nearly full, and cast a reasonable light on the landscape. If something did try and advance on them, they should have reasonable warning.

"Do you think they'll come back for more?" Quartershaft asked.

"Normally, I'd doubt it; there must be easier pickings out here," said the engineer. "But if what Father Martin says is true—that these things are direct challenges to us—then we're bound to face them, or something even worse, soon enough."

"You're starting to believe in the town, then?"

"With everything I've seen over the past day or so, I'd be stupid to dismiss it. I'll still wait for the evidence of my own eyes before I become a fully signed-up member of the Wormwood society, though."

Quartershaft smiled and took a big mouthful of his brandy.

"I'll be honest," he said. "I was far from convinced myself. It sounded a good story, but, well, a bit..." He tapped at his temple with a finger.

"Just a little," Billy agreed. "Though I'd have thought you'd be used to that, from what I've heard of your expeditions."

Quartershaft sighed and decided to break the habit of a lifetime by telling the truth. "Don't believe everything you read," he said. "This is the first time I've left England. The rest of it was all made up, a plot hatched between me and my publisher."

Billy stared at him for a moment and then started laughing. Quartershaft wasn't quite sure how he should take that. "I'm glad it amuses you."

"Oh, it does," said Billy. "It sure does." He patted Quartershaft on the shoulder. "Don't take me wrong, I'm not laughing at you... well, maybe a little... but not in a bad way."

"Oh, good," Quartershaft replied. "Because I do so enjoy being laughed at in a good way."

Billy laughed again. "I guess it's just... well, what a party, you know? A mad inventor and his daughter, a bunch of monks and a fake." He held up his hand as Quartershaft's face fell even further. "No... not a fake, because you know what? You've told the truth, and I respect the hell out of you for it." He patted him on the arm again. "You're a good man, Quartershaft."

"That's not even my real name."

"Oh, Christ..."

"My real name's Patrick Irish."

Billy raised his glass. "Good to meet you, Patrick."

"You won't tell the others?"

"No. But you should probably tell them yourself. Life's too short—especially on this trip—to be anyone but yourself."

Quartershaft nodded. "You may be right."

"Sure I am."

"Can I ask you a question?"

"'Course you can."

Quartershaft thought about it for a moment, summoning up the courage to ask. "Are you scared?"

"Of those things that attacked us yesterday? Of course I am. Only an idiot wouldn't be."

"Not just them. Everything. I seem..." Quartershaft took a drink, not quite believing how honest he was being. "I'm just terrified all the time."

"Fear is what keeps us safe," said Billy. "The trick is to only be afraid of the things that are real. The stuff that's around you. If you spend all your time being scared of things that *might* happen, you'll never draw breath."

"You're right, of course," Quartershaft admitted. "I just wish this country of yours didn't seem so blasted lethal."

"It's not so bad. It's not killed me yet."

"Don't speak too soon."

THE NIGHT PASSED uneventfully. The whole party took it in turns to maintain a watch. The sun rose on Brothers Luke and Conrad, both of whom were fighting to stay awake.

"I think we've seen the last of them," Brother Conrad announced at breakfast.

"Don't believe it for a moment," Billy replied. "At a steady pace, we're all of four hours away from Wormwood."

"So expect the worst in about four hours' time?" asked Elisabeth.

"You got it."

"Father will be ready," she said. "He worked most of the night."

An effort that had clearly taken its toll on the man, by

the time he appeared. He was exhausted and more than a little anxious. "Before we get under way," he said, rubbing at his eyes, "I'm going to need some help."

"You know I'm only too happy to lend a hand," said Elisabeth.

"I know, my dear, but, at the risk of upsetting your noble insistence on equality, this is more a job for Billy and Roderick."

IT TOOK THEM nearly an hour to complete Forset's plans, but finally they were under way, the Land Carriage setting forth on the final leg of its outbound journey.

The flat landscape that had surrounded them thus far began to change as they drew closer to Wormwood, rising to either side of them. They were soon cutting their way through a mountain pass.

Forset and Billy were riding in the engine cab together, their eyes scanning the high ground on either side of them.

"This is where they'll try," said Billy. "Where the cover gives them the advantage."

"And where we can't easily double back on ourselves," Forset agreed. "If this pass gets any narrower, it will be all we can do to keep moving forward."

"According to the map, it should carry on like this for another few miles before opening out again."

"At which point we've arrived."

Billy kept the speed steady, expecting the worst at each turn.

The land itself began to shift around them, the sides of the mountains rippling and cracking. Twice, they had a narrow escape from rocks breaking loose from above them and rolling down towards the Land Carriage. The first narrowly missed their tail end, the second was only avoided at the front by Billy applying the brakes and steering out of its way. There was a terrible grinding sound as they grazed its jagged surface as they passed.

"Another of those and we'll be beyond worrying about the riders," said Billy. "It wouldn't take much of a rockfall to block our way."

But it wasn't rocks that proved to be the obstruction, in the end. They turned past the foot of one of the mountains to find themselves face to face with a large army of the riders.

"Do they think we won't just drive straight through them?" Billy asked.

"Maybe they plan on ensuring there's not enough left of us to try," Forset replied. "Given their firepower, I'm sure they could succeed, too. But they don't know we have a few tricks of our own. Bring us to a stop; we'll want to charge at them, but I need to get into position first."

He turned and began to climb onto the roof of the dining carriage.

"Oh, God!"

Forset turned at the sound of Billy's voice, looking ahead. The riders had parted to reveal a tall wooden cross, nailed to which was the dead body of Brother Samuel. He would hardly have been recognisable were it not for his grey cassock and a single plume of white hair that erupted from the crushed ruin of his skull.

"They think we won't hit him," said Billy.

"And I dare say if Father Martin was driving, we wouldn't." Forset carried on his climb. "As it is, they've just made what I have to do a great deal easier, the heathen bastards."

He moved across the roof of the carriage, taking his position behind a construction covered in tarpaulin. It was this that they had spent an hour bolting into place earlier. Reaching down, he clipped his belt to a pair of chains they had fixed to either side.

"Ready?" shouted Billy. "It looks like they are."

The riders were shifting restlessly, the clatter of their metal parts echoing along the pass as they prepared to charge.

"I'm ready," Forset replied, leaning back against the pull of the chains and reaching for the tarpaulin. "Full steam ahead."

The tarpaulin fell away to reveal a grotesque mockery of a gatling gun, its fat barrel constructed from the severed arms of the fallen riders. Other recognisable sections of skull and limb had gone into constructing the frame, a large tank at its summit filled with all the viable munitions Forset had been able to gather: nails, screws, shrapnel of any kind.

As the Land Carriage surged forward, Forset pressed the trigger and, keeping his aim low, peppered the advancing riders.

Forset shook with the force of the gun, the chains at his belt pulling taut as he leaned on them.

Shrapnel cut through the air, scything into horses and riders alike. The air filled with ricocheting metal, animal screams and the hot spray of blood.

INSIDE THE LAND Carriage, Father Michael was only too glad they couldn't see what was happening. The noise was more than enough. The weapon hammered against the roof above them, the whole carriage shaking with the vibrations as it fought to break free of the bolts holding it in place. The sound of metal tearing its way through stone and flesh echoed back along the pass. The horses screeched as they died *en masse*, the wail of the slaughterhouse or of the very pits of Hell.

He began to cry, pressing his hands against his ears.

* * *

THE STOCK OF shrapnel was beginning to dwindle, but Forset could see he would have no need of it. The effect on the riders had been so sudden, so shocking, they hadn't even had time to offer counter-fire. The Land Carriage tore through the panicked remains of their number, the heavy nose of the traction engine throwing the crucified body of Brother Samuel up in the air before grinding it once more beneath their wheels. It was impossible to differentiate between the snapping of wood and bone.

Forset kept firing, swinging the barrel from right to left, knowing that the fight had gone out of the riders but too frightened and angry to stop.

Eventually the tank of shrapnel was empty, the firing mechanism grinding against itself as Forset's hands clutched the trigger.

"Enough!" shouted Billy as the Land Carriage surged on, the widening of the pass just ahead. "It was a massacre! A goddamned massacre!"

BILLY'S WORDS, SHOUTED at the top of his voice, filtered through into the dining car and Father Michael found himself nodding. *God damned...*

As they rode the last couple of miles to Wormwood, his despair was total.

"Cheer up, father," said Quartershaft. "We've made it!"

"Mr Quartershaft," the monk replied, "in my faith there are certain moral pre-requisites for entering the Kingdom of Heaven. I cannot help but think we have failed in every single one of them."

THE ROAD
TO WORMWOOD

THE CHILDREN
OF DR BLISS

CHAPTER TEN
THE UGLY ONES

ON REFLECTION, THOUGHT Obeisance Hicks, dabbing at his broken front tooth with his tongue, telling Henry Jones which part of his long-dead mother he should bury himself in may have been an error. He always had been quick to cuss when taking a break from talking for the Lord, and this was hardly the first time it had got him in trouble. Though, considering his current circumstances, he supposed it might be the last.

"I asked a civil question," said Jones, cocking the hammer, "and I would appreciate a civil answer."

"I can see that," said Hicks, attempting to add a more conciliatory tone to his voice, difficult now that Jones had forced the gun barrel into his mouth. "And I can only apologise for my un-Christian outburst, but it has been a mightily trying day."

"It's about to get worse," advised Jones' colleague.

"Well now," Hicks replied, "that would be a shame, given that we have an opportunity to turn things around and make matters right between us. My dearest, most holy charge is obviously of interest to you, and he never utters a word without my encouragement." A lie, of course, but Hicks would have told these two he could shit gold if he thought it would extend his life expectancy.

"Is that so?" asked Jones.

"Most assuredly, he's a shy man with his fair share of health problems. Outside of myself, the girl and the Lord God Almighty, he's really not one for conversation."

Thankfully, the object of everyone's attention chose that moment to pipe up again.

"Wormwood!" he shouted. "Out west, the door comes!"

"That's right," said Hicks, "you tell your good friend all about it, so these kind folks can hear."

Hope was holding Soldier Joe as he thrashed around, seemingly in the throes of delirium. "He's burning up," she said, not in the least concerned about the safety of her employer.

"Well, cool him down then," said Hicks, looking up at Jones and smiling around the barrel of the gun. "What say we all start again and see if we can't find some common footing?"

Jones withdrew the gun from the preacher's mouth, wiped the spittle from the barrel in the man's hair and then slid it back into his holster.

Hicks brushed at his hair, as if finishing off an act of grooming that Jones had started, then offered the two gentlemen a smile. "That's better," he said. "A potential friendship is a beautiful thing, and not something that should lightly be cast away."

"I'm not interested in friendship," said Jones. "Just information."

"Well, that's fine," said Hicks, trying not to stare at the patch of skin the man had instead of eyes, turning his broken-toothed smile towards the other who, he assumed, might at least be able to see it. "I can be friendly enough for all of us."

"I bet," the other man said, and for a moment Hicks was confused. He looked closer at the gentleman in question and his confusion deepened. Either this man was a woman, or he had the most beautiful lips Hicks had ever seen, and the preacher was about to experience a hitherto unknown type of lust.

"What's wrong with him?" Jones asked Hope, looking down on Soldier Joe as he writhed on his cot.

"He is so full of the blessings of the Lord that it's lifted his spirit to a higher plane," said Hicks.

Jones turned towards him. "I wasn't asking you. Shut your mouth for a minute, unless you want my gun back in it." He looked back towards Hope.

"Civil War," she said. "He was shot, and left a chunk of brain somewhere near Gettysburg."

"He's a simpleton?"

"He's a war veteran."

"Said like he couldn't be one and the same? Your sense of loyalty is sweet, girl, but not helpful."

"Wormwood," Soldier Joe whispered, beginning to settle back down. "Out west."

"His head is curdled, Henry," said the other gentlemen, moving past Hicks. "He's of no use."

"Maybe," Jones replied, clearly unsure.

"Out west, thirty miles, bear left at Serpent's Creek," said Soldier Joe before promptly falling asleep.

Jones smiled. "Or maybe not."

However much Hope Lane's employer might begrudge this change of plan (and begrudge it he clearly did, sat in the coachman's seat with a face like thunder, necking at his whisky jug as if it had a leak), at least he didn't have to ride in the back with the rest of Jones' party.

She could stomach Knee High, the dwarf. His sanitation

habits were clearly not of note, and he had a habit of scratching at his groin that made her suspect infection was at work, but he showed her no interest and took up little space.

She didn't even mind Toby the Snake Boy. His skin, some kind of medical ailment rather than actual scales, was far from pleasant to look at, but she'd seen worse. The glimpses she caught of his forked tongue—the result of home brew surgery, at a guess—were grotesque, but elicited sympathy rather than disgust.

It was The Geek she couldn't stand. He was surprisingly thin, rattling around inside a pair of dungarees stained with the fluids of his work. His skin was covered in tiny tattoos. "The bill of fare," he explained, his voice cracked and uneven. "When I eat a thing I ain't eaten before, I draws it on there. My memory ain't so good, and it would be a crying shame to forget a single one of them."

She tried not to look, but inevitably her eyes were drawn, taking in the predictable chickens, beetles and worms before stumbling over a cat, an armadillo and a horse.

"I've known lots of people had to eat their horses," she said, "when food got scarce."

"While still alive?" he asked. "It don't count unless they still kicking at the first bite."

The thought repelled Hope, though she had seen her fair share of sideshows in her time. "But why?"

"No geek would eat a dead animal," he said, "'tain't the way it's done."

"But... a horse?"

He grinned, and for the first time she noticed his teeth: polished steel, wedged into swollen gums. "Pretty little smile, ain't it? I lost the originals years ago, snapped off on hoof and bone."

Hope could hardly bear to look at him.

She gave all her attention to Soldier Joe, even though he continued to sleep. Better that than any more conversation with her new travelling companions.

She had always been at home with the sick, since a childhood of nursing her brothers.

"I sometimes think," her mother had said to her just shy of her tenth birthday, "that you ain't ever happy unless you have bandage in one hand and a needle in t'other."

As far as Hope was concerned, there was no better person to be. People had a habit of breaking themselves, and the world would always need those who could fix them. Her skin colour kept her out of any legitimate medical profession. Slavery may have been abolished for twenty years, but anyone thinking that meant the blacks were truly free needed a lesson in reality. Having travelled from the South, she had still lived under an atmosphere of segregation, suspicion and disgust. People hadn't unlocked the chains with good grace; they had lost what they considered a God given right, and the idea of employing a nigger, for actual money, seemed to them to be adding insult to injury. Why else would she tolerate the abuse of Obeisance Hicks? Her life on the road was only a hair's breadth away from the servitude of her parents, but at least she got to see a little of the country and eat regular meals. And then there was Soldier Joe, a man whom she would never have met otherwise. She loved him, of course, though she wasn't dumb enough to think him capable of loving her back. He was comforted by her, he needed her, and that was reward in itself when you were used to so little.

"Wormwood," he said, dreamy and indistinct, the words bubbling up from sleep.

"Yes, honey," she replied. "We're going."

*   *   *

"It seems to me," said Obeisance Hicks, settling back in the coachman's seat and trying to reassert some level of authority, "that we're in the same business."

Henry and Harmonium Jones were sat alongside him, neither of them fools and only too happy to swap the enclosed stink of the caravan for the open air.

"We have very little to do with God," Jones replied, his glasses now back in place so as not to draw undue attention from anyone else they met on the road.

"You and me both," admitted Hicks. "But it's all theatre, isn't it? We both swap cash for a glimpse of the freakish."

"You would be advised," said Harmonium, "to avoid the word 'freak.' It is not one to which we take kindly." She was still dressed as a gentleman, though less concerned, now, to disguise her voice. Hicks, relieved that his lustful instincts had not been in error, took this as a sign of trust. He was quite wrong in that regard; Harmonium Jones had simply decided that it was likely they would kill the preacher before they parted company, so why worry?

"Oh, I mean nothing by it," Hicks replied, quite unaware that his use of the word had brought him closer to death than at any other time in his miserable life. "It's just a word."

"Words have weight," said Jones, stretching his arms out in front of him and working his fingers. He liked to keep them supple, ready to pull a trigger. "Don't use it again. Or we'll shoot you in the head and leave you by the side of the road."

"Fat chance you'd have of getting my little messiah to do his work then." Hicks chuckled. "You need me, friend. Still, I'll mind my tongue. Never let it be said that Obeisance Hicks can't watch his manners."

* * *

THEY REACHED SERPENT'S Creek by dusk, but the dim light did little to improve the town's beauty. It felt, as so many towns did along that trail, like a home that had been abandoned, unloved and ignored. Several of the shops stood empty, their windows boarded up. The street was uneven and dirty, potholes left to gather water and brew mud.

"I've seen more accommodating mule dung," said Hicks as they rode down the main street. "Still, as long as it has a bar and a bed, I guess we can make ourselves comfortable."

"We would prefer to keep travelling," said Jones. "We're not a group for company; people talk, and that is rarely in our best interests. Or theirs." He inclined his head towards Hicks at this point, but the preacher was far too lacking in self-awareness to pick up the hint.

"Well, if you plan on staying in the caravan, you can do it on the edge of town as easy as anywhere else. We'll have few enough places on the road where we can lay our head on a proper pillow, and I don't intend to pass up the opportunity of this one."

Jones sighed, then nodded. "Mayhap it would be sensible to pick up a few provisions, too."

"Now you're thinking straight!" Hicks laughed.

"But the soldier stays with us."

Hicks hadn't anticipated that, which was stupid of him. He cursed himself for his sloppy thinking.

"And what's to stop you just driving off while I'm asleep? I don't think so, Mr Jones, I surely don't. He and the girl will be staying with me. You can keep the caravan. We won't get far without it, so you needn't worry about us giving you the slip." He tried on another charming smile. It wasn't half bad; you didn't get to his station in life without being able to offer the pretence of affability. "Besides, why would we want to? You think there's something worthwhile at this Wormwood place? Hell, I'm a man of the road, and my life is my own. I'm as happy to take a look at it as you are."

"Worthwhile?" Jones smiled, and it wasn't remotely charming. It was the sort of smile an alligator wore when convinced its meat was just about rotten enough to chew. "It's the greatest miracle you'll ever see."

"And miracles are my business, so I'm a happy man."

Hicks stopped the coach and handed Jones the reins. "We'll get off here and you can head out to somewhere more circumspect, miserable and cold with my blessing."

He jumped down and moved around to the back of the caravan.

"I'm surprised at you, Henry," his wife said, once the preacher was out of earshot. "Since when did you get so reasonable?"

"He's going nowhere," Jones replied. "And I'd relish a few hours of silence and privacy while we plan ahead."

Hicks yanked up the canopy at the rear of the caravan, coming face to face with Hope.

"Get him up and out," he told her. "We're taking our leave of these folks for the night." He lowered his voice. "And pass me my satchel, I'd trust these ugly bastards with my gold about as willingly as I'd poke my pecker in a dog."

She didn't argue, only too happy to put distance between herself and their new companions.

Hicks took his satchel—enjoying, as always, the way it pulled on his shoulder—and wandered back to the front of the caravan, leaving Hope to manage the steps and Soldier Joe on her own. That, after all, was what he kept her for.

"I'll even get the provisions," he said to Jones, "so you lot don't have to worry about showing your faces. See what a reasonable man I am?"

Jones nodded and whipped at the reins.

Hope had only just raised the steps; she cried out as they were snatched from her hands by the departing caravan. "I do not like those people," she said to Soldier Joe. "They are not good folk at all."

"Neither are we, darlin'," said Hicks, joining them. "Neither are we."

IT TOOK ONLY a few minutes for Hicks to wonder if they should have stayed in the caravan. Serpent's Creek was silent, and as they walked up the main street, he began to suspect there was nobody in the town at all. He'd seen ghost towns in his time, places that had sprung up at the promise of gold or oil that then dried up, or settlements founded on buffalo herds or horses that were farmed and winnowed out. In the early days of the expansion it seemed that people had set down root at the slightest provocation, not thinking for one moment that the security they clung to could be fleeting. Camps had become towns, the towns had flourished briefly then, as work and money grew scarce, the people began to leave. Once a few gave up on the place, the exodus was never far away. One thing this world had taught people was that home could be anywhere. If things weren't working out, then you upped sticks and tried again.

It seemed to Hicks that towns were like marriages. You either decided to stick them out and make them work, or you cut your losses and ran. He was a man of the road, and he'd been married five times. His feelings on the matter were clear.

"Well now," said a voice from the doorway of the Great Rest saloon across the road. "If it ain't a bunch of tourists. Now I've seen everything."

"Just travellers passing through," said Hicks, heading over, "and much relieved to see this town ain't as empty as it appeared."

"Oh, it's empty alright," said the man, scratching at the dried skin flaking from his bald scalp. Little flurries of white powder fell onto the shoulders of his vest like snow. "Some of us just haven't quite finished packing."

"What happened?"

The man didn't answer, just waved them inside, where they found themselves in a bar that, like the rest of the town, had seen better days. The tables were dusty and disordered, the floor not swept for quite some while. It wasn't altogether empty, though; a woman and child occupied one table.

"Sit yourselves down and I'll pour you a drink," the man said, gesturing vaguely towards a table as he stepped behind his bar. "I don't have much in the way of choice, but I can do you whisky or beer."

"Both sound good to me," Hicks replied, in the mood for softening the night up with booze. He was *always* in that mood. "These two would likely be happy with water. She don't approve of drink, and while he likes the taste right enough, he just can't handle it. One mouthful and he'll be singing for the rest of the night."

The woman stared at them, as if not quite sure what they were.

"Evening, ma'am," said Hicks, doffing a pretend hat in her direction.

"That's my family," the man behind the bar said, filling a tray with drinks. "My wife, Genevieve, and the apple of my eye, George Junior."

The wife looked terrified, as if she had been asked to

dance on the table for the amusement of them all. The kid just stared, working away in his fat nose with a dirty, well-practiced finger.

"I guess that makes you George, then?" asked Hicks.

"It does."

George brought the drinks to the table, then retreated, leaning against the bar with a whisky for himself.

"You're looking at all that remains of the populace of Serpent's Creek," he said. "The town used to be five hundred strong."

"What happened?" asked Hicks.

"The clue, my friend, is in the name."

HENRY JONES TOOK the caravan a mile or two out of town, bringing it to rest within the cover of a pair of ponderosa pines.

Harmonium jumped down and immediately set about rousting the rest of their band. Henry couldn't help but notice how she had taken to leadership during his time in jail. On the one hand, he was proud of her; on the other, there was a small, unreasonable voice that disliked what could be seen as shift of power. Not that he didn't trust her: she had stuck with him ever since they had first met, a pair of young sideshow attractions, their mutual anger and ambition stoking the fire of their passion until it burned dangerously hot.

He loved her. Sometimes too hard. Some men learned moderation through marriage, becoming gentler folk; men who settled and looked for less in life, having found better than they had hoped. Some, like him, found themselves fighting harder and harder. Henry and Harmonium would never have real children, but the sizeable grudges each bore the world had conceived a shared grudge, all the more swollen and angry for their coming together. Sometimes it made him tired, hating so very much.

"You going to sit there all night, my darling?" Harmonium asked, unbuttoning her suit jacket and loosening the corset underneath, relieved to be able to breathe easily.

And that anger that was always a part of him reared its head a little.

He normally controlled it, with her. He'd been scared into restraint by an incident not too long into their relationship.

They had been lying together in the straw, on the edge of DR BLISS'S KARNIVAL OF DELIGHTS, just as they were on the edge of everything. The hard work of setting camp for the night had been done and the acts had eaten. The hot Alabama night was as thick as the soup that had been served, although while it clung to them and made them surly, it won out over that culinary defecation by dint of containing no possum.

A poker game was running at the centre of the camp, just as it would most every night. It was common opinion amongst the acts that Dr Bliss (in reality an angry little man from Michigan by the name of Lieberwitz) kept his business afloat by his skill at cards. An average night would see him reclaiming a sizeable chunk of the wages he had paid out. In fact, when on particularly good form he had even been known to pocket future pay. It was common knowledge that Aquato the Fish Boy would be working for free until the new year, because while he could hold his breath underwater for up to four minutes, he couldn't bluff for shit.

Jones had no interest in the games, even had he been able to 'see' the cards.

He was consistently secretive about how he functioned without eyes, partly because he wasn't altogether sure himself. His aim was impeccable and his speed beat the eye of all but the most experienced onlooker. It wasn't rare that a member of the audience would cry foul, sure that the unbroken band of flesh where his eyes should be must be a trick of makeup. He had taken some convincing not to simply shoot these naysayers (Lieberwitz was a mean old bastard, but even he knew you couldn't make money by killing your audience), and loathed the inevitable examination to which such criticism would lead. He would be sat at the front of his performance area, the public lining up one by one to stare and stroke and poke at the absence above his nose. It inflamed his anger mightily, and rare was the day that he didn't settle back in a foul mood, his gun finger twitching to do more than entertain others.

Harmonium had known he was prone to dark moods, but such was her confidence, her assurance of his love for her, that she rarely paid heed to them.

"You just going to lie there?" she had asked him. "After the day I've had, a girl needs more attention from her man than that."

Her own act consisted of little more than the examination Jones so hated. Lieberwitz had her dressed in a corset and stockings that would make a God-fearing man weep, proffering all her female assets alongside the plaited length of beard. "'Tain't no miracle unless a man can compare," he would say. "Let 'em see the rough alongside the smooth."

Consequently every man took liberties with their hands, and rare was the day when she wouldn't end up bruised from the squeeze of fingers and the slap of palm. The tears she eventually shed after hours of having her beard tugged were from more than just her sore chin; they were an angry vent, as hot and sharp as the twitching finger of Henry Jones.

"I'm sure you've had attention enough," he had said, his irritability making him take verbal shots at her, though he knew how much she hated her performing life. "You can take a few hours without a man doting on you."

The words struck home and she was predictably quick to bite.

"If you knew what you were looking at, you blind fool, you'd be a little more grateful," she said, knowing that you called Jones 'blind' at your peril. Though he was, and would do to accept the fact, in her opinion.

She expected him to shout, maybe continue trading insults, but instead he leapt at her, pinning her down in the straw. "I can see you!" he shouted, before slapping her hard across the face. "I can see all I need to!" And then he punched her and the quiet yelp she gave smarted as hard as if she had returned the blow. He was terrified. She wasn't the first woman he had hit—much as he laid claim to being a gentleman, the label rarely went further than the cut of his suit—but she was the first woman he had loved, and in that moment he was quite sure he had lost her.

"Oh, God," he said, wanting to climb off her but scared that if he did she would just run away and then he'd never see her again. "I'm sorry, darlin', I just lost my mind and..."

She brought up her knee between his legs to show him precisely what she thought of his apology. He rolled off her, curling up next to her as he tried to swallow the pain and sickness in his stomach.

She leaned over him. "That was it, Henry Jones," she had said. "That was the one time you get to lay a hand on me in anger. You ever get the urge to do it again, you'd better make sure you do it hard enough to kill me, because if you don't, I'll most surely kill you."

It hadn't been the threat so much as the realisation of

how close he had come to breaking the one thing of worth he had ever had.

Which was why, now, as much as he found himself riled at her suggesting he was lazy, he bit his tongue and climbed down from the driving bench.

"I was thinking about the journey ahead."

"You and me both," she admitted. "And I'm thinking it would pass a lot easier without that preacher onboard. I don't like the way he looks at me."

"Then you must hate every man," he replied, pulling her close to him. "For I don't know a single one who doesn't look at you wishing they were in your bed."

"Now, now, Henry," she said, though she was smiling, "not in front of the others."

He knew she wasn't so bashful. Many had been the times that they had put on a show of their own, scarcely caring whether their traveling companions saw them or not. Still, if she wanted to make a pretence of virtue, he was happy to let her do so. For a few minutes, at least.

"Toby," he said, "fetch some firewood. Knee High, get to fixing us some grub."

"Hell," said the dwarf, "I always end up cooking."

"You'd rather The Geek did it?"

"Never cook your food," said The Geek. "Takes all the fight out of it."

"You can see to the horses," Jones told him, "and mind you keep your mouth to yourself. I see you've so much as licked those beasts and your next meal will be a bullet."

"And what will we do?" asked Harmonium.

"Whatever we feel like," he said, taking her by the hand and leading her beyond the camp.

They shed their clothes a short distance away and Henry Jones washed away his anger. She had two sweet, bearded holes and his tongue rejoiced at both of them.

He wouldn't say that sex had been the thing he had

missed most while in prison, but its absence had been a discomfort. Most of the prisoners relieved themselves in other ways, either solo or in tandem, but Jones was not a man who would let another see him in that raw a state. He would consider it weakness.

"I've missed you there, honey," Harmonium told him once he was spent. "It fair ached in those months you were away."

He liked to believe that was true.

"I ain't going anywhere again, my sweetness," he told her. "Don't you worry about that."

They lay there for a moment or two, letting a quiet space pass between their lovemaking and talk of business. Harmonium was the first to speak.

"You going to kill that preacher?" she asked.

"Sooner or later," he admitted. "But he may be useful for a little while longer."

"I can't see that anyone would mourn him," she said.

"Maybe not, but while the other two prove useful, there's no point in taking the risk. That simpleton is in touch with something, and I want to know what."

"Maybe he just heard about the town and he's repeating words he doesn't even understand."

"Maybe. In which case we've found ourselves a talking map. Or maybe it's nothing at all, and we're wasting time listening to him. We'll let the next couple of days decide."

"They have money."

"Indeed they do. A fair amount of it, I'd warrant."

"They'll pay their way in the end, then," she laughed. "Dead men have no use for gold."

"They surely don't."

They dressed and returned to the camp. The fire was on its way, a large cooking pan set on top of it.

"I hope you found something edible to put in that, Knee High," said Jones.

"No more than usual," the dwarf admitted.

The sun was vanishing from the sky now, a soft dusk light descending around them as they settled by the fire.

THE GEEK WAS on the hunt. There was nothing in Knee High's pot that was to his liking, he needed food that moved, food that kicked back as you sank your teeth into it.

He kept low to the ground, moving as quietly as he could through the long grass that flourished by the side of the road. The low light made tracking difficult, so he relied as much on his ears as his eyes, pausing every now and then and listening to the still evening, alert to movement around him.

In the distance he heard the sound of hooves; a wild horse, judging by the weight of it. That was beyond him for now. He would never have admitted as much to the darkie nurse, but the horse he had eaten before had been lame, thin and close to death. He had still considered it fair game—if the beast had a pulse, it was fit for the table—but he sincerely doubted he could track and capture one of its breed had it been in the best of health.

There was a rustle closer to hand, something small foraging in the undergrowth. A rabbit, maybe, or possum. Either would do just fine, though the fur tickled your throat something awful until the blood washed it away.

He crouched on all fours and made his way forward, moving through the grass in absolute silence.

He had always been skilled at tracking. It had been the one thing that had kept him alive as a child. Growing up on the farm he had watched the animals, learned to copy them, understand them. Then, when the Comanche came and killed his Ma and Pa, he had been forced to find a way to survive. He knew he would. If God had wanted him dead He'd have let the Indians find him in the grain cellar. God had let him live. God was saying he was special. His Ma had always told him as much, looking up from her bible and ruffling his mess of straw hair.

The first week had been easy enough. There had been enough food in the house to last him, and though he was lonely out there, miles away from the closest town, he had made the best of it. He'd put Ma and Pa in one of the sheds, covering them with a sheet so he didn't have to look at them no more. He knew they weren't really there. His Ma had told him what happened when you died, you left your body behind and went on somewhere better. He kept telling himself that, because it stopped him being sad.

The days were long and he slept more than he should. He knew his Pa would have been angry to see him dozing in the day, but he didn't know what else to do. He fed the animals and swept the yard, but nobody had shown him how to do anything else, so he ran out of jobs by lunchtime.

Then the food began to run out. He tried the animal grain, but that just dried out his mouth and made his belly swell up when he drank water with it. He knew that you could eat the animals, of course, hadn't Ma cooked up a chicken or a hog often enough? He just didn't know how you made it so it looked like she'd prepared it.

Once, a year or so ago, he'd come across a dead rat in the yard, picked it up and brought it into the house, thinking his Ma would be pleased. She could put it in a stew, and she'd think he was the cleverest boy for finding it.

She hadn't. She'd given a scream and clouted him on the side of the head. "Don't touch dead animals!" she had told him. "It's dirty. God only knows what happened to it." He had looked down at the rat, fallen from his hand when she'd hit him. Its eyes were empty, its mouth wide. It certainly looked wrong, its fur dirty and matted, flies buzzing around it. Dead things were not good.

His Ma and Pa continued to teach him that lesson as they drew the flies under their sheet in the barn. Some days he would go in there to talk to them, but he was sure they couldn't hear him, not with the buzzing having gotten that loud.

You couldn't touch the dead animals, which must mean you couldn't eat them either.

He sat at the edge of the pig pen and watched as the swine grunted and squealed at one another. They were funny, like fat old women arguing.

They were quick, too, but he bet he could be quicker.

It took him four days to try.

He sat on the fence, waiting for one of the pigs to pass beneath him. Then he jumped on it, laughing as it gave its silly squeal and snapping at it with his teeth. The pig wriggled and kicked, catching him on the cheek with one of its trotters. He gave a yell and fell back, sure it had kicked a hole right through his cheek, but it hadn't. He was all right. It fetched up one hell of a bruise, but no lasting damage. The pig, however, got away.

Maybe he needed to try something smaller. A chicken, maybe? But he didn't like the idea of those feathers in his mouth; they would be as dry as the grain, and he might choke before he even got a taste of it.

He'd just have to try again.

He sat down in one corner of the pen, being perfectly still, letting the animals get used to him. This they soon did, even the one he had attacked before. That was the one he wanted: it had hurt him, and he decided he didn't like it anymore.

He was patient, waiting for that particular hog. When

one of the others brushed past him, sniffing at him with its snout, he didn't move. He let it explore him for a moment before moving on. He kept plenty of grain in there, he didn't want the pigs getting so hungry they might try and eat him. Sometimes he even sprinkled the grain on himself, drawing them over, letting them get used to him.

Then finally, the one pig, the hog that had kicked him, drew close. He sat with his arms and legs wide and it snuffled its way within reach. It curled against him, rubbing its fat side against his belly, sniffing at his fingers. He moved quickly, grabbing it with his legs and arms, digging his nails into its skin and throwing his weight onto its back. It squealed but couldn't move, his body pinning it down in the dirt.

He was so hungry by now. He bit at its side, and it continued to scream as his little teeth nipped and drew spots of blood. It was so tough! Not like the pork Ma had served. His belly demanded he kept trying, so he kept biting at the animal's side, tearing with his teeth. That first, gushing mouthful of blood nearly made him throw up, but he kept at it, finally able to tear a few chunks of meat away, which slipped down his throat easily. Slowly, the pig stopped fighting back, the dust around them getting wetter with blood. He kept one hand on it and used the other to help pull away at the wound he'd made, trying to grab as much as he could before the animal died.

Then it was still. So he got up, his face and torso soaked red.

The other pigs stared at him. He wondered if they were scared.

He held his arms out to them, like a picture of Jesus he had seen when his Ma had taken him to church. Then he climbed out of the pig pen and went to the house to wash himself.

When he came back out later, the pigs were eating the rest of their dead friend. Pigs were stupid, he decided. They didn't know you weren't supposed to eat dead things.

He'd stayed at the farm for several months, working his way through the livestock. The longer he did it, the harder it got, the animals aware that he was a predator, a danger. So he had to get better at catching them.

Now, all these years later, it was a skill he had perfected.

As he burst through the undergrowth, meaning to catch the animal he had drawn close to, he was startled to find he had competition. The rabbit—for it had been a rabbit, a small one with thankfully short fur—gave a cry as a rattlesnake lashed out from the grass and sank its fangs into it. The Geek acted instinctively, snatching at the snake's neck and pinching hard. He stamped on its tail, strengthened his grip on his neck and stretched the snake before biting at it two-thirds of the way up its body. He bit hard, his metal teeth slicing straight through meat, skin, cartilage and bone. The head he flung away. Rattlesnakes were good, they stayed alive for a while even after you'd taken their heads off. Perfect food that you didn't have to rush.

He stood up, the rest of the snake hanging from his hand, and looked to the rabbit. It was dead, the venom having done its work. No matter, he had meat enough.

He took a large bite. It was pretty bland, certainly not his favourite, a bit like chewy fish. But it did the job and kept his belly from rumbling all night.

He turned to head back towards the camp then noticed that the grass all around him was on the move.

"You been sneaking up on me?" he asked, though of what he could not yet tell.

He backed away, the night suddenly filling with the distinctive rattle of many more snakes.

"How many are you?" he wondered before a host of heads poked from the grass around him and he turned to run.

"THE SNAKES WERE always a problem," said George, taking a sip of his drink. "I don't know why there are so many of them around here, but it was a fool who went to bed without checking underneath the blanket. The scaly bastards just love it around here. They breed at the creek, nests of them building over the years until it got so that they were a fixture.

"'Tweren't such a big deal; snakes are vicious little bastards, but they're easily scared. You just had to be careful. We'd kill 'em and dump 'em, or spice the cooking pot with 'em. They avoided the town, for the most part. Snakes don't like people, as I say. You'd get a few, but it was nothing we couldn't deal with.

"Then they changed."

He took another mouthful of his drink, rubbing his finger around the rim of the glass, trying to be casual but failing.

"They always come at night. You'd step out on the porch and the sound of their goddamn rattles could be heard all over the town. Shine a light on the street and you'd see great rivers of them."

"But what was attracting them?" asked Hicks.

"Who knows? It weren't natural. They weren't behaving right either: they were brave, aggressive. It was like an invasion. They forced their way into shops and houses, attacked people, *killed* people. It wasn't an infestation, it was a goddamned attack.

"'Course, we tried everything we could think of. A group of us went up to the creek and burnt the place out. Old Sam Winston even set a bunch of dynamite charges, damming it up so it would run dry, maybe drive them elsewhere. Didn't make a spit worth of difference. That night the same great shoals of 'em were slithering their way through the town. We dammed up the doors, sealed the windows, whatever we could do to make sure they couldn't get in.

"It ain't easy to seal a whole town, though. Pat David ran the stable and livery, woke up one morning to find he didn't have a single horse left. The snakes had killed every one of them."

"Surely a horse would just trample the thing?" asked Hicks. "I've seen horses spooked by snakes before, but I wouldn't lay a bet in the snake's favour if it came to a fight."

"You ain't seen what these things are like. Like I say, they're aggressive. Damn it, they're intelligent. They go out of their way to attack and kill. It can't be food they're after; the day a rattler tries to eat something as big as a man or a horse is the day of the Second goddamn Coming. They just want to kill."

"And they're coming here?" said Hope. "Wonderful."

"Oh, we've pretty much got this place covered," said George. "We seal it up tight as a drum, you'll be safe enough as long as you keep inside until morning. The snakes leave at first light."

"Why do you stay?" asked Hicks. "If it were me I think I'd have been one of the first over the town line."

"I built this place up," said George. "Took every penny I had. We'll move on soon, but I guess I keep hoping someone figures out a way of putting a stop to them. I don't like to abandon everything just because of some bastard serpents."

Hicks shrugged. "Sometimes it pays to be a travelling man, I guess. When a place gets so it's not comfortable anymore, you just move on."

"And what is it you do?" asked George, prompting Hicks to begin his usual spiel about being a messenger from God, spreading The Word.

Hope stopped listening. She'd heard his speechifying often enough. Besides, she was drawn to George's wife. She acted terrified. The woman had a look on her face that Hope recognised well enough, having seen it on her own mother's face. It was the look of a woman who had been subdued. A woman that did as she was told, knowing that the consequences of doing otherwise would be too much to bear.

Hope did not trust George.

"YOU AIN'T GOING to believe this," The Geek shouted, running back into the camp, "but I swear I have a whole damned posse of rattlesnakes on my tail!"

"Probably heard you've eaten their Ma and Pa," said Knee High. "It was only a matter of time before the animals got organised and decided to get rid of you."

"It ain't a laughing matter," The Geek insisted. "I'm telling you there are hundreds of them, and they're all heading this way."

"Snakes don't act like that," said Toby, offering what he felt was his professional opinion.

Of course, Toby was related to the reptile by stage name only. The skin condition that gave him the look that had, if not earned his fortune, at least kept him fed and watered for most of his life, had come on when he was a kid. His father had taken one look at him and announced, with conviction, 'That boy just ain't right, I want him out of the house before the rest of us catch it.' Such callous parenting had seen Toby on the road and fending for himself before his tenth birthday. Opportunities were slim and kindness rare, as most people seemed to think he had leprosy or some other complaint that they feared they'd pick up. He had been shooed away from homes and businesses and chased out of towns. It was only when he had fallen in with 'Dr Bliss' that he had found security.

"You're ugly as a nine-day old turd," Lieberwitz had told him, "but I don't think you'll do us any harm."

The opposite had been true: after a little aesthetic alteration (getting Toby so drunk he was virtually comatose, then slitting his tongue with a heated Bowie knife), he had become one of the freak show's best earners. There had been a period of dissent when Lieberwitz had forced him to eat live rats and The Geek had complained, but once such little battles were won, he had become part of the weird, dysfunctional family. This didn't mean for one minute that they took his word as gospel.

"What the hell would you know?" asked The Geek. "My dingus is closer to being a snake than you are."

"He's right," said Jones, getting to his feet. "Snakes aren't aggressive unless you invade their territory. However many you say you saw, I doubt they'll come within spitting distance of us and the fire."

"You think that if you like," The Geek replied, "but I've seen the sons of bitches and they are on the rampage."

Jones held up a hand for silence, cocking his head to one side. "I can hear them," he said, listening intently, "...and you're right... there's one hell of a lot of them..."

"Still, they won't come through here, will they?" said Harmonium.

"They're certainly coming this way," Jones replied. He thought for a moment, his senses stretching out beyond their little camp, screening out the sound of the fire and the breathing of his companions, focusing in on the creatures that moved in the long grass nearby.

"Seriously, Mr Jones," said The Geek. "I know snakes, you know I do, and these weren't acting natural. Something's set them off and they're riled and heading right for us."

Jones nodded. "Everybody get in the caravan."

"Ah, Jesus," moaned Knee High. "I was just getting comfortable."

"You can get comfortable in the back of the caravan," said The Geek. "Pipsqueak like you should be the first running for the hills, you're barely taller than a rattlesnake's eyes."

"Shut your face, you lanky streak of piss!" Knee High retorted, never one to take an insult towards his size. "I'm tall enough to kick your ass to hell and back, and you know it."

"Shut up the both of you," said Jones, "and get in the damned caravan."

The evening air was filled with the sound of rattlesnakes, like a hundred angry toddlers advancing on the camp with rattles in their hands.

They gathered up their few belongings, Harmonium whipping them into action while her husband stayed on the edge of the fire's light, facing sightlessly out into the dimming evening.

"Henry?" she called, climbing up into the driving seat once everyone was aboard.

"They're here," he said, turning and running towards the caravan as the line of long grass around them suddenly shook, countless rattlesnakes emerging into the clearing.

"Get moving!" he shouted, jumping up next to her.

The horses had ideas of their own, panicking in their restraints and bolting towards the road.

"Damn you!" she shouted, trying to pull them back as they overshot and plunged into more long grass.

"We'll shake our damned wheels loose at this rate," said Jones, pulling out his gun and firing a couple of shots over the horse's heads. It didn't startle them into a halt as he had hoped, but with both of them grabbing the reins they managed to yank the creatures back towards the road and town.

"Maybe we'll spend the night inside after all," he said.

CHAPTER ELEVEN
NIGHT OF THE SERPENTS

ONCE GEORGE HAD finished his story, Hope decided she'd try and get his wife talking. This proved difficult, but Hope Lane was not a woman easily dissuaded.

"How long you been married?" she asked.

If this was an easy question—and certainly Hope had assumed it to be so—Genevieve didn't agree. It seemed to confuse her terribly.

"Oh," she said, looking to her husband, "I have such a bad head for dates." George was talking with Hicks and unable to come to her help.

The woman hugged her child closer to her and looked at Hope with fearful eyes. "I guess it must be a couple of years now. At least."

Which was interesting, Hope thought, as the child was five if he was a day. She guessed that plenty of people had children out of wedlock—hell, there were sporting girls up and down the country that had borne their fair share—but she found it hard to imagine it happening within this little picture of domestic bliss. She decided to risk questioning her about it:

"Is the boy not yours, then?" she asked.

Genevieve was clearly utterly thrown by that suggestion. "Of course he's mine," she said.

"I'm sorry, my mistake," said Hope. "'Tain't none of my business anyhow. So how did you and George meet?"

This was another simple question that Genevieve found painful to consider.

"You know how it is," she said, flustered, "you just end up falling in with someone."

Hope supposed that could often be the case, but she didn't believe a word of it.

IF HICKS HAD known of Hope's misgivings he would have smiled and nodded. If there was one language he spoke fluently, it was bullshit, and he had been listening to it for some time. George was full of excuses and justifications; he was selling a story and Hicks wasn't buying.

Not that Hicks cared. Whatever George was up to, it didn't affect him.

"Well," he said, "if you're willing to put us up for the night, I'd sure be grateful. I can pay you a fair rate, especially if you'd be willing to throw a meal in."

"I wouldn't send you back out there now," said George. "It wouldn't be Christian."

"That's mighty good to hear, we religious men have to band together."

George reached for Hicks' bag. "I'll take your belongings upstairs and clear out a room for you."

"That's fine," said Hicks, not willing to let his bag out of sight.

Both men had a hold of the heavy satchel and both men tugged.

"You're carrying quite a burden," said George, a curious look in his eyes.

"Ain't we all, brother?" Hicks replied, trying to pull the satchel from the man's grip.

The bag shook and jangled. George held on.

"The religious business must pay well," he said, "to hang so heavy on your shoulder."

"I get by on very little," Hicks insisted. "The rest is prayer books."

George stared at him a moment longer, both still holding the bag.

If Hicks' attention had strayed away from his most important luggage—which it never would—he would have seen that Genevieve was staring at them both, fear in her eyes. He didn't notice, but Hope did, and she realised that they were brushing against the truth of matters. If she had been able to act on her instincts, what followed might have been avoided. Instead, weighed down with her own baggage, she looked to Soldier Joe, who had sat oblivious through the entire conversation, his eyes glazed, his mouth slack.

"I don't believe you," said George and with a speed that Hicks would never have predicted, he snatched the bottle of whisky from the bar table and swung it down against the preacher's head.

JONES AND HIS wife steered the caravan over the town line, finally able to bring the panicked horses to a controlled stop.

The streets of Serpent's Creek were as empty as before, but their attention was firmly fixed on the route they had just taken.

"Any sign of them?" Jones asked Harmonium, his head cocked. "I can't hear them no more."

"We've lost them," she said. "Whatever was making them act like that, they must have quit now. Maybe there was a fire somewhere, something that drove them all out of their nests in panic."

"I didn't smell no fire," said Jones. "And I have a feeling this ain't something so easily explained away."

He thought back to the first time he had heard of Wormwood. Sat by his trailer after a typical day of performing for idiots.

Lieberwitz had picked up a drunk by the name of Alonzo, an ex-performer, so he claimed, down on his luck and happy to earn the price of a meal and place to sleep by doing chores.

"I used to be the talk of the circuit," he had said, "You never saw a better knife thrower. Alonzo the Armless, they called me."

Which raised a chuckle from those acts within earshot, given that the man was in clear possession of both his arms.

"Oh, pay these no mind," he added, waggling said limbs. "I used to bind them up, claimed I'd lost them in the war. Then I'd throw the knives with my feet. It made a better show of it and I was one nimble little bastard. I could split an ant in two from twenty feet."

Jones hadn't believed a word of it; the man was all talk. But if Lieberwitz wanted to have him hang around for a few days then that was up to him, Jones would keep his money locked away and his gun close.

"I'd pay to see you try," someone shouted, but Alonzo just shrugged.

"Can't do it anymore. My legs ain't so supple and my eyes are dim. I can still make myself useful, though. Sweeping up, minding the animals, whatever you need."

Lieberwitz had taken pity on him. There was an unwritten rule on the circuit that you looked after your own, and Alonzo wouldn't be the first old performer to benefit from shelter at Dr Bliss's Karnival of Delights.

He had stayed longer than most, filling his days with whatever spare jobs could be found and his nights in a drunken heap.

The distrust Jones had first felt began to wane. Naturally he could never claim to have liked the man (Jones didn't really like anybody, except for Harmonium), but he grew to respect him a little. Alonzo's claims of his knife-throwing ability may have been exaggerated, but they weren't completely fictional, and Jones recognised something of himself in the man. He had a skill for killing that he wasted on matinees.

And Alonzo treated Jones with respect. He complimented him on his skills, asked no questions about his sight and addressed him with reverence rather than the usual badly-disguised disgust.

"You've got one hell of a hand," Alonzo told him once. "Reminds me of a gunslinger I used to know when I was young. One hell of a man he was, shot like he was simply pointing his finger. Didn't seem to be a thing he couldn't hit. 'Course, like so many of the good old boys, he's dead now. Lost wherever it is old shootists go."

"Hell, I imagine," Jones had replied, never one to fool himself with the notion of divine forgiveness.

"I wonder." Alonzo had been a little drunk, of course; when was he not? But he was at that hallowed stage between laughter and oblivion, where the liquor made you reflective, opened your head to honest thoughts and considerations before the weight of them saw you drink another gutful and wipe them clean.

"I keep hearing stories of a place called Wormwood," he said after a moment. "Probably no truth in it, but... well... you hear a thing often enough, from enough different people, and you get to wonder if there might not be something to it."

"What is it?" Jones had asked, not particularly

interested, but content enough to let the man talk. If he was talking, then he wasn't drinking, and Jones could take his turn on the bottle.

"They say it's a way of getting into Heaven without having to die first."

Of course, Jones scoffed at that, but Alonzo paid him no heed, just continued to sit and think, staring up at the stars on that quiet Georgia night.

"Like I said," the old man continued, "probably no truth in it. Still, the idea of walking into the afterlife and setting up home, well... I like that idea. Ain't that what we all thought we were doing when we came here? Carving ourselves a slice of the promised land?"

"If it's anything like here, then it'll be a disappointment," said Jones, handing him the bottle.

"Maybe so. But I'd sure like to have a word with its President."

It took a moment for the meaning of this to sink in for Jones, not being a man who thought often of God.

"Well," he said to Alonzo, "if you ever see Him, tell Him from me: I don't think much of His work."

"Tell Him yourself," Alonzo had replied. "I'm past chasing after an idea like that. They say the town only appears every hundred years, and the way into it is to pass through Hell itself. They say the world goes mad, get close enough to it. Nature be damned, it's monsters and demons all the way."

"Monsters and demons?" Jones smiled. "I've been called both in my time."

"I just bet you have."

At that, Alonzo had taken his bottle and gone to his bed.

And over a while, the seed that had been planted in Jones' head began slowly to grow.

"'Nature be damned,'" he said now, sat in the quiet,

empty street of Serpent's Creek. "Maybe that shows we're closer than we think."

"Honey, I have no idea what you're talking about," said his wife.

"The snakes," he explained. "The closer you get to Wormwood, the stranger nature gets. Things become different, disturbed... this just might be a sign."

"Well, if it is, I can't say I like it very much."

Henry held up his hand for quiet, cocking his head at a sharper angle. "We didn't lose them yet," he said. "I can hear them out there, their tails shaking."

"Wonderful. So what do we do? Keep riding or take cover?"

Jones thought for a moment. "I'm not a man that takes naturally to running," he said. "We'll find us some cover."

HICKS HAD EXPERIENCED his fair share of encouraged unconsciousness. He had not led what could be termed a popular life and there had been many people only too happy to clout him around the head. In fact, his second wife used to make such a habit of it that he would joke that while some men had hot milk before bed time he partook of a frying pan. It certainly set him up for a full night's sleep, although it didn't take long before the headaches and bruising convinced him it was time to be single again.

He was fairly sure this had been the first time he had been brained with a half-full bottle of whisky. He had known stupid people in his time, but never one so dumb as to waste good liquor. Licking his lips as he slowly returned to consciousness, he had to admit that the method had its benefits.

"Stay still," Hope whispered to him. His wrists were tied behind his back and his ankles bound together. Stay still? What other choice was there? He saw no mileage in wriggling; his head hurt enough as it was without encouraging it. There was one important object of business that he had to attend to, however:

"Where's my goddamn money?" he asked her.

"He's taken it," she replied.

"I am going to bite the fucking legs off that cocksucker," he replied. "Where is he?"

"He's got Soldier Joe," she said, panic creeping into her voice. "He's dumping him outside."

GEORGE CAMPBELL WAS a very acquisitive man. If he liked something, he took it; always had.

Sadly for him, circumstances had been such that great opportunities had never really come his way. When he had set up home in Serpent's Creek, it had been as a barber. He was no great stylist with a pair of scissors, but he could just about set a fringe straight and he kept his mouth shut most of the time. This set him out as an improvement on the Mexican who had held sole rights to the trade before him. That boy would talk like it was Judgement Day. As nobody knew what the hell he was saying this far north of the border, his customers spent most of their time confused, deafened and suspicious that he was insulting them. Actually, he was reciting the stories his mother had told him as a child, because he liked them and it passed the time while he suffered the sullen company of *gringos*.

George's salon had flourished. Yet even a flourishing barber can hardly call himself a rich man, and he spent most of his days sitting on his porch and wishing the things he saw were his own. He particularly wished that about the life of Harry Fowkes, who owned the saloon. He wanted Harry's business (thanks to his cut of the card games and whoring, Harry was a wealthy man), he wanted Harry's horse (a fine gelding, chestnut in colour and the most beautiful animal George had ever seen), and he wanted Harry's wife, Genevieve (George's thoughts towards her were so carnal he could barely sleep at night due to penile distension).

For most of the residents of Serpent's Creek, the snakes had been the worst thing that could have happened. But not for George. Because George had an advantage over most people when it came to rattlesnakes: he was immune to their venom.

When he was a kid, he had been playing in the fields. Throwing a ball for Jack, the family's wolfhound, he had tripped and fallen into a nest of the snakes, twisting and turning as a clutch of them struck. The first his parents knew was when they saw their child running up to the house with snakes dangling from his arms.

It should have killed him. His parents were quite sure it had: he'd been sick in bed for long enough, his skin puffing up into blisters that he retained as scars to this day.

"Sometimes," the doctor said, when the boy was up and around, "God just turns a blind eye."

Not only had he survived the experience, but it had left him with an immunity that went beyond that initial slow recovery. If a rattlesnake bit him, it pained him no more than a bee sting.

And in Serpent's Creek, that had made him king. Though he was forward thinking enough to keep it secret.

In those early days when the town had simply locked its doors and hoped for the aberration to pass, George had taken to the streets. He waded his way through the creatures, ignoring them as they hissed and darted at him.

His first attempt was by way of a test. He picked up a

pair of the serpents and worked his way into the house of old Nora Clooney on the edge of town. She had nothing he wanted, but he was a cautious man, and he believed a good plan needed a dress rehearsal.

He went to her bedroom and dropped the writhing snakes on her sleeping head. She woke up only briefly.

He then prised back the screen on her back door, making it look like the snakes had entered through the gap, and gone home to his bed.

The next morning he joined in the town's gossip and sympathy. Poor old Nora hadn't been secure enough, they all said; she'd missed a crack in the door, and look where it got her.

Satisfied, he set his plan of action. Every night he went to the home of someone who had something he desired, broke in, blamed it on the snakes and helped himself to whatever it was.

Harry Fowkes he had left until last, aware that he had to be cleverer in his planning. The last thing he wanted to do was let snakes into the building while Harry lay there with his wife. Only an idiot damages the thing he wishes to steal in the process of stealing it. Instead, he captured a couple of the snakes, keeping them in an empty jar that had contained hair oil. Then, when he saw Harry heading out one morning to pick up liquor supplies from Elwood, he had asked him if he might fetch him another jar of the oil.

"Take this empty one with you," he had said, "so you can make sure you get the right kind."

He had put the jar in the back of Herbert's cart, the lid unscrewed. He reckoned it would be no time at all before either the jar fell over and tipped the snakes out or they figured out for themselves that freedom was at hand. Either way, Harry would be there and likely to get bitten.

This turned out to be the case, the man's body being brought back some time later, the apparent victim of an accident.

George had watched Genevieve cry for days. She would clutch her young son (a precocious little brat, in George's opinion) and wonder out loud about what the future might hold for them both.

Eventually he had offered his services. Friendly at first, just a man helping out someone in need, and then a clear suitor.

In the meantime, the town of Serpent's Creek was all but cleared out. People had started packing after the first couple of deaths and the exodus had been steady ever since.

Stood in the middle of the main street, the town all but empty around him, he had felt like an emperor. A man that had got the things he needed.

Not that Genevieve hadn't taken some encouragement in the end, full of talk of being a grieving widow and needing a period of mourning. But he had used her feelings for her young son to his advantage. He had made his secret known: if she disobeyed him or tried to leave, he would make sure that little brat of hers was snake food. He illustrated as much by dangling one of the serpents over the boy's bed as the child slept. He kept them locked in their rooms during the day and trapped by the snakes at night.

After that, Genevieve was somewhat more willing to accede to his wishes.

Now, pulling the retarded soldier along by his slack arm, he began to count the fortune he had come into. With the preacher's gold, he figured he could pretty much do whatever he wanted. But could he ever leave? Here he had the advantage, he had a power and authority he could hold over the family. If they moved to another town, he'd be nothing again, and that wasn't a backward step George Campbell was willing to make.

"Sit there, you dumb bastard," he said to Soldier Joe, pressing down on his shoulders and leaving him cross-legged in the middle of the street. "Some friends of mine are coming; they'll keep you company soon enough."

SOLDIER JOE SAT down in the dirt and continued to listen to the noises in his head. Mostly they took the form of cannon fire and screaming.

His awareness of the real word slipped in and out of focus. Sometimes he was as aware of it as a man might be looking at a picture: he could see its shapes and lines, but not his place in it. Sometimes it didn't exist at all.

The sun was setting, but he felt the drop in temperature only through an automatic reflex, the hairs on his arms rising as follicles tightened. The slight breeze moved his hair, but not him. He was just a shell that contained an old war.

His wrists began to bleed, the blood soaking into the legs of his trousers and adding to old stains.

"YOU CAN'T LEAVE him out there!" Hope had shouted once George Campbell had returned to the safety of the saloon.

"I can and I will," he replied. "He's no use to me."

Neither were these two, of course; that much was already obvious to him. But first, he should find out a little bit more about them. There were no horses outside, and yet they could hardly have walked here. He had heard a coach pass earlier. Presumably it had dropped them off. Serpent's Creek was not on the coach run. So where had they come from? Where were they going? And, most importantly of all, did they have any friends that were likely to turn up?

He went behind the bar, retrieved his shotgun and pointed it at them. He had no doubt that it would help them answer his questions truthfully.

JONES HAD STEERED the caravan into a small livery shed on the edge of town.

He looked around. It seemed secure enough. There were no windows and the doors fit tightly.

"It should keep us safe," he said.

"It stinks of horses," The Geek complained, climbing out of the back of the caravan.

"So does your breath," said Knee High.

"So"—Harmonium sat on an empty barrel—"we just wait it out in here? If they keep moving, I guess they'll be past us soon enough."

"No," said Jones. "First we have to find the preacher."

"Why?" she complained. "If they bite him, they bite him."

"He has the soldier and he has the gold," Jones replied. "One of them might survive a snake attack, but the other sure as hell wouldn't. He's no use to us dead."

He unholstered his gun and made for the door. "You stay here. There's little to be gained by us all going out there. If you hear me yell, then you come running."

"IF YOU DON'T tell me what I want to know," said George Campbell, pointing the two barrels of his shotgun at Hope Lane, "I'll happily blow her brains all over the closest wall."

"You'll have to find them first," said Hicks, much to Hope's disgust. "And I'm afraid you have me down as a man who cares. Can't say I'm bothered what you do with her."

Hope didn't fool herself that this was a bluff on Hicks' part. He cared for nothing but his gold and himself.

"Then maybe I'd do better to just point this at you," Campbell replied. "After all, I don't have to kill outright with it. I bet you'd talk ten to the dozen after I'd blown one of your feet off."

"Maybe," Hicks replied. "Or maybe I'd pass out and be no use to you whatsoever. That a risk you're willing to take?"

Campbell was getting more and more frustrated. His rise to power had been lucky, and right now he was losing his grip on it. These people just didn't do as they were told.

"All I want to know," he repeated, "is who dropped you off here and where they've gone. Is that really worth risking a limb for?"

"Well," said Hicks, "here's the thing. I'm a businessman and I know how commerce works. I have something you want and once you get it you'll have no more need for me. That ain't a position I intend to put myself in. You think I'm dumb enough to think you'll let either of us live long once I've spilled my guts to you?"

"There's no profit in my killing you."

"Sure there is. Right now we're a problem, a wrinkle in this plan of yours, whatever the hell it is... and believe me when I say I couldn't give a shit about that. If you want to sit here till Judgement Day with this family of yours, it's no problem of mine.

"So here's my suggestion. You let us go. You walk us out that door and close it behind us. Then we're gone. Problem solved."

"Leaving your precious gold?"

"Well, I won't lie, the idea doesn't sit well with

me. But if it's a choice between that and a face full of shot I guess I can make the sensible decision. We walk away, and then either we survive these snakes of yours..."—and Hicks was still far from convinced he even believed in them—"or we don't. Either way, we're gone from your life, and that's the end of it as far as you're concerned."

Campbell gave this some thought. He didn't trust the man, but night was nearly on them and the snakes would soon be here. Throw these two out the door and life would certainly get a lot simpler.

"Alright," he said. "I can be a reasonable man."

"They'll be dead within minutes," said Genevieve. "You can't just let them go out there."

Hicks wasn't in the mood for her assistance, however well-meant. He had seen one way out of the current situation and one way only. "I guess that's our choice to make as much as anyone else's," he said.

"True enough," said Campbell, looking to Hope. "Untie him. Slowly, mind. Either of you offer so much as an angry glance in my direction and I'll shoot the pair of you and to hell with the consequences."

THE SNAKES FLOWED like water, the rising moon throwing pale white light across the undulating mass as they moved ever closer to Serpent's Creek.

Other wildlife moved before them, alerted by the sound of their tails, a war cry that carried far in the still of the evening. Not everything was quick enough, caught in the fanged mouths that hissed and snapped at anything that moved, including each other. Of course, most of the local fauna had moved on: much like the residents of Serpent's Creek, they knew not to linger where death was a nightly possibility.

The snakes raged, their tiny minds driven wild with a need to attack. The cause was beyond them, a coiled weapon of meat and bone. They simply surged forward, full of fear and rage.

JONES WALKED DOWN the main street, head cocked, listening to the sound of the snakes as they slithered ever closer. The town around him was a map of creaking wood and scuffed earth. There, the nearby sound of raised voices. Nobody else could have understood the world the way he experienced it. He could not *see,* in any literal sense, and yet his sense of place was ever acute. All he had to do was to concentrate, and his environment would fall in place around him. Partly it was elevated hearing, partly some extra sense that was so automatic, so instinctual, that he couldn't really explain it. It would have been like trying to explain smell to a man who had never possessed a nose.

Certainly the world he lived in was a different world from everyone else's. It was a place of echoes and murmurs. He was like a fish swimming in the dark depths of the ocean, aware of everything that moved through the water around him.

When he met a person, he naturally absorbed their particular essence. Hicks was a lump of sweat, old whisky and noise. Hope Lane was sweeter, a delicate fish. Soldier Joe a funky, bloody presence whose heart beat slow just as his breath came laboured.

The last was close now; he could hear the wheezing, smell the wounds that blossomed on the man's arms, hear the slight creak of clothing as he rocked to and fro.

"Where are you?" Jones asked. "What are you doing sitting out here alone?"

"The devil," came the whispered, slightly panicked response. "The devil is here."

Jones didn't know if Soldier Joe was referring to him or not. It was possible. It certainly wasn't the first time he had been labelled in such terms.

He stood next to the man, squatted down and reached out for Soldier Joe's face. "Where are the others?" he asked, only too aware that the man would probably not answer.

"The devil," Soldier Joe repeated. "The devil."

"Yeah." Jones stood upright, his gun firm in his hand. "The devil is here."

"Hicks!" he shouted. "Get your ass out here!"

THE TIMING OF Jones' shout was not good. Hicks and Hope had been moments away from freedom, facing the bolted saloon door. George Campbell was a couple of feet behind them, the shotgun held steadily at their backs. The moment he heard Jones, that calm intent, that conviction of a viable plan, vanished.

"Damn you!" he shouted. "Trying to trick me were you? Got your friends out there waiting to jump me?"

"He ain't no friend of mine," admitted Hicks. He meant it, too; another thirty seconds and he would have been free.

"Yeah, I just bet that's true," Campbell laughed. "You keep your distance!" he shouted. "I've got the preacher and his woman here and I'm a heartbeat away from shooting the pair of them. You just stay where you are."

He moved to the shuttered window, opened it and looked carefully out onto the street. He could see a solitary man stood next to the retard. One man, he could handle. Keep him out there long enough and the snakes would do it for him.

"You been making enemies, Hicks?" the man shouted. "Christ's sake, you've only been here an hour."

Hicks didn't deign to reply.

*   *   *

JONES TURNED TO face the building. He could sense the people inside, five in all. Hicks and the nurse, plus three others. What had the idiot got himself caught up in?

As precise as his senses were, the unfamiliar location and the barrier between them made it hard from him to build an accurate picture, not helped by Hicks' silence.

"You in there," Jones shouted. "Can you hear me?"

"Of course I can hear you," the stranger's voice replied. His voice was different now, coming through the glass of a window. That was good. Jones moved, scuffing his boots in the sand, listening to the echo of the noise come back to him, reworking his impression of the building in front of him, isolating its weakest point.

"And you, Hicks?" Jones called.

"I hear you," the preacher said.

"And what about the girl? She still alive?"

"I am," Hope shouted back.

"Who else you got in there?" Jones asked.

"None of your business," the first man replied. That was all Jones needed to take the shot. He mentally confirmed the angle, the gun swinging up and firing, a fraction of a second's work.

Jones heard the scraping of a chair as one of the other strangers moved. Panicked, no doubt, and probably reaching for a weapon. He fired again, shooting three bullets through the now shattered window, not willing to rely on chance.

"No!" Hope Lane shouted and Jones wondered if he'd been too slow. He heard someone fall to the ground and decided not.

"If you're finished in there," he shouted, "get the hell outside. We need to make cover."

He lifted Soldier Joe to his feet and began leading him down the street towards the livery shed where the rest of them were waiting.

WHEN THE FIRST shot had rung out, Hope couldn't quite believe it. Campbell's head rocked back, blood and brain splattering over the dusty tables of the saloon.

Genevieve, concerned for the safety of her son, had snatched him into her arms and turned to run just as three more shots came through the window, two of them passing both through her and her young boy. She fell, face down, crushing the already dead body of her child beneath her.

"No!" Hope shouted. What the hell was the man thinking? Why had he shot them? What possible threat could they have been? And then she realised. Jones had not even seen them; he had simply known someone had moved and taken the shot.

"If you're finished in there," Jones shouted, "get the hell outside. We need to make cover."

Satisfied he was unlikely to fire again, she ran over to Genevieve. There was nothing to be done. Both she and her son were dead.

"Could be worse," said Hicks, retrieving his satchel. "At least I got my money back."

JONES PICKED UP his pace. The snakes were nearly on top of them, close enough that he could hear the brushing sound their bellies made in the dust.

"You killed an unarmed woman and child," the woman shouted at him as she and Hicks caught up.

"'Thank you' is the expression you're looking for," he replied. "Though you might want to save it until we're behind closed doors, there's a ton of snakes heading our way and they'll be all over us any second."

"Dear Christ," said Hicks, "there's hundreds of them!"

They were in sight now, flooding up the street towards them, hanging off the balconies and porches, slithering beneath the buildings and forcing their way between cracks in the doors.

Hicks turned to run back the way they had come but Jones grabbed his arm.

"There," he said, pointing at the livery shed that was still between them and the serpents.

"Open up!" he called. The four of them made it through the doorway just as the first wave of the snakes reached the building.

Harmonium slammed the door behind them, catching two writhing serpents. They hissed and coiled as the door cut them in half. Hicks, with a yelp of panic, stamped down on their heads.

"He really meant it about the snakes," he said, the outside wall taking a pounding as the things hurled themselves at it, desperate to gain entrance.

"I'm not in the habit of making things up," said Jones.

"Not you," Hicks replied. "The useless bastard that had us at gunpoint."

"Anyone else in this town that's likely to cause us trouble?" Jones asked.

"Nobody else in town at all," Hicks replied. "You just killed the last three citizens of Serpent's Creek."

"Good riddance," said Jones.

CHAPTER TWELVE
THE GREAT SILENCE

BARBAROSSA WAS A town in which nothing ever happened. Its residents took pride in the fact. Many of them chose to live there for that very reason. It was a standing joke in the bar of the Pine Bluff that Barbarossa was where people went to draw breath. A town to retire to after a hard life. A warming glass of spirit after an indigestible meal.

This was certainly true of many of its residents. The sheriff, a lean old man by the name of Garritty, had done his time in the ranger service. He had killed his fair share of men and seen a number of friends die too. He would be a happy man indeed, he told his wife, if the gun he wore stayed forever in its holster. He had no desire to put finger to trigger again.

The doctor, Ellen Quarshie, had been a nurse throughout the war. Hands stained with blood so often she had believed they would never be clean. Now she dished out powders and bound up sprained ankles. She couldn't be happier.

The owner of the Pine Bluff told his customers that he had previously run a restaurant in San Francisco.

This was a lie. He had run a band of horse thieves on the Mexican border. If wanted posters were currency he would have been a rich man. Now he polished glasses and cooked a mean steak. He didn't own a horse of his own. He claimed he had no need of one and had never got on with the damn beasts anyway.

Their stories were mirrored in countless others. People who had done their fair share of violent living, only to survive it and find themselves desperate for peace. And peace they found in Barbarossa. A town where the annual barn dance was the height of excitement.

Then, one day, that changed.

HOPE LANE COULDN'T get the sight of a dead woman and her child from her mind. Whenever she tried to think of something else, she heard the short cry of pain and surprise with which Genevieve had met Henry Jones' bullets, and the vision of her and her son, their blood running together into the floorboards of the saloon, returned.

She had seen violence its equal. She had seen good people die and no doubt would again. But there was something about the sudden, random, pointless death of these two that clung to her. It made her sick in her belly, and her heart despaired. Not even the warmth of Soldier Joe as they lay together in his cage could get the chill out of her.

She had spent a sleepless night in the livery stable in Serpent's Creek. She had lain there, listening to the muted sound of rattling tails and darting heads as they rapped at the wooden walls around them. It seemed that nothing would distract the snakes from their prey, not even a bolted door. She imagined how the serpents were even now coiling around the cooling bodies in the saloon. No doubt sinking their fangs into the lifeless flesh.

It was almost more than she could bear.

She knew morning had come because of the silence. A wave of noise ran past their door as the snakes retreated to the long grass and the dark banks of the creek. Then nothing.

"I think we're safe to find some breakfast now," Toby had said, stirring from out of the blanket he had rolled himself up in.

The Joneses had made themselves a bed in the short hay loft and Hope found herself clenching with fear at the sound of Henry's boot heels descending the stairs.

One day, she thought, that man is going to be the death of us all.

He moved to the front doors and pressed his ear against them. After a moment he nodded. "They've gone."

Even with his assurance, there was a palpable nervousness as he unbolted the door and swung it open.

"Well," said Hicks, "I suggest we head back to the saloon and see what else that bastard had been storing up in there."

"I can't go back," said Hope. "Not with them still lying there."

"Then you'll go hungry," Hicks replied, sympathetic as ever.

THEY WERE ON the road again half an hour later, having raided George Campbell's supplies for food and munitions. There was limited space in the caravan with so many passengers. Harmonium would have preferred they shot the preacher to allow more room, but Henry was still insisting the man could prove useful.

Soldier Joe had said that they should bear left at Serpent's Creek. Following the road they had travelled the previous evening, they were soon back out in open country.

"So how long do we keep driving?" Harmonium asked. "It's about time our talking map earned his keep and gave us a few more directions."

Hicks was only too aware of this, most particularly because his longevity was tied to the usefulness of his charge. "I'll talk to him," he insisted, climbing back into the caravan and Soldier Joe's cage.

"He needs to start talking!" he said to Hope, keeping his voice low. "Has he said nothing?"

She shook her head. "Not since last night."

"Useless fucker." Hicks prodded Soldier Joe, who appeared to be happily asleep. It was alright for him; he was too stupid to know his life was on the line. "Bear left at Serpent's Creek," the preacher said. "And then what?"

SOLDIER JOE WAS dreaming.

Usually his dreams were incoherent affairs, a mess of noise and colour. This was different. He recognised the Tennessee River, its waters flowing pink with the blood of fallen soldiers. The air was alive with shouting and rifle fire. Someone was begging for death, lying back in the undergrowth with an open stomach that revealed a glistening cage of ribs. His cries had turned him from an adult to a child, desperate and alone, driven wild by pain. Soldier Joe couldn't help, knew as much instinctively as he walked through this remembered battlefield like a ghost.

In the trees ahead, a small table was set for tea, its bright gingham cloth and pristine china a ludicrous reflection of blood and bone. At the table sat a man, his clean suit and bright vest a world away from the tattered uniforms of the soldiers that fought and died around him. He smoothed back a stray curl of light blond hair as the shock of a nearby explosion rippled past. It seemed to him no more than a light summer breeze.

"Take a seat," he called, gesturing to the empty chair next to him. "Come and talk to me for a while."

Soldier Joe did as he was asked, never one to question the logic of dreams.

"Take some tea?" the man asked.

Soldier Joe was so used to silence that the sound of his own voice seemed as shocking to him as the carnage that surrounded them. "I guess. Can't say I've ever drunk it."

"You'll like it," the man assured him. "It's somewhat out of fashion these days, but I'm not one to bear a grudge."

He poured a dash of milk into a small cup then added the tea. That arc of glistening amber liquid seemed the greatest anachronism of all. It shone in the morning sunshine, a thing of beauty.

"Help yourself to cake," said the man, passing Soldier Joe the cup.

There was another explosion and the table shook slightly, with a jingle of china.

"Who would live in a place like this?" the man complained.

"Nobody does," Soldier Joe replied.

The man smiled and shook his head. "You do, or we wouldn't be sat here."

Soldier Joe had no reply to that.

The man sipped his tea and looked out at the fighting as if basking in a beautiful view. "So ephemeral," he said. "All these brief little candles of life flickering out one after the other. Why do you always end up at war?"

"God knows."

"If He does, He's not telling. Maybe you can ask Him yourself when you see Him." He put down his tea cup. "Do try the cake, it's quite delightful."

"Who are you?"

The man shrugged slightly, as if this were an awkward

question. "You can call me Alonzo. Beyond that it gets complicated." He smiled. "You didn't ask what I meant when I said about you seeing God."

"We all see Him sooner or later."

"In your case, sooner."

"I'm dying?"

"You all are from my perspective, faster than you seem to think. But no, I mean literally, once you get to Wormwood."

Wormwood. The name triggered a strange sensation in Soldier Joe's head. He suddenly felt as if he was away from this battlefield, lying on his back in a moving caravan. He could see a fat, angry face leaning over him. "Wormwood?" he said, and the face began to smile. "That's it!" the fat man said, "that's it!"

Then he was back in his seat, a tea cup in his hand.

"You're not quite in one world or the other," Alonzo said. "It must be difficult. You spend more time here than there, which is never healthy. Why live in the past, when the future is so small?"

"Where is Wormwood?" Soldier Joe asked.

"You've reached Serpent's Creek, turned left..." Alonzo gazed into the middle distance as if recalling something. "You need to aim north, towards the town of Barbarossa."

"North? Barbarossa?" Soldier Joe suddenly had the sensation of being back in the caravan. He could feel dry straw pressing at the back of his neck. A woman's hand sliding across his brow. The fat man was laughing, getting up and moving away from his line of sight.

He was back at the table.

"Of course," Alonzo continued, "Barbarossa is normally terribly dull. Nothing ever happens there."

"Sounds nice."

Alonzo looked up. Soldier Joe followed the man's gaze

and marvelled at the sight of snow beginning to fall through the trees. It fell on the warring soldiers, evaporating on their hot cannon and soaking up their blood.

"Beautiful," said Soldier Joe.

"Death often is," Alonzo replied. "It appears our little chat is coming to an end. I'll see you again soon."

"I never want to come here again," Soldier Joe replied, looking at the fallen bodies all around him.

Alonzo shrugged. "That choice is yours to make."

With that, he vanished, the cup he had been holding falling to the floor and tipping its contents into bloodied leaves.

"My choice," said Soldier Joe, returning to the prison of his own, tortured head.

"It's unbelievable," said Harmonium Jones as the snow continued to fall all around them. "I haven't seen snow in years."

Not since she had been a child, in fact, growing up in northern Wisconsin. Then she had seen more than her fair share. Ice cold winters that had seized their home and crushed it hard. Her father had worked the timber, and she would always picture him as a mountain of a man, wrapped from head to toe in clothes, buried in fabric, as he headed out the door to chop and saw. One day he had simply never come back. For years she had imagined him caught out in the snow, frozen to death in the forest, bright eyes turned creamy white as they grew solid in his skull. Then, because it was easier, she stopped imagining him at all.

"It's colder than a well digger's ass is what it is," Hicks complained, pulling his jacket tighter around him and taking a nip on the whisky jug.

"Then get inside," Harmonium replied. "'North to

Barbarossa,' you said. We can manage that with your constant complaining, or without. I know which I would prefer."

Hicks wasn't in the mood to argue, he just clambered back inside, glad to be out of the sudden chill.

The weather had appeared out of nowhere, bright skies suddenly filled with grey clouds and thick snow. After their night in Serpent's Creek, the bizarre no longer seemed so surprising, and at least snow wasn't venomous.

For Henry Jones, the weather was having an altogether more unpleasant effect. As he sat there on the driving bench, the world around him slowly but surely began to lose its clarity. The flakes of snow swirling and dancing in the air were too light to register, and as they hit the ground and began to stick it was as if everything around him were being swathed in soft wool.

If this continues, he thought, I really will be blind.

And continue it did.

For all her initial enthusiasm, Harmonium was soon cursing the weather as the snow piled higher and higher around them, the air so thick with it that she could barely see a foot or so of the road ahead.

"Someone fetch me a blanket, for Christ's sake!" she shouted behind her. "I'm liable to freeze to death out here."

"Always complaining," muttered Hicks, but he made sure he was the first to lay his hands on one, just to show he could be useful.

"Barbarossa," Soldier Joe muttered. "Nothing ever happens there."

"Sounds perfect," said Hope, smoothing his hair back from his head.

"Sounds boring," complained The Geek. "Hopefully we'll be passing right through."

"If we can get anywhere in this," said Knee High, peering out at the snow.

"The horses are taller than you, pipsqueak," said The Geek. "They'll manage."

But they didn't. The snow continued to fall, and soon the horses were stumbling and fighting their way through it, each step a challenge.

"What are we going to do, Henry?" Harmonium asked.

But Jones was lost inside his own head, a place that felt smaller and smaller with each passing moment.

His wife roared with frustration, yanking at the reins as the horses drew to a halt.

"Damn you!" she screamed, the fury that was never far from the surface bubbling over as she jumped from the bench. She pushed and kicked at the snow as if it were an enemy she could beat into submission.

"Hello!" called a voice from nearby, the sound flipping through the air on the back of the wind. "Can you hear me?"

"Of course I can hear you!" Harmonium shouted. "Who are you?"

"The name's Garritty!" came the reply. "I'm the sheriff here."

Sheriff. That was not a word to which Harmonium responded warmly. Given their current situation, though, she'd rather worry about the law from within the safety of a set of walls than out here.

"How close is the town?" she asked. "We can't see a thing."

"Tell me about it," the voice replied, this time from right next to her.

She turned to find herself face to face with the man. He was wrapped in skins, his old face looming out from within them, salt and pepper moustache thick with ice crystals.

"As for the town," he said, "you're just about stood in it. Though I figure you folks might still need a hand finding it."

Garritty was a man who took life in his stride. He could not explain the sudden appearance of the snow in the skies above their heads. Certainly, the way it fell so thick and so fast was beyond his previous experience. Still, the simple fact of the matter was: it had, he was wading through it, and there was little point in questioning the existence of something that was freezing your toes off.

He had taken to the street, wrapped in as many warm clothes as he could find, and set about helping those who might struggle with the sudden change in environment.

Within half an hour, it had gotten so that he could barely see the buildings on either side of him.

"Well, damn," he had muttered to himself. "If this keeps up, we'll be buried within the hour."

He had helped old Mrs Keighley, who had been running around her yard trying to gather her chickens.

"They'll freeze their feathers off," she had shouted, struggling to be heard over the wind. "And then where will I get my eggs?"

One by one the birds had been grabbed and shut away in the coop, a pair of blankets thrown over it in the hope of keeping in some of the heat.

Then he had continued on to check on Pat Farmer. Pat had broken his leg a month or so ago and refused to accept the fact. Garritty had lost count of the amount of times he had hoisted him up from where he had fallen while trying to chop wood, or feed the horse, or whatever other damn thing he had set his mind to. The man simply wouldn't sit still. If he'd taken a tumble in this, he would need an ice-pick to set him on his feet again.

"You alright, Patrick?" Garritty shouted through the open window of Farmer's home. "It's snowing like the Arctic out here, you might want to keep the windows closed before you freeze to death."

"Snowing?" came a voice from inside. "You been drinking, Garritty?"

Not yet, the sheriff thought, though if the day carries on this way I may be tempted to start. "Take a look out of your window."

"Well, now," the man replied. "I would, but I seem to have lost my balance."

Garritty sighed, went inside and helped the man up from where he had fallen behind a bookcase. "You just sit still for a while, you hear?" he told him. "I'm going to have a day from hell as it is without having to keep checking on you."

"I'd have got up eventually," Pat insisted. "Just getting my breath back."

Garritty left him to it and stepped back outside. It was getting so he'd have to take cover himself; visibility was low and the wind so cold he'd struggle to stay out here long.

He was thinking of camping out in the Pine Bluff—better to stay central so he could keep an eye on everyone—when he heard the sound of a woman shouting. She sounded fierce as all hell. It made him think of his wife, Maggie, who was likely even now pushing curses out of the window as she looked at the snow. He loved her a great deal, almost especially because she was not a woman shy of working language.

He followed the sound of the woman's shouts and slowly the sight of a caravan and horses loomed up out of the white in front of him. If he didn't get them under cover, they'd be dead of exposure; he'd just have to commandeer a corner of Sam Popewell's shed. Sam wouldn't mind.

After a few minutes, he began to wonder if that was true. This was an unusual band of travellers. He'd seen a few sideshows in his day, though the freak tents had never been much to his taste. It wasn't just the look of them, though, it was their attitude: these people were trouble and he'd stake his badge on it. He failed to see what choice he had, though. He could hardly abandon them just because he didn't take to them.

He'd told Pat Farmer that he expected a day from hell, and that was looking more and more likely with each passing minute.

"Where you headed?" he asked the woman.

"Here," she answered, the snow matting the curls of her beard. "Though God knows why."

"Got a show to put on, have you?" It seemed the likeliest explanation, though he couldn't see the residents of Barbarossa turning out today.

"Just passing through," she said.

She was leading a blind man by his arm, his small, dark glasses whitening with ice crystals as she dragged him through the drifts of snow. He tried to help, but the man shook him away. "I can manage," he insisted, though it was clear to Garritty that he could not.

"We're going to have to leave the caravan," Garritty said, "though we can get your horses shelter."

"I'm not leaving it out here!" shouted a small, fat man. "Anyone could steal it."

"In this weather?" Garritty stared at him. "Son, if we can't shift it, neither can anyone else. Take what you can carry and I'll see about getting some help to dig it clear once the snow stops falling."

The man wasn't happy about that, but Garritty didn't care. He didn't mind helping folk out, but if they were too stupid to know what was good for them, then he wasn't going to argue.

A black girl was helping another wounded man out of the back. A blind man and a cripple, Garritty thought; this is a show that's been in the wars.

He began unfastening the horses. "Someone want to give me a hand here?" he shouted.

"I'll do it," said a young lad with skin the texture of a dried river bed.

"To hell with the horses," came an angry shout. "What about me? I can't walk through this!"

Garritty saw the final member of the party, a thin, tattooed feller, grab the dwarf who had spoken by the scruff of his neck and hoist him up out of the snow.

"Careful!" the dwarf screeched. "I'm not your goddamned dinner!"

"Never eaten a dwarf," the other man said, laughing. "Maybe now's as good a time as any."

These people are definitely going to be trouble, Garritty decided.

IN THE PINE Bluff, Colin Bryson was staying close to his stove, soaking up the heat it kicked out.

He had taken a look outside at the weather, shivered and retired to the warmth. On days like this, he missed his youth in Texas. Texas had heat and knew how to use it. Some men couldn't take it. They would broil under the sun and complain that the state was Hell on earth. Bryson didn't agree. The cold, he felt; that's what the devil would use, if he really wanted to break a man.

The doors opened and Sheriff Garritty came in, leading a whole gang of strangers behind him.

"This weather sure beats me, Colin," the sheriff said. "I think you ought to prepare yourself for a full house."

Garritty shook some of the snow from himself and

moved in alongside Bryson at the stove. "If this keeps up, I reckon we need to get everyone together. This is the kind of cold that kills folks."

"I've got the space," Bryson admitted. "Only too happy to use it."

He looked at the strangers the sheriff had brought with him. "You taking in strays, too?"

"Found them on the edge of town. Couldn't leave them out there." Garritty looked at Bryson and a brief glance passed between them. The sheriff knew Bryson was no idiot. *Keep an eye on these folk*, that look said.

Bryson shrugged. "Like I say, I've got the space."

Harmonium Jones wrung ice cold water from her beard and sat down at a table with Henry. "It's good to get inside," she said. "Be even better if there was a fire going."

"If a couple of you are willing to help me bring some firewood in," said Bryson, "we'll see what we can do about that."

"I don't mind helping," said Toby. "Anything to get warm."

Bryson nodded, looking the kid up and down. "You'll pardon me asking, son," he said, "but you got anything contagious I should worry about?"

Toby looked heartbroken. "No," he replied, "nobody can catch what I got."

"We going to have a problem here?" asked Henry Jones, his confidence returning now that he was away from the snow.

"No problem," said Bryson, calm as you please. "Just asking."

"Only we don't take kindly to people staring," said Jones, a clear note of threat in his voice.

"It's fine," Toby insisted. "I don't mind. He was just asking."

"That's right," said Garritty, "and we don't take kindly to trouble, so what say you settle into a tolerant mood while we all pull together?"

Jones thought about that for a moment then nodded. "Agreed."

Garritty helped Hope lead Soldier Joe over to a chair. "We have a good doctor here," he told her, "if he needs attention."

"Doctors can't help him," she said. "His wounds are twenty years old."

"The war?"

She nodded.

Garritty sighed. "Then he has my sympathy. I fought through it myself."

"Anyone else going to help with the firewood?" Bryson asked, looking directly at The Geek and Hicks. "The more hands we have, the quicker work it will be."

"Sadly I am a martyr to my back," said Hicks, lowering himself carefully into a chair. "If I try and lift more than a glass of water I'm likely to break myself in two."

The Geek sighed. "I'll help."

"Then let's get to it," said Bryson, "before the pile is buried so deep we'll be digging an hour to get to it."

Garritty stared out of the window at the still falling snow. "I'm going to get back out there and start gathering folks together," he said. "All the safer, I reckon." He shook his head, gazing at the blank whiteness. "I'm damned if I've ever seen anything the like of this."

"I DON'T LIKE this, Henry," said Harmonium, once both Garritty and Bryson had left the building. "You think he recognises us?"

Her husband shrugged. "I reckon he wouldn't have given us shelter if he did."

243

Harmonium wasn't convinced. "Shelter? We're as good as locked up in here."

"Along with everyone else in the town. Just keep calm, honey. A cool head is what we need."

"A cool head is sure as hell what I've got," said Knee High, joining them. "Half frozen, more like."

"We'll play it by ear," said Jones. "For now, we need to keep them friendly until this weather passes."

"And when it does?" his wife asked, eager as always for the promise of violence.

"Then I'll shoot up the whole damn town if that's what it takes, ain't no hardship to me."

Though Jones was far from sure this was true. Now he was inside, he felt in control, but he knew that he would be half the man he could be once he stepped outside that door. It had been a long time since he had felt truly powerless, and he couldn't say he liked it one bit.

THEY HAD NOTHING to fear from Garritty, not at that moment. He had more than enough on his plate to keep him occupied.

He had moved from one building to the next, enlisting people to help spread the word and get everyone gathered at the Pine Bluff.

With every passing minute, it was getting more and more difficult to move, and he knew that they had maybe an hour or so before they would be completely trapped. When that happened, he would feel a whole lot more comfortable if they were trapped together. At least then he could keep an eye on everyone.

He called in on Ellen Quarshie. She was gathering as many blankets as she could find, anything to help give warmth.

"I'm trying to get everyone into the Pine Bluff," he told her. "Be better for us all if you were there too."

She nodded. "Makes sense. I'm damned if I'm roaming the streets in this."

She pulled her light grey hair into a ponytail and started gathering her medical equipment. "Where the hell has this come from, Kingsland?" she asked him. "We haven't seen weather like this in all the years I've lived here."

He shook his head. "Damned if I know," he admitted. "Seems like the sky's gone crazy."

He helped her gather her belongings. "We've a band of strangers arrived, too," he told her. "Look like they're from some kind of travelling show. Can't say I warm to them much, though they've got a war veteran with them that might benefit from a little attention."

"First the weather, now strangers," Ellen laughed. "Seems to me like it's a day for the unusual. What brings them here? I wouldn't have thought we're really on the entertainment circuit."

"Say they're just passing through."

"Well, if you don't like them, then I guess that's good to hear."

Garritty nodded. "They're trouble, Ellen, I know it. Just mind yourself with 'em, you hear?"

"I can look after myself, you old woman, as well you know."

He did know that. Still, he worried.

The drawback to a peaceful life, he decided, was that it made you nervous. When you lived your life as if every day might be your last, it gave you a freedom that security didn't. Barbarossa was his home, a quiet, gentle place. The presence of these strangers within the town scared him more than the weather. Ice could be guarded against; these folk were altogether more dangerous, he was sure of that.

*   *   *

BRYSON WOULD HAVE shared Garritty's fears, though he had quickly decided that Toby—despite the look of the lad—was safe enough. He was happy to help, polite and altogether too concerned what people thought of him to be any real trouble. Toby wanted to be liked. The Geek was another story.

Bryson knew enough about life in the sideshows to recognise the man's act once Toby had used his name. He had met a few geeks in his time and they were not men he had warmed to. A man who had got to a stage in his life where eating live chickens was an acceptable career move was a man to be careful of. They didn't have much to lose, and that made them dangerous.

That said, The Geek lifted wood without complaint and they soon had a reasonable supply indoors. It would be enough, Bryson decided, to keep a fire going for a day or so. If the snow lasted beyond then, a supply of logs would be only one of many problems.

Back inside, he watched as the dwarf, Knee High, set to building a fire, only too happy to be involved now the work didn't involve wading through snow the height of his shoulders. Deciding that he could leave that chore to the strangers, he went into his kitchen and set to preparing some food. He figured that once the place filled up, he'd need something to keep people going.

"Any chance of a drink around here?" a voice asked from the kitchen doorway. He turned to find the fat man stood there. Hicks, the others called him.

"Liquor is not something I'm short of," Bryson admitted. "Your back improved?"

Hicks was moving freely, having forgotten to keep up the pretence. "It's fine if I don't bend," he said, feigning a sudden spasm.

"I'll just bet it is," Bryson replied.

He left the beginnings of a stew and walked through to the bar, where he poured the man a small measure of whisky. "Anyone else got a thirst?" he asked, not surprised at the unanimous assent.

He poured out several whiskies, lining them on the bar.

"And who's paying?" he asked, looking directly at Hicks.

"Well," the preacher replied, "I sort of assumed that, given the circumstances..."

"I'm still a business, friend," Bryson replied, "and I'm not so rich that I can afford to keep all visitors fed and watered out of my own pocket."

Hicks nodded. "I'll just organise a whip round then."

Soon enough, the saloon began to fill up, as one by one, the residents of Barbarossa fought their way through the snow to gather inside the Pine Bluff. Every single one of them took a moment to sum up the strangers in their midst, fascinated, as only isolated communities can be, by the sight of new faces. These faces, in particular, rewarded curiosity.

Henry Jones did his best to ignore it, though he couldn't help but be reminded of his days as a performer, a freak to be marvelled at. He knew that it would benefit nobody if he were to lose his temper now. As the building got busier, his ability to centre himself in his surroundings began to struggle. He never did like crowds: they were too loud, too much for his brain to calmly process. He knew his wife would be hating it too. He didn't pass on some of the comments he overheard with regards to her appearance. He knew there was nothing good to be gained from it, even though some of them had him gripping his knee between fingers that were desperate to form a fist.

"I think this is everyone we could reach," Garritty

announced. "The Huxtables are just too far away and they should be safe enough on the farm."

"There's certainly enough of them!" one local wit suggested, to a polite ripple of laughter. "If things get worse, they can always eat Judy!"

Judy Huxtable was a large girl, and several of the gathered townsfolk found this the height of comedy.

Garritty did not. Looking at how heavily the snow continued to fall, he didn't much like the idea of joking about such desperate circumstances. After all, give them a few days and it might seem all too possible.

"There's also the Blackwells and the Furrows," he continued, "and like as not they'll have banded together anyway."

"Don't they always?" The same voice, the same polite laughter. Jones was finding this community spirit suffocating. He could think of nothing worse than living in a town where everybody knew one another and stuck their noses into each other's business.

"Now, I know we're short of space," Garritty said, "but hopefully it won't be for long."

Toby was far from sure of the truth of that. He had been looking out of the window for some time and it seemed to him that the snow was falling even thicker and faster. He couldn't help but imagine what would happen if it got so high it buried the whole building. What would they do then? He asked The Geek his opinion on the matter.

"Well," the man replied, not particularly helpfully, "I sure won't go hungry for a while."

CHAPTER THIRTEEN
BLINDMAN

THE STREETS OF Barbarossa were losing their shape completely.

The sky continued to darken, a false night brought on by the oppressive layer of cloud that sank lower and lower towards the buildings, as if aiming to meet the snow in the middle.

The wind blew, whistling between the buildings and sweeping the still-falling snow into drifts.

It was a world in which nobody could survive for long.

But the storm that was coming inside the Pine Bluff was more dangerous still.

HICKS HAD BEEN drinking steadily. The others could rely on the fire for warmth, if they wished; he took his heat from the whisky bottle.

He had spent the last few minutes talking to a woman by the name of Elsa Jackson. He liked her a great deal. She was quiet, young and possessed breasts he wanted to rest his balls on. He was telling her as much, laughing at the look of disgust that passed across her face at the suggestion.

He was aware that some of the other townsfolk were getting uncomfortable at the tables around them, but if there was one surefire symptom to his drinking whisky, it was an inclination towards single-mindedness.

"If you know a better way of keeping the cold out," he told her, "feel free to mention it. But I reckon what we both need is a good bit of physical exercise." He leaned in close. "Half an hour with your thighs as a muffler and I reckon I'd be as toasty as hellfire."

"I think you need to watch your manners," said a voice from behind him. Hicks turned to find himself face to face with Colin Bryson.

"And you need to mind your own fucking business," the preacher replied.

"You don't know how we like things here in Barbarossa," Bryson said, taking Hicks by his collar. "We offered you shelter, and you owe us a little respect."

Through the whisky, Hicks mulled over a little idea. The idea pleased him, so he acted upon it. He punched Bryson in the stomach and rose unsteadily to his feet. "If you want another where that came from, I'm only too happy to oblige," he told the bar owner.

A number of the townsfolk got to their feet around him. Jones, sensing the way the mood was turning, also rose, pulling his gun from its holster.

Garritty, who had been waiting for just such a move, already had his gun in his hand.

"You want to place that gun on the table in front of you," he said. "And I'd like the rest of your folks to do the same."

Jones contemplated the suggestion. After all, he had been the one advocating a cool head earlier. But Henry Jones' head never did run all that cool.

"I don't give up my gun for anybody," he said, turning it towards the sheriff. "Now I might consider not firing it, because I think we all need to take a little step back and think about this situation before it gets a hell of a lot worse. But I don't think I'll be giving it up; no, not for anyone in this room."

"You tell 'em!" said Hicks, drunkenly. "About time these people learned to keep a civil tongue in their head. Nobody messes with Henry Jones, am I right?"

He was not. No sooner had he finished speaking than Jones had been grabbed from behind by three of the other townsmen. His gun was taken from him.

Harmonium reached for hers, but they were surrounded and she was no further than hoisting her skirts before she too was taken hold of and a rough hand finished the job for her, taking the small pistol from her garter holster and pointing it right at her.

There was a general sound of pistol hammers being cocked, and it was clear to the entirety of Jones' party that they were at the mercy of the residents of Barbarossa.

"It's always the same with you people," said Garritty. "So full of piss and wind that you think you can take on anything. Well, not here. This town likes to stick together. We have rules. We have principles. We have a peaceful life. I think it's time you all stepped outside."

"Outside?" screamed Hicks. "Are you out of your fucking mind?" He grabbed an empty bottle from the table and held it up like a club. "I'd like to see you try and make me."

"Idiot," said Harmonium. "I knew we should have just killed him."

"Allow me," said Garritty, before shooting Hicks dead-centre of his forehead.

For a moment, the preacher looked confused. Then he

toppled backwards, tipping up a table and chairs and falling to the floor.

"I will happily do that to each and every one of you," the sheriff said. "Or you can take the chance to walk away."

"Out there?" asked Toby. "We'd be dead within five minutes."

"Not my problem," Garritty replied. "We do not tolerate your kind here. You won't be the first we've run out of town, and I dare say you won't be the last. Barbarossa is a peaceful place, and it stays peaceful because every single one of us is willing to do what it takes to keep it that way."

"Please," said Hope, holding on to Soldier Joe. "We haven't got anything to do with the rest of them, we wouldn't cause any trouble."

"All of you," Garritty said. "Now."

"Jesus wept," said Harmonium, looking around at the several guns pointing at her and her husband.

She and Henry walked towards the door, followed by Knee High, Toby and The Geek.

"He'll die," Hope begged, hugging her Soldier Joe. "Please... I couldn't bear that..."

"Then you should mind the company you keep," Garritty replied. "I don't know a single one of you. I don't trust a single one of you." He looked to the rest of the gathered townsfolk. "But I'm happy to put it to the vote. All in favour of letting them stay?"

There was silence.

"I guess you have your answer."

"You'll wish you killed me," said Jones. "Mark my words, old man. Because I am going to come back here and shoot every single one of you. Just you watch."

Garritty stared at him, then came to a decision. "Colin, you want to wrap up and step outside with me? I think we should make sure these folks cross the town line and don't come back."

THEY MOVED IN a procession, Garritty leading them down the main street and towards the edge of town.

The sheriff was sad but resolute. No matter how many times he hoped he would be able to avoid violence, it seemed that others would make the decision for him. It had been the same with the Lansdowne boys, talking up rough every night; the Casey kid that had helped himself to a bottle of liquor when Bryson's back had been turned; the Popwell twins; Sam Laker; Wade Cruse; Gard Galloway... the list went on. When would people just learn to obey the rules?

He cursed his own softness in bringing these people into the town in the first place. He had known they were trouble from the word go; hadn't he told everyone as much? It would have been easier and fairer on them all if he had just shot them as they first got out of their caravan. But Garritty was a man of principles, all the men of the town were. You gave people a chance... just one... and let them be the best they could be.

He had some misgivings about the girl and the soldier. They might have been safe to stay, but who was to tell? They travelled together, didn't they? How was he to know whether she would have been trustworthy or not? No. The town was everything, and he wasn't going to take any risks. The life they had was worth fighting for, always had been.

HENRY JONES HAD fallen off the world. He stumbled forward through an unchanging landscape of emptiness, with no idea whatsoever of what was around him. He was vaguely aware of someone to his right—he thought it might just be his wife—but they were far enough away that he couldn't be sure. All he knew for certain was the icy wind on his face and the crunch of his boots in the snow beneath him.

Once again he had let his temper get in the way of common sense. That said, he wasn't convinced the sheriff would have treated them any differently had he agreed to give up his gun. The man had been waiting for an excuse and, as loathsome as Hicks had been, if it hadn't been him that wore out their welcome, it would have been someone else. Barbarossa was no different from the rest of the world. He and his band didn't belong.

And now, not for the first time, someone was out to kill them because of it.

He certainly didn't imagine Garritty intended to let them just walk away. If that had been so, then he wouldn't have needed to come out with them. No. He meant to make sure of things. A bullet in the back. Problem solved.

Jones had been in situations as dire before, but with the snow, with his damned blindness... he wasn't sure how best to handle it. People had often made the mistake of assuming him incapable because of his handicap; in fact, that had often been to his advantage. Unaware of how clearly he perceived the world around him, people thought he was easy to beat. Those people were now dead. But this time he really was blind. Utterly. Even had his eyes worked, the snow was so thick that nobody could see further than a few feet. Nobody.

And with that thought came his only real chance of survival.

"That's about far enough!" Garritty shouted behind him. They were seconds away from a bullet and the only alternative would result in his becoming even more powerless than he was now. But what choice did he have?

"Harmonium!" he shouted. "One way or the other I'll find you, honey. Now, run!"

He flung himself forward, rolling into the deep snow before clawing himself forward on his hands and knees. A gunshot sounded, muffled and made distant by the wind and snow but surely no more than a few feet away. He had to keep moving. If they all scattered and kept running, then Garritty and the barkeep would lose sight of them, probably already had.

Keep shifting direction, zig-zagging and hoping that they were as blind as he now was.

He collided with someone, tumbling into the snow to find himself nose to nose with Knee High.

"I need you!" he said, grabbing the dwarf and pulling him onto his back. "I'm blind."

"Tell me something I don't know, boss." Knee High replied, though he held on tight. He was no idiot; he stood a better chance of getting through the snow on Jones' back than he did wading alone.

"Just tell me what you can see, you little shit," Jones replied, running forward, lifting his legs as high as he could to try and clear the deepening drifts around them.

There was another gunshot and someone cried out. A man's voice. Not his wife. Never let it be his wife.

He would find her. Somehow he would find her.

GARRITTY AND BRYSON were shooting into thin air. They could barely see each other, let alone their targets.

"Leave it," the sheriff said. "They don't have a chance out here. If they manage to make their way back to town, we're more than a match for them."

He kept his revolver in his hand, just in case, and the two of them returned to the warmth and peace of Barbarossa.

*   *   *

"Run!"

Hope hadn't needed telling twice. She pulled at Soldier Joe and the two of them veered off to one side, pushing their way through the snow as fast as they could. She hoped that Garritty and Bryson would shoot at the others first. It made sense. After all, how much of a threat were she and Joe? If the others kept them occupied for long enough, they just might get away.

"Got to keep moving," she told Soldier Joe, the man shaking in her arms, his legs unsteady and his mind elsewhere as always. "Got to stay ahead."

"Ahead," Soldier Joe replied. "Ahead to Wormwood."

"To hell with Wormwood," she said. "I'm trying to make for the caravan."

She thought she was heading in the right direction, but it was impossible to be sure. She could make out nothing around them but the never-changing curtains of snow. As far as she could remember, this was the direction they had come from.

She wondered how long they could both last out here, if she was wrong. Hope had come from Texas: snow was something she had heard about, but never seen with her own eyes. She had heard stories of people dying of exposure, and she had no doubt that was what awaited them if they didn't find cover quickly. Every breath made her throat feel as if it was bleeding. Her body was shaking against the cold, her legs weak and unsteady already after only a few minutes. If they could just get as far as the caravan, then she might be able to wrap the both of them up. Maybe climb into Soldier Joe's cage and surround themselves with blankets, wait the storm out.

And if the townspeople come looking while you're all

shut up in there? That was a problem she'd just have to deal with when the time came.

JONES WAS SLOWING down already, but he forced himself to keep going. The harder he moved, the warmer he would stay and the longer he would survive. Knee High was silent on his back, the man's head pressed against his shoulder like that of a child. He considered dumping him; he would get further on his own. He couldn't do it. All of them had looked after one another over the years. Certainly nobody else had. That had to mean something.

After they had left the employment of Dr Bliss, they had done everything together. They had robbed together, killed together, and when Jones had found himself on the wrong side of a set of prison gates, they had come for him. He wouldn't repay that by leaving him to die. Jones was determined to be a better man than that.

Besides, they would both be dead soon anyway. There was no way they could last out here much longer.

Harmonium. If he died, he was damned if he was going to die without her.

Jones shook Knee High. "Wake up, damn you!" he shouted. "Wake up! I am Henry Jones, wanted in nine states, killer of more men than I can count and the biggest bastard this piss pot of a world has ever seen. I am not going to lie down and die. When I go, it will be screaming. It will be in fire and bullets. It will not be face down in the snow."

"Good for you," Knee High murmured. "Wish I could say the same."

"You will, you little bastard," said Jones. "You will."

And with the anger that always burned so brightly in him, he fought his way on.

*   *   *

HOPE WAS LOST. However far they walked, the caravan refused to appear. It was all snow. Never changing, never slackening, just an empty, infinite wilderness.

"I think we're done," she said, pulling Soldier Joe close to her as her legs began to give way. "Yes. I think we're done."

She fell to one side, pulling him with her. Both came to rest, nestled deep within the thick blanket all around them.

"Not so cold," she said, her face covered with a thin sheen of ice. She turned to face him. "Not cold at all."

She cupped his face in her hands and looked into those sad, old eyes of his. "I love you, Soldier Joe," she said, kissing him on the lips. "Sorry if I haven't done right by you."

She buried her face in his chest and held him tight, slipping out of consciousness and into the darkness beyond.

Soldier Joe lay there, his wrists beginning to bleed, blood trickling slowly into the perfect white around them.

Then he stood up, cradled Hope Lane in his arms and began to walk.

HEAVEN'S
GATE

IF YOU'D ASKED me what it was I expected to see when we reached the legendary Wormwood, I'd have been hard pressed to tell you. I guess I'd been too busy not dying to give it much thought. Had I tried to predict it, though, I'm sure I would have been wide of the mark. The old man had said that the town was due to arrive soon, so I suppose I would have imagined nothing but an open plain, somewhere we would sit and wait, legendary survivors of a heroic journey. Actually, we found ourselves in the middle of the biggest camp I had ever seen.

You couldn't move for people. Most were gathered around their caravans or tents, but some had even been there so long they had erected ramshackle homes.

"When you get to my age," one of these house-dwellers told me, a woman the very spit of my grandmother, all thick, homespun cotton and long white hair, "you can't move as fast as you'd like. I wasn't going to miss this, not unless the good Lord chose to let me in early. I've been here six months."

Her son, a retiring type who was obviously used to doing what he was told, just smiled and went back to fixing loose floorboards.

On one edge of the camp was the most amazing machine I'd ever clapped eyes on. It looked like a train that had given up on its tracks and found itself some fat wheels. It had clearly seen some hard travelling: the paintwork was chipped and burned, some sections heavily damaged.

"Looks like it came through a battlefield," I said to a man sat in front of it. He was in his early fifties, I'd say, bald and with the pink, slightly chubby skin of a drinker. I knew that look well enough, having grown up around my father. The stranger had none of Pa's fiery temper, though; he just smiled and nodded.

"That it did, and I for one am still finding it hard to believe we got here in one piece." He held out his hand. "The name's Patrick Irish. I'm a writer."

"Elwyn Wallace, bank clerk in waiting."

"Where we're going, I'd be a bit disappointed if we still needed banks." He laughed, pulled out a notebook and jotted down my name. "I'm trying to keep a record," he explained. "A writer's job. We're surrounded by stories, here, and I'd like to get a few of them on paper."

"But how will they finish?" I asked. "Seems to me the best is yet to come."

"Well, yes," he agreed. "Though sometimes the journey's the thing. Whatever happens to us in a couple of days' time, it will be a fresh start. A new chapter!"

Given that I had been working my way across the country in search of just that, I took a degree of comfort from the idea. "That sounds good to me."

"You and me both," he replied. "When you have the time, maybe you could sit down with me and tell me about your journey?"

"Happy to," I said, "though you might not believe all of it."

He laughed again. "Ask around. You're surrounded by miracles and magic. We've all seen things we would never have believed possible, and now we're sat waiting for the arrival of Heaven. We're beyond skepticism at this point. I'll believe anything you tell me."

He was right about that. In the days to come, I'd hear countless stories to match my own.

The old man and I made camp on the far edge of everyone else. Predictably, he wanted to keep his distance.

"Did you expect so many people?" I asked him. "I mean, there must be hundreds here."

"No," he admitted, taking the saddle off his horse and setting to building a small fire. "Word has certainly spread more than usual."

"More than usual? You've done this before?"

He nodded.

"But I thought Wormwood was only supposed to appear every hundred years? You're old, but..." Then I realised I was being stupid. There was no point in judging the old man by human terms; if there was one thing I had learned over the few days in his company, it was that. He might look like one of us, but that didn't make it so.

As much as he wanted to avoid the rest of the camp, people were naturally curious and eager to hear about our journey.

"Surely they know," I said to the old man, after having being asked so many times.

"I told you," he replied. "Everyone's journey is different. The challenges we face are personal."

As the sky darkened, I began to see the truth of his words. Every now and then new people arrived at the camp, but they didn't simply walk out onto the plain. They appeared from all over the place. The air would shimmer, much as it had done in the desert we had crossed, and then someone else would appear. I had no doubt that to them, as had been the case with us, the passage seemed natural. The camp appeared ahead of them as they came to the end of whichever road had brought them here. From this side, they just emerged from nowhere.

I talked about it with the party next to ours. Hs name was Clarke, a doctor from Montana traveling with his wife.

"We heard the town was going to appear in Oregon," he said. "From a Chippewa medicine man who had been travelling through our town."

"Oregon? We're miles away from Oregon!"

Clarke shrugged. "Maybe, but that's where we went, and we're sitting here now just as you are."

He didn't seem altogether happy to be so. He and his wife had a sad way about them. As the night wore on, I soon found out why.

"We're hoping to see our son," he said, "lost to us these five years now. He was helping me fix the roof. The damn rains had been getting in, and I never was one for that sort of work. Show me a human body that's in need of fixing, and I can do the job, but when it comes to wood and nails..."

He looked out across the crowds of people. "Though sometimes I can't fix everything."

His wife held his hand and there was a warmth from the two of them, then, that burned harder than the fire.

"I tried everything I could," he continued, "but Jack was..."

He didn't want to finish the sentence. "I should never have let him up there, but he always had such a good eye for that kind of thing. God knows where he got it from. He could make anything."

"We'll see him soon," his wife said. "Together again."

He nodded and looked to us. "Are you here to be reunited with someone?"

I shook my head, feeling guilty for some reason. "I just kind of fell into this," I admitted. "He led and I followed."

The doctor looked to the old man. "You?"

"Old friends," he said but, as usual, refused to go into detail.

"You should come and see me in the morning," Clarke told me. "I've got some cream that'll help take those burns down."

I told him I'd do just that. The desert had taken its toll, and my face was still pink and blistered.

Later, as we prepared to sleep, the old man pulled me to one side. "We should be careful," he said, "I can't control my appearance when I sleep. And as you know, people don't always take kindly to it."

"If you lie in front of the fire," I suggested, "people probably won't even notice."

He nodded. "But if they do... be ready."

For what, I could hardly guess, but it didn't turn out to be necessary.

I woke to the sound of kids laughing. There were a couple of them, hunched down by the old man.

"He's glowing!" one of them said. "Like magic!"

The old man woke with a start and sat up, that light in his throat swallowed away as he got control of himself.

"Oh!" the other kid moaned. "Bring it back! I want to see it again."

The old man looked at me, confused.

"Don't mind them," said a woman's voice. "They're a mite too inquisitive for their own good." She appeared in the faint light of the fire and took hold of her kids.

"I wouldn't have hurt them," the old man said.

She smiled. "I never thought you would. We've seen

enough things on our journey here to be a bit more open minded. This world is filled with all sorts, and if you're here, then I guess God wishes it."

"Please show us again!" one of the kids asked.

"Now come on," the woman said. "Let the man get his sleep."

"I don't mind," he said, and I swear it was the first time I had seen him appear in any way uncertain. He closed his eyes and opened his mouth and the fire glowed. Both kids laughed and clapped their hands.

He opened his eyes again and the light in his mouth dimmed.

"Well, mister," she said, "if I have as much problem lighting a fire tomorrow as I did tonight, don't be surprised if I come over and ask you to breathe on it." She laughed and led her children away.

I looked at the old man, his face a perfect picture of confusion. I couldn't help but laugh. "Yeah, you can face down killer towns, but you're lost when it comes to kids."

He gave me a scathing look. "Go back to sleep."

"Don't mind if I do."

As dawn broke over the camp, it was clear that even more people had appeared during the night.

"Much more of this," I said to the old man, "and we're going to have a city of our very own."

We had breakfast—with more of his wonderfully lethal coffee—and afterwards I decided to take a walk. Drop in on Clarke, and maybe pay a visit on the writer and tell him about Wentworth Falls; I was pretty sure he'd like that one.

I found Clarke after a few minutes. He had set up a temporary hospital. So many of the people that arrived were in need of attention that he and a couple of the other members of the camp who were medically trained had decided to get organised. There was a row of bedrolls, filled with patients in various states of disrepair. A couple particularly drew my eye.

"What the hell happened to them?" I asked.

One was a man whose eyes appeared to have vanished, a smooth band of skin running from above his nose to his hair line. The other was a dwarf. Both were in a bad way, their skin red and bruised, some places turning almost to black.

"Exposure to extreme cold," said Clarke. "They appeared in the night, both so close to death I can hardly believe they're still breathing." He held up the man's hands. The fingers were raw and swollen. "Even if he does pull through, I can't imagine he's going to be playing the banjo anytime soon."

"Harmonium," the man said, suddenly convulsing.

Clarke held him down, straightening the blankets he had covered the man in. "He keeps saying that. God knows what he's talking about. Maybe the others will know."

"Others?"

He led me over to another bed where a man lay holding onto a black girl. He held her so tight it was a wonder she could breathe. They had the same signs of damage from the cold.

"It may not look like it," said Clarke, "but they're in better shape. They'll pull through soon enough."

"Soon enough to see Wormwood?"

"That's the question. Everyone seems to agree it'll appear tomorrow afternoon, so I guess they have time yet. Whatever happens, though, they're lucky to be alive."

He gave me some cream for my burns and I left him to it, heading back out into the camp and over towards the large train.

Irish had company today. A whole row of seats had been

set up, and he was joined by a young man and woman, the first wearing rough work clothes, the second looking mightily out of place in a long, expensive dress.

"Well," said Irish, "if it isn't the banker. Pull up a chair."

I did so, sitting between him and the young couple.

"These are two of my travelling companions," he said. "Billy Herbert, our fine engineer and driver, and Lady Elisabeth Forset, a jewel plucked from England's crown and dropped here to glitter in the dust."

"You can tell you're a writer," I said.

"Never use one word when four will do just as well." He laughed, and the other two shook my hand.

"You look like you've marched across Arizona," said Billy. "I've eaten steaks less cooked than that face."

"It smarts some," I admitted, "but it didn't kill me, so I guess it don't matter all that much."

"We've all been through our fair share of trouble getting here," said Lady Forset. She looked out over the camp. "All of us."

"Yeah," said Billy. "And here was I thinking I was traveling with the only handful of lunatics that had heard of Wormwood."

I admitted that I'd thought the same, and we all joked for awhile about the fact that we were sat in a place that none of us had ever believed could exist.

"Of course," said Billy, "there's no guarantee it will appear. Tomorrow evening we could all be feeling pretty stupid."

"It'll appear," said Lady Forset. "I've no doubt about that anymore."

"No," said Billy, "I guess not. Then God help us when the rush begins."

"I'm sure Heaven has plenty of room," said Irish. "Certainly most of the people I know would be going to the other place!"

"Hell?" Billy asked. "Seems to me most of the folks here have already ridden through it."

Which led into my telling them my story, Irish writing down notes as I went.

At one point we were interrupted by an old man in monk's clothing.

"Father Martin," said Lady Forset, "meet Elwyn Wallace, the only man I've ever met to have been attacked by a town."

He looked at me and his lower lip trembled. He looked momentarily terrified. Suddenly he seemed to get himself under control and managed to offer me a weak smile. "Forgive me, my son," he said. "It was your face; it reminded me of something... someone. I seem to see it everywhere I look, of late."

With that he excused himself and returned to the privacy of one of the carriages.

"Don't mind him," said Billy. "He's struggling with his conscience at the moment."

The engineer told me the story of how they had fought their way past a grotesque tribe of Indians to arrive here, saved only by the invention of Lady Forset's father.

"You'll meet him soon, I'm sure," she said. "He's always working on something or another."

At that moment there came the sound of a small explosion from the rear of the train.

"That would be him now," she said.

AFTER A FEW hours I left them to it, returning to our section of the camp, and the old man. He was sat in silence, looking out over the camp, in a world of his own.

"Only one more day," I said. "Then it'll be here."

He looked at me, a dreamy look on his face that showed he hadn't quite been listening.

"Wormwood," I explained. "Everybody says it'll be here tomorrow."

He nodded. "I can feel it."

"I was wondering," I said. "If things are supposed to get stranger and more dangerous the closer you get to the place, how come here it's all so peaceful?"

"The journey's done," he said. "This is a charmed place at the centre, the eye at the heart of the storm."

"Not that I'm complaining," I admitted. "I'm only too happy to catch my breath."

We sat and watched the people. A new family had appeared in the middle of the afternoon, a mother and father and so many children I could only imagine the nights got cold where they lived. It was like watching a Sunday School picnic, the way they all set about their chores and prepared their food. It seemed so delicate and normal.

The religious crowd were here in full, of course. Several congregations had developed in the camp and, as night fell, hymns erupted from all corners as they began their worship.

"If you want to go and join in," I said to the old man, "don't let me stop you."

He gave one of those rare half-smiles and set about preparing some food for his horse and my mule. He was as relieved as I was, that old nag. I don't think he expected to make the journey either. Now he was content to eat and lie down next to the old man's horse. I think he was in love.

The night passed quietly, but for a brief commotion from the hospital tent. Someone was shouting. An argument, maybe, or a grieving family member. I thought about the man with no eyes; perhaps he had woken up and was causing trouble? If so, I had no doubt Clarke could handle it. The man had been nothing but bruises and wounds, I doubt he could put up much of a fight.

*   *   *

THE NEXT MORNING, the camp was buzzing with anticipation. The hymn-singing of the night before was early to pick up again and it was like working your way through a carnival as I made my way over to the hospital tent.

"Morning," said Clarke as I entered. "Don't tell me you need more cream for your face. You were supposed to rub it on, not eat it."

"I'm fine," I said. "Just wondering if you needed some help. I heard some fuss last night and thought I'd check to make sure everything was alright."

"It was nothing I couldn't handle. Our blind friend woke up, and was surprisingly active, given his condition. Apparently he lost his wife on his way here; he wanted to go back and find her. Easier said than done, as I told him. Besides, even if he could work out how to retrace his steps, he's hardly fit to go running off back into whatever freezing hell he came from."

"He seems quiet enough now," I said, walking over to where the man lay.

"I injected him with veterinary tranquilisers," said Clarke. "It was the only way I could shut him up."

"What about the rest of his party?"

"Still out for the count, thankfully. My favourite kind of patient."

As THE DAY drew on, the mood got even more excited, people shouting, laughing and praying. A couple of fights broke out, but nothing that got too out of hand.

I stopped by the train again, finally getting the chance to meet Lady Forset's father.

"I might have something for those burns," he told me,

peering at my face as if it were the most fascinating thing he'd ever seen.

"Stick to the cream," Lady Forset told me. "The last medical cure he offered nearly blew a man's leg off."

Finally I headed back to the old man and sat down to wait for the thing that had brought us all here.

It was just shy of four o'clock when people first started shouting and pointing to the sky out west. The air seemed to be flexing, the clouds beyond it twisting and bending as if viewed through distorted glass. Then there came the rain. It fell warm and peculiarly coloured, a sort of faint purple, lasting about half an hour before the ground itself started shaking.

"Keep steady," the old man said, taking hold of my arm. "It can get pretty violent."

At first it was hard to tell whether what we were seeing was just distortion again, but slowly, a distinct shape began to form about half a mile away. Lines resolved themselves into gutters and roofs, joists and gateposts. Over a period of about an hour, a town solidified out of nowhere. I thought of Wentworth Falls. It had that same false, perfect quality. A town that had never really been lived in.

People began walking towards it, and I couldn't help but join them, the old man following more reluctantly at my side.

There was a creaking, grinding sound as if the town had only just gained weight, pressing itself down into the earth beneath it.

We surrounded it, looking along its streets, trying to peer through its windows.

I saw Irish in the crowd, his notebook in his hand. I waved at him, but his attention was elsewhere.

Nobody seemed willing to cross the town's threshold.

Then a bright light surged out from the centre of the

town, pulsing through the streets and shooting straight up into the sky above. People panicked, backing away and crying out, worried that the whole place might be about to explode. It didn't.

A figure appeared, a tall, blond-haired man in a smart suit and vest. He walked towards us (though I later heard that he appeared to walk towards *everybody*, whatever side of town you were facing) and came to a halt on the edge of the town.

"Welcome!" he shouted, his voice carrying perfectly over the crowd. "My name, as some of you already know, is Alonzo. And I'm here to welcome you to Wormwood." He smiled, the most charming smile I had ever seen. "You've all been through terrible ordeals to get here, and some of you have travelled thousands of miles to reach this point.

"Well..."—he clasped his hands together, as if in prayer—"what can I say? What has come before was nothing. *This* is where your adventure really begins."

And in that, he was quite right.

ACKNOWLEDGEMENTS

WHEN I WAS a child I loathed Westerns. That was because I had never seen a Sergio Leone film. Once the dollars trilogy and—most especially—*Once Upon A Time In The West* had been crammed into my naive eyes I saw the west in a different way and fell in love. This series is the resultant child, a hobbling bastard with a hybrid set of genes. Leone, Corbucci and Il Maestro, Ennio Morricone all played their part.

As did Alex Cox, that wonderful curator of unloved movies for many seasons of *Moviedrome*. He knows why the Italians made the best narrators of the savage west and his enthusiasm and recommendations led me to treasure time and time again.

It's a story I've wanted to tell for many years and I can only thank Jon Oliver and David Thomas Moore time and time again for letting me tell it. Their support, enthusiasm and wise editorial nudges have been a real boost. It's been wonderful to finally storm Fort Solaris, it only took four stocks of dynamite and a barrel of hooch to do so.

As always I must also thank Debra. She puts up with my being a moody varmint when working on a book and is always the first to read the result. She is lovely and more precious than all the smuggled Civil War gold in the world.

Mum is the second reader and equally valuable for that. She knows when not to ask 'how's the book going'? and always points out the way to Sierra Madre. I love her lots and, like many sons, probably never tell her enough. Given that nobody reads the acknowledgments but mothers and lovers anyway at least I've told her now.

Finally, all the chapter titles are the names of Spaghetti Westerns. While you're waiting for the next book in my crazed oat opera you would do worse than to track them down and watch them. Trust me, you'll be glad you did.

ABOUT THE AUTHOR

GUY ADAMS IS a no-good, pen-toting son of a bitch. Responsible for over twenty penny-dreadfuls and scientific romances such as *The World House* and the *Deadbeat* series. He has also worked with the Hammer Books Gang creating novelisations of their foul kinematographs and has been known to operate under the alias of John Watson M.D. writing novels featuring that pansy-ass detective Sherlock Holmes. He is wanted in several states and a reward is offered for anyone quick enough to slip a noose around his crooked neck. Further evidence of his crimes can be found on his Wild Western Waystation:

www.guyadamsauthor.com

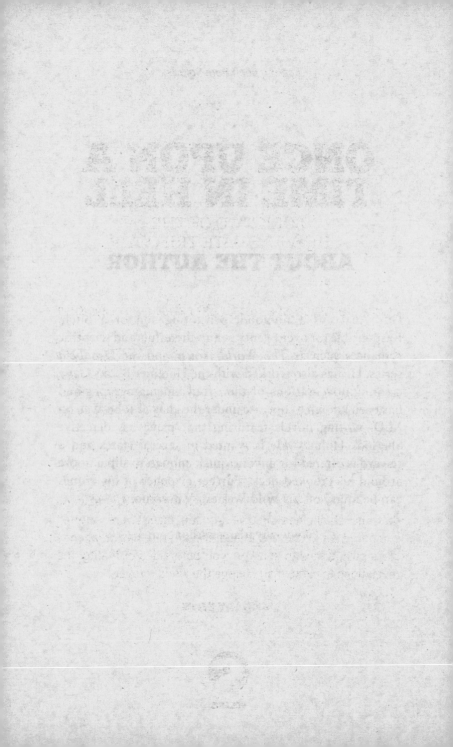

ONCE UPON A TIME IN HELL

BOOK TWO OF THE HEAVEN'S GATE TRILOGY

UK ISBN: 978 1 78108 155 6 • US ISBN: 978 1 78108 156 3 • £7.99/$7.99

"Heaven? Hell? There's no difference. Angels, demons, we're all a bit of both. This could be the most wondrous place you ever experience, or so terrifying it makes you pray for death.

"Not that death would help you, of course; there's no escape from here..."

Wormwood has appeared, and for twenty four hours the gateway to the afterlife is wide open. But just because a door is open doesn't mean you should step through it.

The few who have travelled to reach the town are realising that the challenges they've already faced were nothing compared with what lies ahead. The afterlife has an agenda of its own, and with scheming on both sides of reality, the revelations to come may change the world forever...

JANUARY 2014

SOLARIS

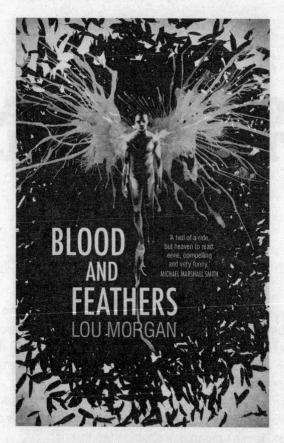

BLOOD AND FEATHERS
LOU MORGAN

'A hell of a ride,
but heaven to read:
eerie, compelling
and very funny.'
MICHAEL MARSHALL SMITH

UK ISBN: 978 1 78108 018 4 • US ISBN: 978 1 78108 019 1 • £7.99/$9.99

Alice isn't having the best of days – late for work, missed her bus, and now she's getting rained on – but it's about to get worse.

The war between the angels and the Fallen is escalating and innocent civilians are getting caught in the cross-fire. If the balance is to be restored, the angels must act – or risk the Fallen taking control. Forever. That's where Alice comes in. Hunted by the Fallen and guided by Mallory – a disgraced angel with a drinking problem he doesn't want to fix – Alice will learn the truth about her own history... and why the angels want to send her to hell.

What do the Fallen want from her? How does Mallory know so much about her past? What is it the angels are hiding – and can she trust either side?

BEN MACALLAN

DESDAEMONA

UK ISBN: 978 1 907519 62 8 • US ISBN: 978 1 907519 63 5 • £7.99/$7.99

Jordan helps kids on the run find their way back home. He's good at that. He should be - he's a runaway himself. Sometimes he helps the kids in other, stranger, ways. He looks like a regular teenager, but he's not. He acts like he's not exactly human, but he is. He treads the line between mundane reality and the world of the supernatural. Ben McCallan's urban fantasy debut takes you on a teffifying journey.

 WWW.SOLARISBOOKS.COM

BEN MACALLAN

PANDAEMONIUM

'Smart, witty, and full of surprises, it grips until the very last shock.'
— Suzanne McLeod, best-selling author of *Spellerackers.com*

UK ISBN: 978 1 78108 051 1 • US ISBN: 978 1 78108 052 8 • £7.99/$8.99

Desdaemona's done a bad, bad thing.

A thing so, so terrible that she has to run away from the consequences. Again. Where better to look for shelter than with the boy she was running from before?

But trouble follows. And if it's not Jacey's parents who sent the deadly crow-men, the Twa Corbies, in chase of her, then who is it? Deep under London, among the lost and rejected of two worlds, answers begin to emerge from Desi's hidden past. Answers that send her north in a flight that turns to a hunt, with strange companions and stranger prey. Dangers lie ahead and behind; inconvenient passion lays traps for her, just when she needs a clear head; at the last, even Desi has to beg for help. From one who has more cause than most to want her dead...

 WWW.SOLARISBOOKS.COM

Follow us on Twitter! www.twitter.com/solarisbooks

'difficult to put
down... a thoroughly
entertaining novel that
I would recommend
to those looking for a
summer blockbuster'
Sacramento Book Review
on Age of Odin

New York Times Best Selling Author
JAMES LOVEGROVE

UK ISBN: 978 1 907992 04 9 • US ISBN: 978 1 907992 05 6 • £7.99/$7.99

POLICING THE DAMNED

They live among us, abhorred, marginalised, despised. They are vampires, known politely as the Sunless. The job of policing their community falls to the men and women of SHADE: the Sunless Housing and Disclosure Executive. Captain John Redlaw is London's most feared and respected SHADE officer, a living legend.

But when the vampires start rioting in their ghettos, and angry humans respond with violence of their own, even Redlaw may not be able to keep the peace. Especially when political forces are aligning to introduce a radical answer to the Sunless problem, one that will resolve the situation once and for all...

 WWW.SOLARISBOOKS.COM

Follow us on Twitter! www.twitter.com/solarisbooks

UK ISBN: 978 1 78108 049 8 • US ISBN: 978 1 78108 050 4 • £7.99/$8.99

BLOOD ON THE EASTERN SEABOARD

The east coast of the USA is experiencing the worst winter weather in living memory, and John Redlaw is in the cold white thick of it. He's come to America to investigate a series of vicious attacks on vampire immigrants — targeted kills that can't simply be the work of amateur vigilantes. Dogging his footsteps is Tina "Tick" Checkley, a wannabe TV journalist with an eye on the big time.

The conspiracy Redlaw uncovers could give Tina the career break she's been looking for. It could also spell death for Redlaw.

OCTOBER 2012

'Ingenious, gripping, and full of pleasures on every level. Exceptional.'
- Mike Carey, NYT Bestselling author of The Unwritten

BABYLON STEEL
GAIE SEBOLD

UK ISBN: 978 1 907992 37 7 • US ISBN: 978 1 907992 38 4 • £7.99/$8.99

Babylon Steel, ex-sword-for-hire, ex... other things, runs The Red Lantern, the best brothel in the city. She's got elves using sex magic upstairs, S&M in the basement and a large green troll cooking breakfast in the kitchen. She'd love you to visit, except...

She's not having a good week. The Vessels of Purity are protesting against brothels, girls are disappearing, and if she can't pay her taxes, Babylon's going to lose the Lantern. She'd given up the mercenary life, but when the mysterious Darask Fain pays her to find a missing heiress, she has to take the job. And then her past starts to catch up with her in other, more dangerous ways.

Witty and fresh, Sebold delivers the most exciting fantasy debut in years.

 WWW.SOLARISBOOKS.COM

Follow us on Twitter! www.twitter.com/solarisbooks

UK ISBN: 978 1 78108 079 5 • US ISBN: 978 1 78108 080 1 • £7.99/$8.99

Babylon Steel, owner of the Red Lantern brothel – and former avatar of the goddess of sex and war – has been offered a job. Two jobs, really: bodyguard to Enthemmerlee, a girl transformed into a figure of legend... and spy for the barely-acknowledged government of Scalentine. The very young Enthemmerlee embodies the hopes and fears of many on her home world of Incandress, and is a prime target for assassination.

Babylon must somehow turn Enthemmerlee's useless household guard into a disciplined fighting force, dodge Incandress's bizarre and oppressive Moral Statutes, and unruffle the feathers of a very annoyed Scalentine diplomat. All of which would be hard enough, were she not already distracted by threats to both her livelihood and those dearest to her...

NON STOP.
ONE WAY.
STRAIGHT
DOWN!

The very British spirit
of Hammer Horror
rises from the grave
in Christopher Fowler's
rattling, roaring yarn.
- Kim Newman,
author of *Anno Dracula*

HELL TRAIN
CHRISTOPHER FOWLER

UK ISBN: 978 1 907992 43 8 • US ISBN: 978 1 907992 44 5 • £7.99/$8.99

Imagine there was a supernatural chiller that Hammer Films never made. A grand epic produced at the studio's peak, which played like a cross between the Dracula and Frankenstein films and Dr Terror's House of Horrors...

Four passengers meet on a train journey through Eastern Europe during the First World War, and face a mystery that must be solved if they are to survive. As the Arkangel races through the war-torn countryside, they must find out: What is in the casket that everyone is so afraid of? What is the tragic secret of the veiled Red Countess who travels with them? Why is their fellow passenger, the army brigadier, so feared by his own men? And what exactly is the devilish secret of the Arkangel itself?

Bizarre creatures, Satanic rites, terrified passengers and the romance of travelling by train, all in a classically-styled horror novel.

 WWW.SOLARISBOOKS.COM

Follow us on Twitter! www.twitter.com/solarisbooks